BRAD PIERCE

CAPITAL MURDER

AETHON THRILLS

aethonbooks.com

CAPITAL MURDER
©2024 BRAD PIERCE

Aethon Books
www.aethonbooks.com

Print and eBook formatting by Kevin G. Summers.

Published by Aethon Books LLC.

Aethon Books is not responsible for websites (or their content) that are not owned by the publisher.

This book is a work of fiction. Names, characters, places, and incidents are the product of the author's imagination or are used fictitiously. Any resemblance to actual events, locales, or persons, living or dead is coincidental.

ALSO BY BRAD PIERCE

COLIN FROST

Capital Murder

Echoes of Deception

Check out the entire series here! (Tap or scan)

A lie that is half-truth is the darkest of all lies.
—Alfred Tennyson

WASHINGTON D.C. SNOW CLEARANCE ESTIMATES

Snow Performance Measures – Penguin Chart

| Storm Type | Accumulation | Major Streets | | Residential Streets | |
		Time from storm end	Percent of streets passable	Time from storm end	Percent of streets passable
Freezing Rain	Coating	12 hours	85%	12 hours	85%
Snow	0 to 2 inches	4 hours	85%	8 hours	85%
	2 to 4 inches	6 hours	85%	12 hours	85%
	4 to 8 inches	12 hours	85%	24 hours	85%
	8 to 12 inches	18 hours	85%	36 hours	85%
	12 to 18 inches	36 hours	75%	48 hours	75%
	over 18 inches	36 hours	75%	60 hours	75%

SOURCE- HTTPS://SNOW.DC.GOV/SITES/DEFAULT/FILES/DC/SITES/SNOW/SNOW%20PERFOR-

MANCE%20MEASURES%20–%20PENGUIN%20CHART%5B3%5D.PDF

To my wife.
You supporting my wildest dreams is everything.
-Brad Pierce

PROLOGUE

17 Years Ago

Death had come to the snow filled streets of Washington D.C. More specifically, Susan was sure death had come for her. As Christmas lights twinkled from the leafless trees and fluffy white powder poured from the frozen black sky, it seemed the only cheer she could find was that of the faint hope of survival she so desperately clung to.

Susan Frost held the key to her survival concealed within the lining of her purse. She tried to forget this as she pushed her way through the graffitied movie theater door into the onslaught of the winter storm, but that was easier said than done. Wind and snow hit her like a wall of ice, trying to push her back inside. Crystalline flakes pelted her eyes and nearly blew the two younger brothers she was traveling with back inside. Snow fell in such thick squalls that one could be forgiven for thinking they were walking around in a snow globe. Susan and her younger brothers had just finished a Christmas Eve screening of *It's A Wonderful Life* at a local theater.

"Take my hands!" Susan yelled over the wind, looking back at James and Colin. She felt two gloved hands take her own as she started down the street. In her mind, she was unsure if they were two beacons of warmth at her side or a possible source of heat for the internal furnace that had been relentlessly pushing her forward over the past few months.

The faint yellow, glowing orbs of streetlights could be seen through the flurry of falling snow around them. Further out, snow and night were only broken by the occasional light of a bar or twenty-four-hour convenience store open late on the holiday. The group of three proceeded down Connecticut Avenue for another block huddled against the wind before turning down a side street whose name was obscured by a patch of snow sticking to the sign. This didn't matter to Susan, as Washington D.C. was her home and she knew the route well.

Their house was about a twenty-minute walk. Usually, with the boys, Susan would have called for a cab, but the snow had ground most of the capital to a halt. The boys, however, would not be deterred from the family tradition, as it reminded them of their parents. When they had died three years earlier, the care of the boys had fallen to Susan.

Try as she might to keep her little brothers' lives normal, she could not be both parents and an older sister at the same time. But she made every effort to make the holidays a happy time for them. To that end, she had called the theater and asked if they would still be doing the showing in this weather. A slightly annoyed sounding man answered yes, so she bundled the boys up and ventured out into the storm.

Their boots crunched the snow that blanketed the sidewalk, the Christmas movie a faint memory for her already, as they walked up the ever-darkening block. They were moving further off the main strip now toward a block of brick row houses that looked cheerful with their Christmas lights twinkling under the snow. The boys were quiet, having eaten their fill of the theater's buttery popcorn and special mint cocoa that the theater only served for the Christmas Eve show. She hadn't partaken in the treats, which were usually a favorite for her, subsisting on nothing but coffee and nerves for the past two days.

Susan felt the knot of anxiety in her stomach pulling every muscle tight within her body. The unbreakable tension kept her looking around, playing it off to the boys that she was taking in the Christmas lights, but really checking her surroundings. She didn't like being alone in the dark these days. Usually, the hustle and bustle of the city kept this feeling at bay, but the eerie quiet of the snow seemed to muffle even the howling wind. Darkness, it seemed, was all around her.

Susan was several years older than the boys. She had always been the prodigal child to her parents. Staying up late to study, never getting in trouble, and always going out of her way to take care of her younger brothers. Their parents had died in her last year of college at Georgetown. After their death, she abandoned her dorm room and came home to take care of the boys, managing to finish her degree in the small amount of free time she had. Her hopes of being a lawyer seemed to have been dashed. Though their parents had left them a fair bit of money, she had no hope of finding the time to go to law school, even locally. They had no family to speak of, and Susan didn't trust anyone else to raise the broken boys but herself.

Her father, however, had a friend who thought he could help Susan out. He was the newly appointed Assistant U.S. Attorney of Washington D.C. and had offered Susan a part-time job, with the flexibility to take on as much new casework as she saw fit in her free time. This way, she could keep earning experience until the boys were older, when she could make the time to go to law school. Susan had been apprehensive at first but ultimately accepted the reasoning that she could allow herself this one thing.

The job, which had started great, was now the source of her terror. While working cases in her free time, Susan had stumbled upon something. Being inherently curious and with the mind of a young lawyer, she had begun peeling back layers and making connections. Although Susan had not identified the full depth of the conspiracy, she was getting close. There was something bad happening, but she wasn't sure how all the pieces fit together yet.

It was then that she had begun to feel it. At first, she thought it was paranoia. It was the kind of feeling someone got when walking up the basement stairs with the lights off behind them, or a child running away from someone they knew must be inches behind them. But for all of her gut feelings, she had no proof.

Days had stretched into weeks, growing darker and colder as winter closed in. The boys football practices, playdates, and small family dinners were the only respite she had, but she always felt like she was shielding them from what she had found. Or, she thought, what she had unleashed.

Then she had found something. She wasn't entirely sure what it was other than a string of numbers, but she knew it had to be important. She had copied the information onto a compact disk, which she now kept with her at all times, scared in her paranoia that someone would steal it from the house.

They turned another corner onto an even darker street. This one had several shops and restaurants, all of which now appeared to be closed. The streetlights here were even fewer, and several of them seemed to not work at all. Susan quickened her pace, dragging the boys along slightly, as they were getting sleepy and tired of walking. She checked behind her again and thought she might have seen someone standing near the corner they had turned moments before. She tried to wave it off as a trick of the light, with the snow cascading through it.

The feeling, however, wouldn't abate. They walked several more paces before Susan turned around again. This time, she definitely saw it. Standing at the corner was the silhouette of a large man. He didn't move. Susan thought that maybe he had just stepped out of a building to have a cigarette. She turned and kept walking this time, physically pushing the boys ahead so they would move faster. She wished she could say this was a new thing, some fluke where she could call the police and say some strange man was following her. But it had been going on for weeks and getting worse by the day.

She knew no one would help her but herself. The police were probably involved, she reminded herself. An inner voice had told her to drop it and move on. That same voice drove countless numbers of people to quit when things got hard. She had even applied to Georgetown Law in a fit of self-described weakness, when things had gotten really bad a few weeks before. She had their answer in a thick envelope in her purse. One she refused to open, as it might cause her to give up the fight. But she couldn't go on much longer. The danger was becoming more palpable by the day.

Ten more steps along, Susan turned again. Her stomach dropped. The man, it seemed, had kept pace with them and had stopped before she turned, continuing to stare at them. Alarm bells clanged in Susan's head as primal instincts screamed to her that a predator was near. She looked forward, frantically searching for a place they could step inside.

A snowflake stuck to one of her eyelashes, partially obscuring her vision. She reached up to brush it away, temporarily dropping Colin's hand. She grabbed it again and continued to hurry forward. Up ahead, she finally saw the open sign of a late-night bodega. She checked over her shoulder to see where he was. The figure was closer than ever now, a mere fifteen feet behind them. It stopped again, seeming to wait for her. She could have sworn she saw a smile. Every fiber of Susan's being demanded that she run as fast as she could, but a motherly instinct for her young arose within her.

Thoughts raced through her mind on how to react as she now stood rooted to the spot. She had a choice. Send the boys to the bodega for help, or risk them becoming collateral damage in her fight. The decision was clear. She bent down, pulling the boys close.

"Colin, James, I want you to run to that convenience store over there. Tell the clerk inside that there is trouble and to call the police."

James looked confused and started to protest. Colin, however, looked from her eyes around her to the figure standing mere feet behind.

"But—" James got out before Susan cut him off.

"Go!" she demanded. James continued to look bewildered, but

5

Colin, looking her once more in the eyes and seeming to understand something there, grabbed James and took off toward the store.

Susan took a deep breath and stood up, watching the boys run down the street. She was perspiring from extreme fear and adrenaline. She turned to face the figure, suddenly feeling brave in the face of the terror she was now confronted with.

"What do you wa—" she tried to scream but was cut short. The figure had charged, closing the distance with incredible speed on the slippery snow-coated ground. He hit her with such force that the wind was knocked out of her, and she went flying to the ground. She landed on her back a split second before smacking her head on the freezing pavement. Stunned, she lay there, blood dripping from a large gash at the back of her head into the white snow.

The figure casually stood up, lazily brushing snow from himself, watching the boys enter the bodega down the street as he did so. *Plenty of time*, he thought. He reached down and picked up one of her legs, dragging her into a nearby alley with little effort. Once he deemed them far enough within the alley, he picked up her bag. She tried to hold onto it, but the man wrenched it from her grasp, an ember of excitement and anticipation flaring in the darkness of his gut.

Good, she still has some fight in her, he thought, smiling again. He rifled through the contents of the purse, not finding what he was looking for. Remembering tradecraft, he upended it, dumping the contents on the ground. He reached down and pocketed the cash from the wallet before feeling the lining of the purse. Another smile. He pulled a knife from a sheath at the small of his back and slit it open, finding the compact disc inside. He pocketed the disc and turned to his prey.

This was his favorite part. Whatever the mission was, or whoever he was working for at the time, was gone now. This was between him and his victim. He was God now. Somewhere, through the many missions, something had become unhinged inside of him. He began to enjoy every part of the rush of killing. His stalks, his hits, everything about his demeanor had been carefully designed to inspire maximum terror. Those who might employ him thought of him as the best way to send a brutal message; they had no idea he enjoyed what he did. If they knew it was so personal, they never would have hired him.

He bent down next to her. She tried to speak but merely sputtered incoherently as a result of her severe concussion. She looked pale and sweaty. He wasn't sure if this was from nausea related to her head injury, or her fear. Slowly, he went to work. It didn't take long for her to pass out. When he was done, he dug the knife in, cutting her throat from ear to ear. He crossed her arms and straightened what hair wasn't matted with blood on her head.

For a moment, he stood there, admiring his work. He could hear police sirens in the distance now as snow floated past his eyes toward the ground. Their response time would be slower because of the weather, he thought. How much time he had, he could not say. Be that as it may, the man couldn't resist one more look down at his victim. A deep sense of satisfaction overtook him. He looked toward the entrance to the alley. Standing there was one of the little boys. He must have run back from the store to check on his sister. It didn't matter; the boy couldn't do anything. His employer was safe, the last vestiges of guilt swept away inside of this girl's rapidly dying mind.

Colin stood at the end of the alley, staring at the figure who was standing over his sister. It stared back, then slowly cocked its head to the side and smiled. Yellow teeth caught some of the dim streetlight from where Colin was standing. The man then turned and took off into the darkness down the other side of the alley.

He stood there for another moment, then cautiously walked toward his sister's body. When he arrived, he found her nearly peaceful, except for the horrific carnage done to her head. Sirens blared in the background as he stared down. The corpse stared back, eyeless, tongueless, and dead. A mixture of non-understanding and rage built within Colin, his small mind barely able to take in what had happened, not wanting to believe it. He wanted to kill the man with the yellow teeth, he wanted revenge.

1

Present Day
Washington D.C., Monday, 4 p.m.

S enator Rand took his seat at the dark wooden table. Dim light from incandescent bulbs shining through emerald glass fixtures overhead blanketed the wood paneled walls in a feeble sort of way. This being one of the oldest secure compartmented information facilities in the Capitol building meant that it hadn't been updated since nearly the 1970s. *Rooms that don't technically exist don't get updated very often,* thought Rand.

A strange quiet overtook the group that sat there. Whether from the thick concrete walls that blocked all electronic signals or the gloomy mood in the air, Rand wasn't sure. Arrayed around it were three other senators from different states and parties. One chair sat empty amongst them. Rand felt the absence sharply, and he could tell by the swollen bags under his colleagues sleepless eyes that they did too. The group represented a very secret investigative arm within the Senate intelligence committee. Their task was to investigate and ferret out potential treason and espionage within the highest echelons of the U.S. government.

Investigations like these could put traditional law enforcement in tricky situations where favor wrangling, political status, and organizational funding might compromise the integrity of those involved. The committee was created under President Kennedy when the West seemed to be under a never-ending assault from the Communists. Fear that this assault would eventually place a Soviet agent in Congress or another position of power solidified support for its creation.

The group was made up of experienced senators from both parties who were chosen by the vice president and ranking member of the committee, who was deemed to be at no risk of losing re-election. This ensured that there was less risk of partisanship or corruption among the committee and that no one was unfairly investigated. These matters usually came to this committee's attention through the vice president. A post that conveyed extreme power but kept one out of the everyday limelight that other more senior positions enjoyed.

Senator Rand placed a mug of coffee down on the wood and gold coaster emblazoned with the seal of the United States Senate. He looked around, taking in the solemn faces of his colleagues.

"I know we're all shocked and upset at Anthony's murder," he began in a Carolina drawl. Senator Marks, a woman in her late fifties with short-cropped gray hair, wiped a tear from her eye. Senator Rand gave her a reassuring look and continued, "Our fearless leader, taken from us in an attempt to scare us off the truth."

"Well, it worked," interrupted Senator Miller with a thick New York accent. "I am scared. We all are," he said, looking around the table, to nods of agreement from everyone except Rand, who intentionally never allowed himself to be read. "And Anthony was a huge part of our investigation. If he hadn't been approached, we wouldn't even have known that this treason existed. And the way he was killed! My god!"

"I know everyone is scared," said Senator Rand, "but all this has done is show us that we truly are on to something!" He shook his fist with emphasis on the last few words.

"We should turn this case over to the FBI," interrupted the third senator in the room. "We have enough evidence. All we need is the missing link, and they're better equipped to handle it."

The room seemed to nod in consensus. Senator Rand nodded himself, placating his colleagues, and continued, "I have thought of that and agree we need to hand it over to the professionals, but not just the FBI."

The other senators in the room looked at him with curious expressions on their faces. He took the expressions in, enjoying being at the leading edge of his colleagues' thoughts, even if he did find it tiresome. Politicians always had to be dragged along; blazing one's own trail in Washington was too risky. He continued, "I've spoken with the vice president, and he agrees we need to bring in the cavalry but feels we need to get a little more creative.

Traditional law enforcement will move too slowly, and time is of the essence. There's also the not so small matter that the investigation's target has a fair bit of influence over the FBI... to say the least. The Vice President suggests bringing in an Echo Unit codenamed Alien. They will link up with the FBI's special agent in charge and get the ball across the goal line."

"Military units aren't allowed to operate offensively on U.S. soil," interrupted Senator Miller.

Rand shot him a look that said "obviously" and continued, "An Echo Unit isn't 'technically' in the military. In fact, it doesn't 'technically' exist within any organizational structure within the government. Its operators come from a whole heaping pile of three-letter agencies, military units, and well, other organizations. They are 'not so technically' speaking, passed around to whichever agency needs them. The idea is to keep them both independent and free of red tape. Command authority comes exclusively from the very top of the food chain and nowhere else. Their skillset is uniquely suited to our current situation, said Rand with a shrug of his relaxed shoulders.

"What exactly is that skill set?" interrupted Senator Walker; he had only joined the committee four weeks ago and was new to this. Rand could tell from the look on his face that he'd never even heard a rumor of such a unit. *He is still young and naïve,* thought Rand.

He indulged his more junior colleague. "Counterintelligence, among other things. Or, more specifically, currently at least, to find and interdict Chinese agents in Afghanistan. Which, as you know, given our friends from the east's expected involvement in this, would be critical in identifying that missing link." The group around the table remained quiet for a moment, thinking the situation over. These were seasoned political operators who took time to calculate every decision they made.

"How do we make it legal for them to take on the investigation?" asked Senator Marks. She was exceedingly sharp and quick on the uptake.

"After this meeting, provided you all agree, the echo unit will become part of the FBI. Temporarily at least," said Rand in his relaxed southern drawl. The group considered this for another moment. Rand let them think it over and let his eyes wander over the dark wood paneling of the room. The U.S. Capitol Police had swept the S.C.I.F. earlier for bugs. One could never be too careful when operating in circles as powerful as these. One foot out of line, and you'd find yourself crushed.

The third senator in the room broke his long silence. "I think it's a good plan. We need to move quickly, though. The murder of a U.S. senator is a brazen act of war. Especially if we can prove that a foreign government was involved."

"How soon can they start?" asked Senator Miller.

Senator Rand smiled in the charming way that got him elected so many years ago, taking in the nods of agreement from around the room, and doing his best to quell any doubts they might have. He loved it when a plan came together. Now he just needed to see it executed without a hitch; his reputation was on the line here. "I'll have things in motion within the hour."

2

Present, Tuesday, 6 a.m.

The Gulfstream G650ER banked left and settled in on its approach over the Potomac to Reagan National Airport. Thick gray clouds obscured the water as the jet dipped lower on its descent. This plane wasn't typically used for government charters due to its high cost and blatant opulence, but it was the only one available on such short notice with the range and speed to get Team Alien back to D.C. from the Middle East in such a short period of time.

Colin Frost reflected on this luxury, pressing his hand against the freezing window and staring around at the five-star finishes adorning the cabin—deep soft Italian leather seats, dark grained wood, plush carpets, and gold-plated seatbelt buckles were just a few of the things that added to Colin's sense of non-belonging.

Colin could hear the faint sounds of one of his team members snoring behind him. He chose to let him sleep, as another drop in their altitude signaled to Colin that he was almost home. Coming home was always a strange experience for him. Home brought him back to a place where much of his family had been taken from him as a child. A place where he had crawled his way back from the brink to piece his life back together. The truth was, Colin tried to avoid home as much as possible.

He couldn't help but run through it in his head. Parents dead in a plane crash, sister savagely murdered, brother god knows where. He tried to put this out of his mind like he did when he left to join the army at eighteen, looking for a sense of purpose, but loss seemed to follow him. Colin had enlisted as an Eighteen X-Ray—a special program that allowed new recruits the chance to try out for special forces after completing basic training and airborne school. Six months after making it through special forces selection and joining Operational Detachment Alpha, his entire team was killed on a routine mission to help train partner forces in Africa. Colin was the sole survivor, again.

It was then that he was offered the chance to join the Echo program. Lost, broken, and unsure of where to go next, he agreed. His death was faked, his identity was erased, and he was put through a year of brutal training. Two years had passed since then, and now a year had passed since he was given command of a team. But the fear of losing them too was constant.

Colin sighed, rubbing his tired blue eyes, pushing the thoughts from his head, and wishing for a cup of coffee. A young thirty-something of South American descent with smoking dark eyes and a body that men couldn't help but notice came walking toward him down the aisle, bracing herself against the descent on seats as she went.

"On the ground in five, boss," she said. She was no flight attendant. Her skill set was far more suited to procuring weapons and gear than drinks and peanuts. Sarah was Team Alien's head of logistics. Before joining the team, she had worked for DEVGRU, formerly known as Seal Team Six, making sure they had supplies in some of the worst places on earth. She was supremely qualified, and Colin trusted her with his life. He nodded at her. "Thanks, Sarah."

It had been weeks since he had a proper night's sleep, and the fits and starts he had received since getting on the plane had been interrupted by a never-ending stream of satellite calls. This mission had so much red tape slapped on it initially that Colin thought it would never get off the ground. Then, almost without warning a few hours ago, it all disappeared. This didn't make him feel any better. People in much higher places than Colin were clearly extremely nervous, which was why Colin was on a plane and not kicking in doors halfway around the world.

The other thing that kept nagging at Colin was the lack of media attention. A sitting U.S. senator had been savagely murdered, and no one outside of the people on this plane and a few people in Washington had any idea about it. The sheer logistics of that being orchestrated were mind-boggling. Yes, it was nearly Christmas, and yes, Congress was out of session, but still, Colin was so sure that the story would break any second. He felt like he was standing in front of a tsunami. However, the vice president himself had called to assure them that he would keep the story behind them.

"This is some gruesome shit," said the man sitting across from him, watching the live news feed on the flatscreen next to him. The operator next to him, known as Jester, was a tall man with dark, parted hair and a full, bushy beard. A tan face, leathery from months in the desert, concealed green eyes with a fierceness most men wouldn't choose to challenge.

"I'll make sure there's a flight attendant next time," replied Colin, looking back down at the tablet in front of him. Jester, who was watching highlights from Monday Night Football, was Colin's second in command and had become like his brother over what seemed like an endless amount of missions. The two had gotten to the point where they could virtually read each other's minds.

The jet finally broke through the thick cloud layer, and a dull light entered the cabin through the windows. Colin caught a glimpse of his own face as he stared down at the Potomac below. He was tan from the months in the high mountains of Afghanistan. He had trimmed his beard back to something more civilized earlier in the flight, and the darker undergrowth clashed with his blonde hair. Frosted blue eyes continuously probed the ground, taking in the familiar sights of home. Old Town Alexandria was flying past while the plane made its final descent into Reagan. Colin saw snow flurries already beginning to race past the plane's windows.

"I thought swamps were supposed to be warm, Snowman," said Jester, using Colin's call-sign instead of his actual name. Call signs were more than just funny nicknames on Team Alien. They helped protect operators' anonymity. This was more important now than ever in the age of social media.

"Remember that saying about hell freezing over?" asked Colin.

"If the Chinese did have a hand in executing a U.S. senator, it might explain the weather," Jester said back, only half-joking.

"Amen to that," replied Colin, locking the tablet and putting it back into the tactical style backpack at his feet.

The plane touched down, blowing high-speed gusts of snowflakes across the tarmac. Reagan was almost completely shut down. Even a small amount of snow tended to paralyze D.C., and this was supposed to be far worse. A Nor'easter was blasting its way up the coast, taking advantage of an extreme cold front. Meteorologists were predicting eighteen to thirty-six inches of snow in the next two days, calling it everything from a once in a lifetime event to the perfect storm. Colin wasn't sure if this would play to their advantage or not. On the one hand, the city would be paralyzed, and any opposition would likely be holed up in the same place. On the other hand, the storm would strain support resources and most likely make it more challenging to pursue leads.

They taxied up to a hanger toward two waiting unmarked Suburbans, and after a few thank-you's to the pilots, Colin and Team Alien disembarked into the falling snow.

"You Snowman?" called a serious but incredibly beautiful woman stepping out of the Suburban.

"Who's asking?" Colin said back, speaking loudly enough to be heard over the engines powering down behind him.

The woman walked forward to shake Colin's hand. "Special Agent Alexandra Smith."

"Nice to meet you. This is my team," said Colin, motioning to the people behind him. The two shook hands, and she glanced past him at his five teammates getting off the plane.

"If your team wants to load your gear into the SUVs, I can take you to FBI headquarters. We have a room set up for them to work out of there."

"Negative," said Colin. "My team will work out of here. Sarah, have the pilots bring the plane in, and you and Charlie get set up. Sheriff, Witch, get the gear ready. I want to go discrete but have everything we need to rock 'n roll within reach. Jester—"

"Excuse me!" interrupted Agent Smith. "This is my investigation. You may have been brought in to grab the reigns, but I'm still the SAC here," she said, using the acronym for Special Agent in Charge.

"And we're going to follow your lead in the investigation, but my team needs to remain independent and move as quickly as possible. Getting set up in a federal government building compromises both of those," said Colin, only half lying. The truth was that he didn't want to set up in an FBI building if the ultimate target of their investigation was involved. They needed to maintain the element of surprise.

Agent Smith didn't know this, of course. She knew that a senator had been murdered and that she had been tasked with investigating it and protecting three other senators deemed to be under threat. She also knew that she was to share responsibilities for this investigation with this team of individuals in front of her and report nothing up to the traditional command structure. Colin was sure these were probably the most confusing orders she had ever received in her time at the FBI. He needed her to focus on the investigation, though, and not on how unusual this situation was or who was in charge.

She stood there, staring a bit bewildered at him, and he could tell she was thinking of the best path to take with her next words. She was extremely athletic-looking with green eyes and blonde hair. Colin couldn't help but think she looked cute when she was flustered. He pushed the thought from his mind. "Listen, I know this is a bit unorthodox, but I promise it's for a good reason," he said, trying to put on an appeasing expression.

"Where should we start?" Colin asked, handing her an olive

branch. She seemed to take this in stride, and her face eased up a bit. "Senator Carson's townhouse is in Georgetown. The scene's been secured and the body removed, but we haven't had the chance to pick through it thoroughly yet. Fair warning though—you'll need a strong stomach," she finished.

"Have you looked through his computer yet?" Asked Colin.

"No, the team hasn't had the chance to thoroughly search his belongings yet."

Colin nodded, sensing a clear path forward. "Okay, agreed, let's head there first," he said, turning around to where the team was gearing up. "We're on the move in five."

3

The SUVs tore out of the airport using a private exit that led them to the George Washington Parkway. Snow careened off of the windshield while gusts of winter air buffeted the SUV around the highway. The mood in the car was tense, Agent Smith's hands were turning white from gripping the steering wheel so hard, and Colin could feel the overheated air prickling his skin. "You all right?" he asked.

"Fine," she shot back, a touch of determined focus and aggravation at being questioned in her voice. Colin raised his eyebrows in a conciliatory way. He sat in the front seat with Agent Smith, while the operator, Sheriff, a former member of the FBI and current member of Team Alien, sat in the back. The second Suburban followed closely behind with Agent Smith's partner driving the rest of the team, which consisted of Jester and the last tactical operator on the team, call sign Witch.

Agent Smith seemed like she needed to focus, so Colin busied himself reviewing a file Agent Smith had sent to him on his tablet. Inside was necessary information the FBI had on the case so far and many grizzly crime scene photos from Senator Carson's townhouse. Colin's team had been briefed on the plane, but he wanted to see if any details had been left out. So far, he couldn't find any.

The photos did, however, look intimately familiar to Colin. His team had found similar scenes all over Afghanistan. They expected involvement by the Chinese equivalent of the CIA, the Ministry of State Security, also known as MSS. That was because, in every case, the people murdered were former warlords with ties to the Taliban and ISIS. These men had fought a never-ending battle against U.S. forces in Afghanistan. As the U.S. forces slowly dismantled the organizations that funded the warlords, they needed new sources of capital.

Luckily for them, Afghanistan shares a border with a country that isn't very fond of having large U.S. military forces close to them. The Chinese had stepped up to fill the funding void and had been sowing chaos in Afghanistan ever since. This was until things started improving in Afghanistan. The weight of American power and U.S. dollars had finally started turning the country around, and even the warlords were noticing. Slowly, one by one, they began to lay down their arms and ally themselves with the United States backed new government.

The Chinese, however, who had invested a lot into removing U.S. forces from the country, couldn't allow this to happen. They sent in a specialist to inspire fear and terror among anyone who would think of stopping the crusade against the American military.

Colin and his team had been in theater for two years. Initially, it was just hunting Chinese spies who were trying to steal U.S. military secrets. Then, about a year ago, bodies had begun turning up, and fear spread like wildfire among the warlords of Afghanistan. The country destabilized, and the attacks against U.S. forces were stepped up both in ferocity and frequency. Catching those responsible became Team Alien's number one priority.

Then disaster struck. The U.S. began its withdrawal from Afghanistan, and the chaos deepened. The crime scenes got more gruesome, and the warlords, who were deeply religious men, had begun referring to the killer as Azrael, or the angel of death sent by Allah to take those who would end his jihad against the West. Hunting Azrael became an obsession for U.S. commanders left on the ground, but they had run out of time, and the country had been lost.

Their combined obsessions with catching Azrael, however, were nothing next to Colin's, because he had seen this before. His sister's death was all too similar in almost every way to the ones occurring in Afghanistan and now back in Washington. At first, when the killings had started in Afghanistan, Colin was convinced they must be from another source. His denial, though, vanished with every gruesome scene the team walked into. All of them were horrific, yet all of them were meticulous in a way Colin couldn't get past. Time and the knowledge that Susan's killer had never been caught wore down on him until he had no choice but to accept the truth of it. His sister's killer was Azrael. Did this mean that she had been involved with some deep-seated conspiracy before she had been killed, he asked himself?

Colin pushed the thought from his mind and tried to bring himself back to the present. "Something on your mind?" asked Agent Smith. Colin realized his face must have gone blank upon reviewing the file.

"No, just linking this up with what we know currently," said Colin, only half lying. He had never told anyone about his sister. As far as anyone knew, she had died in a tragic accident when they were young. The SUVs were heading over the Arlington Memorial Bridge now into Georgetown. Colin saw that the statues at both ends now had a coating of snow on them. The Lincoln Memorial stood tall in the distance, but he could only make out the outline through the falling snow.

The roads were so quiet that one could hardly believe this was their nation's capital. It snowed so rarely in D.C. that when it did, the whole city would typically be shut down for days. This morning was only the first day of a possible multi-day Nor'easter event. Colin had been so engrossed with reviewing the file and thinking about his past that he had almost found the lack of traffic on the George Washington Parkway unremarkable. It was remarkable.

"How long until we're there?" he asked.

"Ten minutes," Agent Smith replied. Colin noticed she was white, gripping the wheel even harder now.

"Have you ever driven in the snow, Agent Smith?" asked Colin, not unkindly.

"Yes," she said indignantly. "I just don't like it."

Colin nodded. "Would you prefer if I drove?" he asked.

"Would you prefer to walk?" she shot back.

His earpiece chimed. It was Charlie. "Overwatch is up."

Colin replied, "Acknowledged."

Colin heard a faint muttered curse word from his left as the SUV fishtailed slightly on a right turn. He decided to try and get her talking rather than stressing about the drive.

"What's your read on the scene at the Carson townhouse?" he asked Agent Smith. She paused and took her eyes off the road for a second to fix him with a ghastly stare. "I've never seen anything like it."

4

The SUVs pulled up in front of a newer-looking townhouse development and took a side entrance around the rear of the houses. Most of the houses looked to be still under construction, with only the first row boasting siding or windows. Piles of wood, pipe, and various other construction supplies littered the development, all with ever-accumulating snow on top. Almost all the other units seemed to be vacant.

Agent Smith pulled around to the garage of the last house in the row, where one other black SUV was already parked outside. Snow formed a thick blanket over the vehicle and seemed to suck the ambient noise from the air around them. Colin scanned the area behind the house and saw a thicket of pines to the rear that was obscuring the houses on the adjacent street. Footprints in the snow ran from the SUV into the garage of the townhouse.

"Your people?" asked Colin, looking from the trail of footprints to the SUV and noticing the U.S. government license plate.

"Yeah, two crime scene technicians. They've been ordered to report nothing up to the traditional chain of command," she said, catching Colin's look of disapproval. He thought about this for a moment and decided they would help things move more quickly. He made a mental note of this and told Sheriff to sync up with Charlie to monitor the tech's communications for the rest of the day as they walked into the house.

Colin's first impression upon entering the garage was that it was too clean. There wasn't a tool in sight, and apart from a set of golf clubs, Colin saw nothing else. They proceeded through the garage into a kitchen on the first floor. Colin noticed the temperature didn't change at all, and he understood why a second later. The smell of death was potent, and someone had been trying to keep it under control by keeping the house near freezing. The room was clean in a modern sort of way, and everything he looked at seemed to be some shade of gray or white. He doubted very much that the senator had picked anything out himself. Being a younger senior senator who was also single made this man an eligible bachelor, but Colin saw no sign of a woman anywhere. He walked through the kitchen into the family room, which clashed brilliantly with everything else he saw in the place. This was due almost entirely to a large amount of drying blood on the floor and yellow crime scene markers around the room.

Two men stood in the room, one photographing the blood, while the other seemed to be dusting for prints. They looked up as the team entered the room. "Who the fuck are you guys?" asked the man dusting for fingerprints. He was a large man with a mustache and bright rosy cheeks from the cold outside.

"Agent John Doe, FBI," Colin replied.

"Sounds made up," said the man bent over the body. Colin shot the man a "so what" kind of look before examining the body more closely. What struck him immediately was how peaceful it looked outside of its gruesome appearance. The senator's arms were folded over his chest, and his facial expression was that of a person who was in a deep sleep, but the utter carnage done to the man clashed brilliantly with this.

The throat was sliced under the chin from ear to ear, but it appeared the blood had been wiped away from the wound, as the neck was clean apart from the incision. Empty eye sockets stared up at him, but Colin saw no signs of blood here either. He wasn't sure if a person bled when their eyes were removed from their sockets, but the thing that struck him as even more strange was that the eyebrows seemed once again to be in a relaxed position, as if the man was sleeping.

Wouldn't a person tense up when this was happening to them? he thought, especially since they knew most of the victims to have been alive when this happened to them in the Middle East. The contrast between the carnage and the strange, relaxed look was stunning. The senator's mouth was closed, the lips creased flat as if, once again, he were in a deep sleep. Colin looked at the tech.

"Open his mouth, please."

The tech looked from him to Agent Smith, a bit bewildered.

She looked similar but nodded. "Do what agent Doe says, please."

Colin watched the technician as he reached both of his gloved hands to the man's jaw to pull it open. He couldn't help but notice the man's look of surprise as he put his fingers in the body's mouth and pulled the now blue lips apart. It was as if something normal had completely changed. Colin felt this was strange given the likely hundreds of dead bodies he had probably dealt with. "What is it?" he asked.

"Rigor mortis should have set in by now, which should be making the process of getting this man's mouth open more complicated. I've dealt with thousands of bodies in my time at the Bureau, and this is the only time I've seen a stiff so, well, loose."

Colin had never picked up on this before and suddenly found himself thinking back to the bodies in Afghanistan, trying to remember if they had been loose as well. He couldn't remember for sure. The technician peered inside and saw a crumpled up piece of paper. Carefully, he removed it from the mouth and began to pull its moist edges apart.

Witch came up to the man and reached out a blue-gloved hand. "I'll take that," he said before the technician could get it all the way open. The man handed it over begrudgingly, with a look that said he was clearly disappointed he didn't get to see what it said. The tech recovered his professional demeanor but still looked a bit indignant at having the note taken away. Taking out a flashlight from a small tool bag next to him, he pointed it inside the mouth. As Colin suspected, it revealed an empty cavern. The tongue had been cut out as well.

Colin stood up as the technician grabbed a camera and began photographing this new development. Agent Smith waved him into the kitchen and pulled him aside. "Are we dealing with some kind of serial killer here?" she asked.

"In a manner of speaking, yes," said Colin evasively.

This wasn't missed by Agent Smith. "Look, you can dodge my questions all you want, but there is no one better in the world at catching serial killers than the FBI. Your expertise may be stopping attacks, or whatever it is, but at least let me call in a team of experts so we can catch this guy."

Colin looked at her thoughtfully for a moment. "We have plenty of experience with this kind of thing, and as far as experts go, I have you."

Colin wasn't wrong. Agent Smith may have been young and beautiful, but her record spoke for itself. Her expertise was serial killings, and she had caught quite a few of them to date, which was the reason she was already a Special Agent in Charge, and also the reason she had been chosen. It had been Colin's choice who would be their liaison, and it was pure dumb luck that Agent Smith had been located in the area they would be operating in.

Colin wasn't quite ready to read her in yet, though. He wanted to gauge her reactions and take a measure of her before trusting her with more information. If there was indeed a compromise in the FBI, he couldn't be too careful when it came to operational security. Lives and the protection of the United States depended on it.

"I can't be of any help if I have no idea what's going on," she said.

"Look, Smith I—" Colin was cut off before he could finish his sentence.

"Hey, Boss, you need to check this out now," Witch called from the kitchen.

5

C olin stood with Witch in the kitchen, staring at the note that was carefully unfolded on the quartz countertop.

You have taken from us, and now it must stop. Five lives must die before the last tick of the day's clock. Unless what is set in motion ceases where power is struck with the stroke of a pen. All of this will happen again.

"He's changing his MO again," said Witch in a frustrated voice.

Colin continued looking at the note, not responding, lost in thought. This doesn't fit with what we know about Azrael, he told himself. Or at least what we thought we knew.

Every psychological workup they had done on the killer said he was a profoundly religious man who most likely sat most of the jihad in Afghanistan on the sidelines. For some reason, he was incapable or unwilling to fight. But he grew furious at those who were able to fight and gave up. The profile surmised that he was most likely a coward with deep personal trauma, likely sexual or violent in his past, and hated to see his cowardice reflected in others he deemed to be his heroes. It was his anger at seeing himself in his heroes that drove him to such acts, but his own personal trauma that executed them with such extreme violence. Religion seemed to be the convenient vale that framed the way he carried them out.

For all of this, though, Colin wasn't sure he agreed. The killer was too meticulous a planner, and there was too much evidence that he was carrying out these acts for Chinese Intelligence. This all screamed prior military experience to Colin, but there were a few sticking points in Colin's mind. The first was the way the acts were committed. Extreme violence could be a tool to send a message, but there was a difference between that and the downright gruesome atrocities the killer had committed. Professional intelligence services didn't typically hire unhinged assets and let them loose; it was sloppy.

The other thing that kept nagging at Colin was his sister Susan's death. He had put it out of his mind for so many years before he started trying to catch Azrael, but the similarities between the way she had been murdered and these incidents were too much to ignore. For all of that, though, he had no evidence of a link between the two. The memory of her death was fuzzy at best, having blocked it out for so many years. Now it only came in flashes of occasional nightmares that woke him in a cold sweat.

He had shared his theory, minus the details of his sister's death, with the team. Their leading hypothesis now was that the killer was an intelligence asset, but why they had hired such a meticulously gruesome asset, they still did not know.

"This fits with our working theory, though. He's clearly trying to send a message," he replied to Witch.

"The question is, what is the message? Usually, we get a verse or page from the Quran that reflects the sins of his victim," said Witch, crossing his arms.

Agent Smith chimed in, having clearly been listening to their conversation, "Well, it's definitely a warning, and even more than that, a taunt. He's telling us he is going to take five lives before today ends; he's daring us to stop him."

"That's all well and good; he knows we're after him, but he's changing his message, and we need to know why to catch him.

'Where power is written with the stroke of a pen' must mean Congress," said Colin, stroking the hair on his trimmed beard deep in thought.

"What would the Chinese want to stop in Congress?" asked Witch.

"There's nothing I can think of that's on the floor for a vote right now," replied Agent Smith.

"No, but tensions have been high as of late," said Colin. The group stood in silent contemplation for a moment, thinking. Colin keyed his earpiece and raised the team back at the hangar. "Charlie, Sarah, we're sending you a note we found on the senator from Azrael. We think it means they're trying to send a message to stop something in Congress. Run an analysis on the note and dig through any upcoming legislation that the Chinese government may want to stop. If you don't see anything blatant, dig into the intelligence and defense committees, there must be something going on."

A few seconds passed when he heard Charlie's voice reply, "You got it, boss. Have you found the senator's laptop yet?"

As if in reply, Sheriff came walking through the door of the kitchen with a MacBook in his hand. "Found it!"

Charlie's voice came back over their earpieces. "Good, turn it on and plug in Lockpick. I'll start receiving the data shortly."

Sheriff keyed his earpiece. "Roger that." He placed the laptop on the counter, opening it and powering it up. When the password screen appeared, Sheriff pulled what looked like an external hard drive from his backpack and plugged it into the USB-C connector on the laptop. Instantly, the screen went black, and Colin heard the fans begin to spin up on the computer. Lockpick was a top-secret NSA tool that had been developed over the last ten years. It worked using a combination of an advanced deep learning net and the world's smallest quantum computing chip, which, in layman's terms, could think circles around even the fastest commercially available computers before they could even start thinking.

"Receiving the data now," said Charlie.

"What is that?" asked Agent Smith.

Colin shot her a grin. "That's classified."

She gave him a look that said screw you, but Colin could tell she was still curious. She began walking over to the device to take a closer look, but Sheriff stepped in her way.

"How about you get your goon out of my way," she said.

"The goon stays," replied Colin. "It's just an external hard drive," he finished with a hint of playful boredom. She gave him another look that let him know how unimpressed she was with him.

"Hate to interrupt," Charlie chimed in. "I've got something."

"What is it?" asked Colin.

"There's a malware file hidden deep within the system archive. He must've downloaded it from an email attachment. He never would've known it was there, but it certainly knew everything he was doing. It looks like they could access his camera and microphone, as well as read all of his keystrokes. In short, they were spying on him," said Charlie.

"I got that much," replied Colin. "Just tell me they can't hear us right now."

"No, I disabled it. But I think you'll like what I have to say next even more. I traced where they're sending the data back, and I have a location for you; it's about a twenty-minute drive from the senator's townhouse."

"Where?" asked Colin.

"According to my IP trace, 800 F Street NW. And Colin, you'll never believe what that address is."

Colin was in the middle of a wrap it up and move out gesture to the team when he curiously replied, "What?"

"The old Spy Museum."

6

Team Alien had been driving for nearly thirty minutes. The progress was brutally slow as the two-Suburban convoy made its way closer to Chinatown through mostly empty streets. Snow was beginning to stick to the sidewalks, and gusts of wind kicked up small ice tornadoes on the black asphalt streets. It was remarkable how quiet the city could become when it snowed. What was less remarkable was the city's ability to handle even the slightest winter storm.

Snow preparedness goals for the plow crews in the city called for only 75 percent of main roads to be passable in snowfalls above eighteen inches within thirty-six hours, and nearly twice that time for side streets. This storm was projected to dump almost twice that amount on the nation's capital, and Colin shuddered to think what their operational tempo would slow to in these conditions.

The one good thing about this weather was that the streets were clear of civilians, and Colin expected the cover of the storm to aid them in keeping a low profile. He also thought it might make it more difficult for the bad guys to see them coming. The SUVs turned down another street, and Colin saw the thematic arches of China Town ahead through the falling snow.

"Three mikes out," he said into his earpiece. From a hip holster, he pulled his Colt M1911A1. The weapon had been heavily modified by special operations gunsmiths and came equipped with a custom grip that sported a laser targeting system, tritium night sights that were raised slightly to see over suppressors, and a Picatinny rail sporting a tactical flashlight. Colin dropped the magazine from the weapon to check that it was loaded and, once satisfied, reloaded it, placing the weapon back in its holster. Colin was a marksman by trade and preferred the heavier .45 caliber's stopping power and accuracy over more popular nine-millimeter alternatives.

The SUVs pulled up to the front of the museum, and the operators got out of them and immediately proceeded to the trunks to kit up with long guns. Typically, they wouldn't have been so blatant by parking out front of a target building, but there were no windows here, and time was of the essence. The team, including Colin, pulled suppressed MP7s with various modifications from cases in the trunk and filled their pockets with extra magazines.

The Spy Museum was a marvel of intrigue and experience, seamlessly blending both popular culture and the history of espionage. When the first iteration of it opened, it was hard to even get in the door, and the exhibits were always teeming with tourists and locals alike. But for all of its splendor, the museum was far too small to compete with the massive museums in D.C. Luckily, however, the museum made enough money to build a new state-of-the-art facility that was almost twice the size and offered even more in the way of thrills.

The old facility would, for the time being, serve as storage for old exhibits while the museum was fully transitioned to its new home. The windows were covered in paper, and large signs on the building told eager tourists to check them out in their new home at 700 L'enfant Plaza down the street. For all intents and purposes, this building was abandoned for now, or at least it seemed to be from the outside.

"Agent Smith, you and your partner will pull security on the vehicles and the front door while me and my team clear the building. Shoot anyone who comes out of the door who isn't wearing an FBI windbreaker," ordered Colin. Agent Smith began to pipe up in confusion almost as much as annoyance, but then she saw Jester unzip a duffle bag and begin to toss blue windbreakers with yellow FBI letters emblazoned on the back to his three teammates.

"I cannot allow you goons to run around shooting up the city, pretending to be FBI agents," she said, stepping forward.

"Who's pretending," said Jester, pulling a set of FBI credentials from his many pockets and holding them up to her face.

"We are whoever we need to be to get the job done, and I'm not arguing with you. Don't believe me? Check the bags," replied Colin, moving away and leading his team to the door.

Agent Smith walked up to the bag they had pulled the windbreakers from, too stunned and annoyed to care anymore. Inside was a smaller bag with dozens of sets of credentials from different law enforcement and intelligence agencies, all with different first names, and all with the last name Doe, like some kind of bad joke. Worse yet, they all appeared to be 100 percent legit.

Who the fuck are these guys?

Colin and his team stacked up on the door. He whispered to Sheriff, "Scan it." The man stepped out from behind them, pulling a large tactical-looking tablet from a backpack he had and ran it over the four sides of the door. The device was a micro x-ray scanner looking for explosive devices, and soon, Sheriff gave the OK signal to Colin, stepping back into the tactical stack at the door.

Colin pulled his pistol and screwed a suppressor on to the end of it. He listened for a second and waited for a particularly violent gust of wind. When it came, he pressed the trigger and shot the lock off of the door. The falling snow dampened the sound of the shot almost more than the suppressor did. He kicked the door and moved to the side so that the team could move in and clear the lobby. It took mere seconds for them to get inside, Colin following, having already holstered his sidearm, his MP7 up, and scanning for bad guys.

The lobby was mostly dark except for the glow of an emergency exit sign above the door they had just come through. The room was clear but a bizarre sight all in itself. It almost looked like the abandoned lobby of a movie theater, with a light box above a ticket counter that displayed the names of interactive exhibits instead of feature films. Except there were odd murals and quotes of spies painted on the walls. Colin took a second to assess the situation.

At the far end of the lobby, there were silver elevators, and to his left was the glass door of what looked to be an old gift shop. Colin knew elevators were a tactical no-go and that all museums tended to end in the gift shop. So he opted to proceed left through the gift shop. He signaled as much to the team, and they moved in that direction. It was odd to see a store with nothing in it, made even more creepy by the mannequins and the faint light coming through the brown paper over the windows. Empty off-white shelves filled the space, creating too many obstacles that bad guys could hide behind for Colin's liking.

They moved methodically through, clearing as they went. Colin could hear the intense wind outside gusting against the windows, its cold trying to penetrate the dark space they now moved through. This was eerie, Colin thought, as if no other word could describe their current environment. Like a startling clash between the world they really lived in and the commercially portrayed world of spies in movies.

They reached the other side of the gift shop and stacked up on the door to the next room. It was even darker in there because it lacked windows, unlike the gift shop. With the slightest signal, they proceeded swiftly into the next section, clearing a rectangular room with an exhibit space in the middle that no longer held anything. Colin decided to run point with a single tactical flashlight in order to minimize their target signature should a firefight ensue. He cursed the last-minute preparations for this trip. He was sure there were night vision goggles in their gear back at the hangar, but in their haste to get started, they had not brought them. He made a note to have Sarah bring them to the team the first chance she had. In the meantime, they would just have to make do.

They cleared room after room, all filled with empty facades and everything from fake houses and glass display cases to screens and even a car before finally seeing some light up ahead. It seemed to be an artificial blue light that came from a screen. They heard nothing except possibly the scurrying of rats in the mostly abandoned space. Colin clicked off his flashlight and proceeded forward, hearing the soft footsteps of his team behind him.

He did his best to mute his own footfalls, the soles of his Origin boots padding softly against the carpeted hallway. The faint, dull hum of the building's heating kicking on through the vents above them pierced the silence like a gunshot. The tension was palpable as they approached the room where the light was coming from. Finally, when they reached the entranceway at the end of the dark hallway, they saw a small work station had been set up among a sea of boxes. Power came from an orange extension cord running off into the darkness. Slowly, the team fanned out to secure the room while Colin and Sheriff approached the workstation.

Colin pulled security for him while he examined the station, keeping his Colt low and ready to meet any oncoming threats. He saw Sheriff once again take out the Lockpick Module and plug it into the computer tower located beneath the makeshift workstation. Colin chanced a whisper into his earpiece, "Charlie, plugging into a workstation now. Prepare for system download and analysis."

Charlie replied, "Copy that, boss. Waiting on our end."

A series of clicks in Colin's earpiece alerted him that the floor was clear of hostiles, and Jester's voice on the radio confirmed it. "Floor clear, boss. Should we chance some light?"

"Do it. Search the floor for any other signs of these guys and stay frosty." A few seconds later, a dim light came from the sealing as Jester turned up the dimmer switches at the other end of the room. "Elevator's over here," said Witch over the radio. Colin's eyes took a second to adjust to the new light. The space's complete lack of windows added precious seconds to this process, but immediately he noticed something was off. Lockpick was causing the computer's fans to spin up once again, which had made Colin look down in that direction.

Odd wiring ran over the back of the computer tower and up under the desk. A fingerprint scanner sat next to the keyboard. Sheriff seemed to notice something was off too because he stood up and backed slowly away from the computer, trying to get a better look under the desk it was on. A blinking popup on the computer screen caught their attention. A timer counting down from twenty seconds appeared with a fingerprint icon next to it.

It clicked in Colin's head just as Sheriff yelled, "Oh fuck! Everybody out now!" Everyone sprinted for the elevator as fast as they could, thinking a stairwell would be nearby. There wasn't. Witch, who had realized this, had instinctively hit the down button on the elevator as soon as he heard Sheriff's panicked yell. The team got to the door just as it opened and dove inside. Colin jammed his finger into the 'close door' button, praying it would close.

The detonator in the explosive ignited the RDX and PETN chemicals inside the Semtex explosive just as the elevator doors closed. An inferno of chemically accelerated high-explosive shockwave ripped through the floor of the building, blowing the elevator doors a foot inward and sending the elevator careening downward, where it slammed to a stop with the help of its emergency brakes on the lobby floor.

Agent Smith stood by the vehicles pulling security with a sour look on her face when the ground shook beneath her and several windows blew out on the building in front of her. Even the incredible storm all around them did little to hide the cacophonous explosion. She was momentarily stunned into inaction. Then fear came. She was worried that she had just lost the four operators she was tasked to work with. *What the hell am I involved in*, she thought, goose bumps prickling up her arms and anxiousness filling her stomach. When she recovered and regained her wits, she was about to charge into the building to see if anyone was still alive when the four operators emerged coughing, dazed and covered in soot, but otherwise unharmed with the exception of a few cuts and bruises.

"Are you okay?" she yelled through the wind.

It took Colin a second to respond. His ears were ringing, and everything seemed dead quiet to him now. "Fine," he said, taking deep breaths to steady himself.

"What the fuck happened?" she demanded.

Colin looked up to respond but noticed people peering out from apartments in the building across the street. "It looks like we were set up," replied Colin matter-of-factly, his composure coming back to him.

"Somebody just blew up an entire building in Washington D.C. trying to kill you," she said, as if trying to hammer some point home he was missing.

"Somebody knows we're here," said Jester, more to Colin than Agent Smith. "I doubt a regular FBI investigative team would have gotten that treatment," he finished. Colin nodded in agreement.

"I'm calling this in," said Agent Smith. "This is well past what we signed on for here. People are going to get killed." She began reaching for her phone.

"People are going to get killed if we don't figure out where these people are," said Colin. "And you're not going to call this in. We'll handle that." She looked irate, but Colin paid it no mind. "Charlie," he called into his earpiece.

"Yeah, boss? You guys okay?" he replied through his earpiece, having clearly seen the explosion from the drone feed overhead.

"Fine. Call in a gas explosion to the local authorities and make sure there is someone there who's friendly to hamstring any kind of investigation. It's going to be obvious to anyone who knows anything that that is not what happened."

"Roger that, boss," said Charlie. Colin yelled to the team over the wind. "Let's EVAC. Too many eyes on us here."

They got into the SUVs and prepared to take off, but Agent Smith refused to get in. Colin was annoyed, in a rush, and did not want to deal with someone so high minded right now.

"Agent Smith, I need you with us. Frankly, you're valuable in trying to catch this guy. But don't get me wrong, I will happily go way the fuck up my non-existent chain of command, find someone who asks way fewer questions, and leave your ass in the snow if you don't fall in line."

She stared at him for a minute and finally got in the SUV. Clearly fuming, she put the car in gear and started forward, the SUV sliding slightly on the accumulating snow as she went. Colin couldn't help but wonder what the hell he had gotten himself involved with either.

7

Team Alien had been driving for another twenty minutes when the convoy came around another corner and proceeded down another entirely empty street. Colin couldn't help but think they had nothing as they drove aimlessly past dark houses in the pale morning light. And if they had failed, innocent people were going to die. At least my ears have stopped ringing, he thought. Which was saying something given the size of the explosion at the Spy Museum they had just left behind. "Well, boss, what the hell—" Jester started, but Charlie came back over their earpieces and cut him off. "Boss, I've got something over here."

"What is it?" asked Colin in return.

"Before Lockpick was unceremoniously blown up, it started transmitting files back to us. Specifically, it started sending malware, which I've managed to isolate before it infected everything. I recognize some of the code. It's similar to the work of Kong, who is someone we've dealt with a few times now in Afghanistan." Colin remembered Kong as a Triad hacker they had run into several times now. He was almost definitely paid by Chinese Intelligence, but they had never actually caught up with him yet, as he usually operated inside China's borders.

"So alert another team and have them try and scoop him up," he said. "We can't grab him now, but at least we know this definitely involves China in the plot," he finished, catching a look of pure curiosity on Agent Smith's face.

"Hang on, boss, the signal to blow that computer didn't come from a timer—it was just meant to look like it did. Lockpick got in too fast to have triggered any kind of authentication alarm. In the files, I did get a line of command code that came from an external port that stuck out at me. It got bounced around using a pretty high-end VPN, but we've got some pretty awesome tech over here that can narrow in on that. It's actually pretty cool how it works. It—"

He cut him off. "Sounds cool, Charlie, but we're in a hurry, so can we get the quick version?"

"Sorry, boss. I'll put the nerd aside for a minute. The signal came from D.C. It's a building under construction in Navy Yard owned by a Chinese company called Zen Corp. that we think is a shell company for the Triads."

"Send us the address," said Colin, not believing this stroke of luck.

"What if it's another trap?" asked Agent Smith, making a U-turn and heading in the direction of Navy Yard.

"Traps are what we do, Agent Smith," he replied.

Twenty minutes later, they arrived at the building and Colin was wiggling the Mithril experimental body armor to make sure it was secured tightly to his chest. They were standing in a back alley, one warehouse over from the address Charlie had sent. The building they were supposed to be hitting had been under renovation for about a year and a half. This construction site was suspected of being an electronics-smuggling waypoint and had been under surveillance for quite some time. But today, all looked quiet in the ever-increasing snowfall.

There were two large bulldozers out front, as well as a crane and several dumpsters all in a row and piled high with scraps of wood, metal, and wire. The building itself was five stories and was supposed to become apartments when it was finished in another year. On the first walk around Colin and Jester had taken, they had seen no signs of any construction occurring today. Whether that was because of the snowstorm or because of illegal activities occurring, they weren't sure.

He and Jester stood at the back of the suburban, going over the building's plans on an iPad. They were taking a few extra minutes so as not to blindly walk into another trap.

"Now, these blueprints aren't up to date with the construction, so we have no idea what we're going to get when we go inside," began Colin. "From what Jester and I could tell on our walk around, there are only two entrances to the building currently accessible. One larger entrance in the front that has no doors is wide enough to drive a pickup truck through. The other entrance is around a corner, about a hundred meters away from the main entrance.

Now normally we'd scope this out a bit more, but because of the storm and the fact that we don't want this guy to have any warning that we're coming, we're doing it quietly by ourselves. So Witch, Sheriff, and Agent Sunderland, you guys are going through the side entrance and straight up this stairway to floor two to clear it." Colin said, pointing at a staircase on the blueprint.

"Myself, Jester, and Agent Smith will clear the first floor and rendezvous with you guys at this stairwell here on the other side of the second floor," he continued, tracing his way over to the other side of the building. "That is the only stairwell that goes up to the upper three levels. We'll then sweep the upper three levels together. You guys got it?" he asked.

After some debate over some minor details, the plan had been settled. He grabbed the MP7 out of the trunk of the SUV, dropped, and checked the magazine. He grabbed two extra magazines and added them to his pockets. All of his nerves from the day seemed to subside. This was what he was trained to do.

The clear earpiece in his ear chattered to life as Witch's voice came over it. "Everyone got me?"

Colin heard the other two respond, then responded in kind, "This is Snowman. Good to go."

Jester and Colin moved swiftly and quietly between the dumpsters, with Agent Smith trailing slightly behind them, her Glock-17 down in a low ready. The only sound was the whipping wind around their ears and the crunch of the snow beneath their boots. He peered around the fourth to last dumpster and saw the main entrance to the building. He signaled to Jester that the coast was clear, and they both continued to move. The snow was really starting to pick up now, colliding with Colin's face with greater frequency.

They finally turned the corner around the last dumpster and saw their door. It was approximately sixty meters in front of them. They continued moving quickly, his weapon trained on the door and Jester's up at the building. They reached the end of the dumpster and the gap between the buildings and realized there was no more cover. Jester trained his weapon down the gap while he bounded forward toward the building. When Colin made it to the building, he turned and covered Jester and Agent Smith as they came across. He called into his earpiece, "We're in position."

———

The boy's phone began to noisily vibrate on the metal table next to him. He was annoyed at the loud buzzing, as he had asked not to be disturbed. He was sitting on the second floor of a construction site on his laptop. Currently, he was listing credit card numbers for sale on the dark web. He cursed his handler's caution in not even being able to put him in a safe house on this mission. At least it was over now, and he was heading home.

Their plan had worked perfectly, and the American team of operators who had plagued their existence for months was now dead. The phone vibrated again, almost in unison with the dull hum of the space heater next to him. "Fuck," he cursed, reaching out and sliding the button on the ancient jailbroken iPhone to the side to answer the call.

"Kong, this is Dao. They haven't removed any bodies from the Old Spy Museum. And I just overheard the fire captain saying 'thank god there was no one inside,'" the man finished in a heavy Chinese accent. The eighteen-year-old of formidable build, extreme intelligence, and excellent training in martial arts hit the end button on the call and stood up.

"Let's go—we're leaving now," he said to the two burly-looking Chinese men playing cards at a table across the room. He feared capture by the American team in the event they were still alive. Worse yet, he knew if they were still alive that the legendary hacker working with them, known by his screen name Wonka84, had likely already figured out where he was.

Witch had just communicated back that they were a go, and Colin turned the corner, bringing his MP7 up, scanning for targets. He moved quietly into the large entrance, checking his corners as he went. Jester moved on his left, scanning the opposite side of the building as they moved deeper inside. About twenty feet in, he noticed that there was a white Range Rover Evoque with its front covered by a brown tarp that made it invisible to the outside. He was about to communicate with Witch to tell him that they had located a vehicle when his radio crackled in his ear. "Snowman, this is Witch. The staircase on the blueprint no longer exists. We're moving to you now."

He was going to respond when he looked over his head. The second floor above him had been cut away, likely to make a large, elegant atrium. The second floor began again, about eight feet from his current position next to the Range Rover. He looked over at Jester and brought his finger up to his lips, motioning for him to be silent. He listened very closely to the open floor above him. He heard a hurried movement that sounded like packing.

Colin saw Jester looking at the open floor above him and heard the noises as well. They closed the rest of the distance to him, and he motioned for them to head up the stairs at the far end of the building. The team moved silently to the stairwell, careful not to disturb the slightest of objects that might alert their targets to their presence. They reached the stairwell, and Colin went first, moving sideways up the stairs, his weapon trained above him. He finished moving up the first set, turned left, and continued the rest of the way up, moving slower this time. He was unsure what he would find at the top but was relieved to see a slightly closed-off area with an open door.

The team finished up the stairs and stacked up outside the door. Colin stole a quick peek around the corner and saw the three men. He turned to the team and motioned to them that there were three men, two of them armed. The team nodded, and Witch pulled a flash-bang. Colin smiled and nodded, happy that someone had come prepared. Colin nodded at the team, and they nodded back, acknowledging they were ready.

Kong looked over to see what had noisily clattered to the ground in between the two other men. He was annoyed that one of them would carelessly drop an expensive piece of computing equipment. Before he could even finish the thought, however, a large flash and an immense noise deafened him and stunned his vision. He staggered back, knowing in his head what had happened.

The effect of the device was sensory overload, meaning that the amount of light that the flash emitted and the decibel level of the sound that occurred literally overloaded one's ability to perceive what had happened. He turned and tried to run away toward the balcony, but tripped over his own feet and fell hard on his face. The fall helped to shake the effect slightly, and he could see better now. He hoisted himself to his feet in an instant and ran toward the opening to the first floor.

The team burst through the opening. "FBI! Get the fuck down on the ground!" Agent Sunderland screamed. The two larger men were holding their heads in agony, clearly completely stunned. Both saw the team and raised weapons. They didn't get far—shots came from both Jester and Sheriff, making two smoking round holes appear in each of their heads and blood spray everywhere.

"Fucking stop! Don't move another inch!" Colin screamed, his weapon aimed at the younger Chinese man who had just fallen. Realizing the boy wasn't going to stop, he went racing after him. Colin was quickly gaining on the subject when he jumped from the ledge.

"Shit!" Jester yelled, beginning to chase after the pair of them. He heard the boy land on top of the Range Rover, not seconds before he cleared the ledge as well. He briefly, while in the air, thought about how stupid of an idea it had been to jump before slamming onto the top of the vehicle.

He snapped out of the pain of landing on the car just in time to hear the car door close and the engine start. Fuck, he thought, not good. He heard a slight shift, and all of a sudden, the wheels began to spin out in the dirt. The car lurched forward with incredible speed and power. The brown tarp flew up, catching on his head momentarily before flying off in the wind behind him. The snow and freezing air whooshed past his face as the car exited the warehouse and made its way outside. He grabbed on to anything he could as the boy desperately swerved, trying to throw him from the top of the vehicle.

The bright white of the outside temporarily blinded Colin as he tried to think of a way to stop the SUV. Snow careened past his face, catching his open eyes. The Range Rover hit a large bump and threw him up in the air. He landed another foot back on the car, his legs now dangling off of the back of it. He reached out, his Oakley Pilot Glove–clad hands trying desperately to pull himself forward. The force of the wind and kinetic energy of the car's motion, however, were too much for the little grip he had on the car's smooth top.

Colin looked forward and realized that the car would have to slow down to make the sharp right turn to exit the lot. If he timed it right, he could slide forward. The car accelerated again, making it more and more difficult for him to hold on. The car leveled out its speed momentarily, and he used the opportunity to grab his MP7 from its sling around his back and bring it forward. He flipped the selector switch to full auto and tried to dig the handle into the top of the car to give him more grip.

They were approaching the turn, and he prepared to make his move. He lifted the weapon at the precise moment of the slowdown and began to slide forward. Aiming the MP7 at the engine block, he fired a sustained burst as quickly as he could before using the force of the turning car to throw himself off of the side into a hopefully soft snowbank.

Colin slammed into the pile of wood covered in snow just as the Range Rover lost control and hit the side of another building. Everything seemed momentarily quiet as the deafening rush of wind had stopped with his sudden departure from the car. Rolling off the pile of lumber in extreme pain, he attempted to get to his feet. He ran as quickly as he could to the crashed SUV, drawing his pistol as he went. As he did, the door opened and out staggered the boy, bleeding from a small but significant cut to his head. He was clearly ready for a fight, however. He was sick of this kid and wanted to beat the shit out of him for trying to kill him. He took a deep breath to calm himself, feeling the pain in his back from the collision.

"Fuck you!" yelled the boy as he charged forward. He thought about shooting him but decided first that it would be bad to kill their only lead in the investigation, and second that the gun barrel was likely loaded with snow from his recent fall. He quickly holstered the weapon and brought up his hands. He was in a defensive stance and ready. Colin had been trained extensively in hand-to-hand combat in the special forces. He even did side training to improve his skills. He was an expert in Jujitsu, Krav Maga, and Systema, three combat systems beloved by special forces operators around the world. One for body control, the other for practical rapid killing blows, and the final for smooth flowing attacks.

The boy threw his first blow, and Colin violently swept it away with his left arm. He then stepped back to create space between him and his attacker. The boy charged once again and threw another series of punches that he blocked in kind. The boy's mistake came when he attempted to throw a kick, which Colin had anticipated. He caught the kick between his left arm and body and threw a hard punch into the boy's right eye. He fell backward and quickly scrambled up.

He seemed more unsteady now to Colin, so he decided to strike. He moved in with incredible speed and precision, allowing the boy to punch, which he correctly judged would put him off balance. Instantly, he gave a hard kick to his lower back, dodging the punch at the same time, sending the boy falling forward. He wasted no time in tackling him as he was falling in mid-air. He put one knee in the small of the boy's back, effectively immobilizing him. Grabbing both of his arms, he wrenched the boy's hands behind his back and bound them with riot cuffs. He stood up out of breath just as Jester and the rest of the team came bounding up next to him.

"Holy shit, you all right?" asked Witch.

"I'll be fine," he panted. "Just get this fuck ready for transport. It's time to get some answers."

8

The man sat hooded on the loading dock while torrents of snow cascaded down around him. He was tall, well over six feet, but one would scarcely know this because few people ever looked at him long enough to know this. His baggy, nondescript clothing hid his muscled frame, and the lid of the baseball cap he wore hid his empty eyes. Small snowbanks formed in the creases of his clothing, but he remained still. There was a serene sense of calmness in the silence of the snow for him.

He marveled at the fact that anything so chaotic could be at such peace with itself and smiled a dark internal smile, as if comparing himself to the blizzard around him. He pulled the small wooden pocketknife that he had acquired so many years ago from his pocket. He rubbed his thumb over the small engraving toward the hilt. The letters *J.S.* brought back memories from another life, from another him. He flicked the knife open and pulled up his sleeve. He felt a sudden flash of anger that the snow muted the sound of the blade moving against the wooden handle.

He placed the blade back into the hilt and flicked it open again next to his ear. This time he heard it and felt intense satisfaction as the old blade moved against the worn wood. Slowly, he touched the tip of the knife to his inner arm. He worked the blade deliberately in a circle, applying all of the pressure of the tip at one point in the skin. A hole began to open in his skin.

Blood ran down his arm in fast-flowing crimson rivers. The pain was an intense satisfaction to him, marking a new target in his deadly game. When the kill was complete, a line would go through the circle carved by the same old knife. It allowed him to savor the fear and pain of his victims for hours and sometimes even days. He looked at the rest of his arm as he pulled the lighter from his pocket. Flicking it on, he began heating the edge of the blade. He loved to look at the massive number of scars covering his arm. It made him feel an intense sense of power. The blood that continued down his arm was now dripping into the snow. When the knife began to glow orange, he extinguished the lighter and pressed the searing hot blade to the red circle. The pain was immediate, and he gasped out loud as it shot up his arm almost in an equal amount of pleasure and agony. Soon, he would come for them. Soon, this circle too would be complete.

The pieces on his chessboard had been placed masterfully. His employer's orders would be accomplished on schedule, of course. More importantly, though, his legacy would continue to grow as he satisfied his deep-seated need to free people from their earthly bonds —by sending them to the afterlife.

9

Colin had never thought in his wildest dreams that they would throw a black bag over someone's head and render them to a secret site inside the United States. Much less that they would have done it a few blocks away from Capitol Hill. The team would have preferred to interrogate the Chinese hacker at the construction site, but there was too much of a chance that the gunfire would have attracted unwanted attention. Rather than stay, Jester had secured the hacker, and the team had left the area again as quickly as possible.

They were now in a government safe house several blocks away from the shootout after having once again anonymously called in to report trouble in the area they had left. The stealth surveillance drone Charlie had up over the city had reported that both areas now had official authorities at them, but the response seemed extremely slow and subdued due to the storm.

The hacker was zip-tied to a chair in the center of the room with a black bag over his head. A pair of headphones was over his ears, blasting death metal to keep him disoriented from his surroundings. Technically, what they were doing was beyond illegal, and Agent Smith had let them know this from the look on her face and her tightly crossed arms in the kitchen. The team, however, was unbothered by her silent protest.

Witch, who had spoken very little since the day had started, was busy taking vitals from the Chinese hacker. He was a medium height black bald man with an intense, almost evil look about him. Most people they dealt with had no idea his given codename was supposed to be ironic, because he was considered by many to be one of the kindest people they had ever met. But the man had a switch that turned on a dime when dealing with bad people.

He had actually received his codename from a German GSG 9 operator who, during an interrogation, had remarked that he reminded him of the witch from Hansel and Gretel, luring them in with candy, then trying to cook and eat the children. The name had stuck, and to his credit, he had embraced it without hesitation.

When he had taken a few notes on the hacker's vitals, he opened a black plastic case and injected something into the boy's arm. Colin watched impassively as Witch worked, his arms crossed as he took everything in.

"Enjoying the show?" Colin heard Jester ask Agent Smith.

"What's he injecting him with?" she asked in return.

"Truth Juice," he replied matter-of-factly.

"Sodium pentothal is considered a human rights violation," she began, flaring up again.

Jester cut her off, smiling. "Nah, that's old school, Smith. In case you haven't noticed, you're running with the new school now."

Colin could tell by the look on her face that she knew she wasn't going to get anywhere with him. "You're enjoying this, aren't you?"

"Shit, I've got the best job in the world. Private jets, guns, shooting bad guys, and hot girls. I'm practically the American James Bond," he said with a wink at her. She took it in stride as typical male operator ego and was more annoyed than offended. Just as she was about to reply, Colin responded to Jester, taking his eyes off of the working Witch.

"Maybe more like the American Austin Powers,"

"You know, boss, I'll take that title happily."

Witch interrupted. "Good to go, boss. We can start when you're ready." Colin nodded back.

Witch walked up to the hacker with a lamp and shined it right at the eyes of the hood. He placed it down and pulled the headphones off the hacker's ears. He then ripped the black bag off, and Kong blinked, wildly rolling his head around, disoriented.

"Where am I?" he demanded in a thick Chinese accent. Witch wound up with a cupped hand and slapped him hard over his right ear. The hacker reeled in pain, whimpering and dizzy from the blow to his equilibrium.

Witch grabbed him by the chin and straightened his head. "Listen to me, and I won't hurt you again." The boy's head continued to roll, and his eyes kept blinking wildly. "I need you to understand me. Is your name Kong Chang?"

The boy looked up defiantly. Witch wound up as if to slap him again, and the boy nodded in fear. Agent Smith started forward as if to stop what was going on, but Colin grabbed her shoulder and kept her where she was.

"Now I need you to listen to me, Kong. Did you feel me inject something into your arm a minute ago?" The boy nodded again. Colin saw the boy was sweating profusely, which seemed odd as it was still very cold in the safehouse, but Colin knew Witch had something special in store for the boy.

"That was a mixture of tetrodotoxin and a cocktail of various other chemicals that are degenerative nerve agents. Now, I'm short on time, so we skipped all the truth serums and other bullshit. This compound has one very simple use. It chemically burns every nerve in your body and eats away at the fluid in your spinal cord. Over the course of the next ten minutes, it will slowly but permanently paralyze you for the rest of your life, unless I administer the antidote. Now, in order to receive that antidote, you need to answer my questions honestly and quickly."

The hacker didn't say anything, and Witch pulled out his cellphone and turned it around so he could see it. The timer read seven minutes and thirty seconds. He started squirming uncontrollably and begging for the antidote. This hacker, really more of a young twenty-something boy, was no soldier. He did this for the money. The fact that his country was the one that was paying it was really more of a coincidence to him.

Agent Smith started forward again, outraged that this would happen. This was no less than torture, and she intended to stop it. Colin grabbed her and forcefully led her back to the kitchen as Witch began to ask questions. They could hear the hacker blubbering speedy answers all the way back to the kitchen and out the rear door of the house where the SUVs were parked. Agent Sunderland stood guard over the vehicles, brushing snow off the windshields every few minutes.

"You need to stop this right now. Administer him the antidote, and we will take him back to a real facility and break him," she demanded.

"Calm down," Colin said. "He's in no danger at all."

"You're melting his fucking nerves and paralyzing him forever— don't give me that fucking bullshit. You and your team are on a fucking rampage through this city, shooting everything in sight and breaking laws that I don't even think they've fucking written yet. This is America, not some backwater shithole across the world where you can do whatever you want. Give him the antidote and give him to us, and we will take and break him the proper way."

"That's not going to happen, Agent Smith. And for your information, Witch was lying to him. The compound he administered was niacin, which people use to clear toxins like drugs out of their bloodstream to beat drug tests, and something to make him feel nervous. It burns just enough to make him scared, and the nervousness-inducing drug makes it seem way worse. The only danger that kid is in is passing his state administered drug test, or at the worst, Witch slapping him across the head again."

Colin paused for effect, hoping he didn't need to explain himself to Agent Smith anymore. Part of the reason he had been chosen to lead Team Alien was his patience and diplomatic skills. Echo Teams were all the same in that sense. They generally operated so far outside of the bounds of legality that when they were brought in to interact with government agencies or military units, they very often needed someone to keep everyone's heads cool, mission oriented, and not to get lost in the bureaucracy they were brought in to circumvent in the first place.

He could tell from the look on her face that she didn't feel wrong, but she didn't feel like she was in the right, either. Now that she was out of the immediate situation, it seemed highly unlikely that they would have administered some far-fetched, most likely fake, torture drug to a twenty-something-year-old computer geek.

The gears behind her eyes were turning and Colin could tell she was starting to think that she might not have an accurate picture of who she was dealing with when he heard someone shout an obscenity from inside and heard a loud bang! Immediately, gunshots began to echo from the front of the house. They were unsuppressed, so Colin knew immediately they weren't from his team. Agent Smith went to race back into the house, but Colin grabbed her shoulder again. "No! Follow me."

They raced around the side of the house up a narrow alley and bounded for the front. Colin was happy to hear the retort of at least one silenced weapon as they went. Someone was firing back. It had sounded like a flash bang to Colin, and he hoped that his team was stunned but okay. He crouched in the snow behind a set of metal trashcans near the front of the alley, his Colt M1911A1 at a low ready to begin engaging hostiles. Agent Smith stood behind him, and Agent Sunderland pulled security at the back of the alley, protecting the vehicles from any other possible assault.

Colin poked his head around the wall. He saw at least ten bad guys, all dressed in black with balaclavas and assault rifles and firing into the house. At least three of them saw him, and Colin just got his head back behind the brick wall when a hail of 7.62 mm rounds slammed into the bricks of the brownstone next to the safehouse. He flattened himself against the wall. *Fuck, bad positioning,* he thought. *We're going to get smoked if we stay here.*

"Ten hostiles heavily armed with AKs!" he yelled to Agent Smith. He pivoted out from the wall at a low crouch and fired four controlled shots, two for each and in rapid succession. "Two down!"

he yelled back as another storm of bullets impacted the wall behind him. He knew he needed to do something and quickly. If they didn't regain the tactical advantage, they were all going to lose their only lead, and worse yet, they were probably all going to die. There was only one thing to do.

"Cover me!" he yelled to Smith over the deafening fire from the assault rifles. She nodded at him and button-hooked around the wall, keeping low. He heard the sound of her Glocks magazine being emptied as he bounded forward out of the alley and toward a parked car on the street. Her gun fell silent just as he dove for the rear tire well of the Honda sedan. He hoped it was because her weapon had run dry and not because she had taken a bullet. In any event, he didn't have time to think more deeply about this as rounds began slamming into the sedan and the car windows shattered above him. He popped up and fired three rounds into the closest attacker before ducking to reload and reengage.

Just then, he heard tires spinning out on ice and snow and turned his head around the car just in time to see two Sprinter vans taking off down the street. One body lay in the few inches of snow on the street, blood oozing from a headshot into the white snow. The other two Colin hit must have gotten into one of the vans wounded. He thought about engaging the vans as they drove away but remembered they were in a neighborhood, and there was too much risk that there were kids playing in the snow somewhere down the street.

He looked back at Agent Smith. "You all right?" he asked. He doubted she had been in very many firefights in her time at the FBI. Today, she had already been in two. She nodded, out of breath from the sudden and rapid exertion. "Go check on Sunderland," he ordered, pointing down the alley. It was best to keep moving and not think too much when you were new to this level of violence. She complied, running down the alley. Colin ran over to the body of the fallen attacker and kicked the weapon away from his hand. While he went to check him for pocket litter or anything else he may have, he communicated with the team. "Everyone all right?" he asked.

Jester replied, "We're whole, but the kid's gone. They grabbed him right out from underneath us."

Fuck, Colin thought.

They had just lost their only lead and had nothing else to go on. Their only hope was that they had gotten something out of him before he was taken.

10

Capitol Hill Neighborhood

The fire danced and crackled on the old, worn bricks of the fireplace in Senator Marks study. The two large windows which looked out onto a pleasant garden in the back seemed almost dark in the dim morning light. Thick snow squalls fell past them and joined millions of other flakes accumulating beneath the windows. The firelight played off many old leather books and an old-looking mahogany desk in the corner. Two smartly wrapped green leather armchairs sat before the fire, and in one of them was Senator Marks.

She was an older woman in her mid-sixties with short-cropped gray hair and a slight build. Her house usually smelled of good southern cooking and was a happy place. Today, however, was different. It was scarcely eleven in the morning, and already, a glass of bourbon sat on the table next to her. The cheerful Christmas decorations that hung about the house looked downright gloomy with the mood she was casting about them.

A particularly loud pop from the fire made her jump, and she reached for the glass of bourbon next to her again. Her close friend, Senator Carson, had been savagely murdered this morning. The committee was monitoring the Echo Team's investigation closely, but she was fearful of reprisal at this point.

The note which they had found in the senator's mouth was seared into her brain. She loved America, but the thought of being martyred by a psychopath carving up senators didn't appeal to her. Senator Carson had been a mentee of hers since he was a junior senator, and she thought of him almost like one of her children.

Her children were coming into town later this week to spend the holidays with her. They were now grown up with kids of their own who adored their grandmother. She secretly wished they were here now. They might help to make the empty house feel safer. She had guards, of course—two Capitol Police officers assigned to protect her. She usually wasn't high-ranking enough to merit protection, but two had been assigned after the other senator had been murdered. One was currently in the kitchen of the house, sipping coffee, while the other was walking the exterior of the house, checking for any abnormalities. Occasionally, she heard them checking in with each other from her study. She felt happy they were there, but she wasn't sure she felt any more secure. They were strangers to her. Quite capable, she was sure, but strangers nonetheless.

A shadow darkened the faint light coming from one of the windows. Slightly drunk and very distracted, she barely even noticed. She figured it was either the snow or the other Capital Police officer outside. Taking another sip of bourbon, she stared deep into the fire, thinking once again of her family and her friend Senator Carson, whose life was extinguished so violently.

Officer O'Malley finished his cup of coffee and walked back to the pot to get some more. The senator's kitchen smelled of the rich, dark roast from a local coffee shop down the street. It was good, and he was happy it was better than the shit coffee they usually had on protection details. While he filled his mug up, his radio chimed. "All clear out here. Heading back in through the front." It was his partner,

Officer Pelerito, who had just finished doing a sweep of the property. O'Malley decided to radio back in a situation report to command. He had no idea why the senator had merited protection so last minute and during this massive snowstorm, but she must have been receiving threats in the mail or something.

"Command, this is protection two-six," he said, using their anonymized protection detail code number. "All is clear here and is proceeding normally."

His orders were to report to command every hour. Per protocol, they swept the outside of the house every hour as well. Officer Pelerito and he had been rotating walking the perimeter in the snow every hour. He hated weather like this, originally being from Virginia Beach. It never snowed here, and that was why he lived here.

Every time it did, work turned into a nightmare. It was very likely they wouldn't even get relieved today because the rotating team wouldn't be able to get here. It was incredible how incompetent the local government was when it came to snow. A few inches could paralyze the city for days. A few feet, though... O'Malley wasn't sure if he wanted to know how long it would take for the roads to be clear. At least they had been assigned an SUV out of the motor pool today.

He heard the front door open and close again. "How many inches do you think we have so far, Nick?" he asked Pelerito. No response. He figured he was just shaking the snow off and hanging his jacket up near the door, but walked over to check on him, looking down the hallway toward the senator's study as he went. All seemed clear. When he got into the hall to check on Pelerito, his stomach sank, the blood drained from his face, and the hair instantly stood up on the back of his neck. There was no one there.

He reached for his weapon in a flash, turning around as he went to go down the hallway toward the senator's study. This is very wrong, he thought. Raising the gun, he moved quickly down the hall, radioing Pelerito as he went. "Pelerito, where the fuck is—"

A dark figure leaped out of the dining room with incredible speed, driving a six-inch blade into his throat as he went. O'Malley never even got a shot off as he fell to the floor, dying, blood spurting from his neck onto the chestnut hardwood floor. The shock kept the pain at bay. His vision began to fade, and he felt the warm blood pooling around his ear. All he could see were a set of wet footprints he had missed leading from the front door down the hallway and the coldest eyes staring dead into his.

The senator heard a dull thud in the hallway. "Mike?" she called, using Officer O'Malley's first name. No response. She sat up a little straighter, listening, and then stood to see what had happened. There in the dark hallway stood a figure dressed all in black. A black baseball cap was positioned low over his eyes, so all she could see was a wide, deranged-looking smile with yellow teeth. Fear took her, for she knew death stood at her door. "Mike!" she yelled again. The man's smile vanished, and he shook his head slowly from side to side. The senator ran to her desk to grab the landline she still kept there. She picked it up to call for help, but the steady beep, beep, beep told her the line was dead.

She looked up at the man standing there. Her heart rate quickened, and her hands began to shake. The sudden realization that the bourbon she had consumed was slowing her responses made her even more upset at her own weakness. She was trembling as she put the phone receiver back down on its cradle. Her fear was palpable, and he seemed to savor this, slightly cocking his head to the side as if he were a dog trying to understand a child. She screamed at him, "What do you want?"

He did nothing, continuing only to stare. She cursed the fact that she didn't keep the cellphone her granddaughter always wanted to FaceTime on closer to her. It was useless in her purse in the kitchen. She took four steps to the table where her glass of bourbon lay. Picking it up, she hurled it across the room at him.

It missed and broke into pieces, splattering it and him with the remnants of her drink. This seemed to infuriate the man instantly. He crossed the room in three quick, powerful strides, picking her up by the neck with one hand and lifting her into the air. She tried to resist, kicking and desperately grabbing at his hand wrapped around her throat, but there was nothing she could do in the face of his strength. He slammed her down onto her back with a righteous fury, and the world as she knew it went dark.

He was angry, so furious that she had done that. That she had dared to mess up his killing ground. His obsessive-compulsive disorder flared him into action. He would have to clean up the mess to preserve the scene.

All in good time, he told himself, trying to calm down. He took a deep, calming breath, closing his eyes and envisioning what needed to be done.

For now, he needed to reap his reward, to cross off another circle on his arm, to take from her everything. He went to work, doing his usual to her. Leaving her looking peaceful but for the terrible carnage done to her. Leaving the message that his masters had requested. Then he cleaned up the bourbon staining the wall and disposed of the glass.

He left satisfied, having taken three more victims. I will have to take at least one more, he thought. Odd numbers infuriated him to no end. However, he was confident he would have a plethora of souls to take by the end of the day. Two of these people had been inconsequential collateral damage, nothing he could help, and more for his employers to deal with than for him. But the senator, she had been everything he needed to keep the rush going.

11

"What a fucking nightmare," Colin said to no one in particular, shaking his head. It was midday now, and the thick snow clouds made it seem as if it was just about night outside. Six inches of snow had fallen so far, and the storm seemed to be only getting worse. An alarm had gone out from central dispatch when the Capitol Police team guarding Senator Marks had failed to report an hour ago. The storm slowed Capitol Police response times considerably, though, and gave Charlie enough time to route the team to the senator's house before additional units could arrive.

"Charlie, we didn't exactly have time to get a lot out of him before we got hit by the Chinese," Colin argued over his earpiece.

"I know, but I need more to go on than that. It would be one thing if Kong were a part of 61398. I'd have more of an idea of their plans and capabilities. But he's not," Charlie said, referring to the well-known Chinese People's Liberation Army Unit 61398, which was responsible for many of the world's most significant cyber-attacks.

"This kid wasn't a soldier. He's a hacker who was in it for the money. I know it's not a lot to go on, but if anyone can do it, it's you.

"To be clear, all you got out of him besides that he was working for the Chinese government and that there was some plot going on was his username to his laptop and half of his password."

"Roger that," replied Colin.

Charlie sighed. This is why he had sent them into the field with Lockpick. It would have cracked the laptop in seconds. But in typical Team Alien fashion, it had been blown up only hours into their mission. "I'll send Sarah to meet you and pick it up."

The team rolled up to Senator Marks's house a few minutes later. Colin stepped out of the SUV and down onto an unplowed street. In front of him were two Capital Police SUVs. One stood empty the other had a middle-aged officer with curly gray hair and rosy red cheeks standing outside of it attempting to call something into his radio which didn't appear to be working.

Colin knew Charlie was jamming radio and cell phone communication within a hundred-yard radius of the team. Colin did a once over of the house and took in its gray stone Victorian façade, with ivy growing up its front. It was large, but not in an ostentatious sort of way that said someone powerful lived here. It almost looked cheerful in the snow, but he had a feeling that what they would find here was anything but. He and Agent Smith walked over to the Capitol Police Officer, Agent Smith flashing her credentials as they went. The man looked weary. "Who are you?" he asked.

"My name is Agent Smith. I'm with the FBI. Where are the other men guarding the senator?"

"Dead," he said frankly, "and so is the senator. I've been trying to call it in, but I think the storm is screwing with my radio and cell reception, and the other units that are supposed to be here haven't shown."

"Have you cleared the house and perimeter yet?" Colin asked.

The man turned to him and gave him a "who the fuck are you" look and said, "Yeah, I did. One of my guys is down in the back, one in the entrance hallway, and the senator in her study. I've never seen anything like it. Fucking brutal."

Colin turned to the team behind him and pointed at the house. "Clear it."

The team took off, splitting into two elements. Witch and Sheriff went into the house—room-clearing was best done in pairs—and Jester took the perimeter.

"Hey, that's an active fucking crime scene," said the officer, flaring up.

"What's your name, officer?" asked Colin.

"Lieutenant John Mazetti."

"You're a bit high ranking to be in the field, aren't you?" inquired Colin.

"I live near here and was off for the storm. They called and asked if I could come and check it out. Want to tell me why you're here now? 'Cause I'm pretty sure I didn't call the FBI."

Agent Smith went to answer, but Colin cut her off. "We're with the FBI's Counterintelligence Directorate. We're investigating the threat on the senator's life and got a tip about an hour ago that it may have been more credible than we thought. We were coming to ask the senator some questions," Colin said, only half lying.

"If you're with the CD, then that means a foreign government is involved. Shouldn't we have been informed about something like that?"

"The higher-ups were informed, hence the extra security. But the details of our investigation are highly classified. What I'm about to tell you is even more top secret."

Colin made a mental calculation that this guy could be useful to them. He had no skin in the game, and Colin felt it was a fairly sure bet that he wouldn't have been involved in the conspiracy if he hadn't even been working on the day it was enacted. He also knew that the Capitol Police were one of the few law enforcement agencies that reported directly to Congress, not the Department of Justice. "There's a mole inside the U.S. government suspected to be very high up in the Justice Department. We're operating outside the bounds of the traditional hierarchy here to stay off the radar of this person. We believe the Chinese are working with this mole, and that they are the ones behind the attack on Senator Marks."

"Interesting theory, but I did twelve years as a homicide cop on the Metro PD before this, and I ain't never seen anything like what I saw in there. That wasn't some regular hit. The scumbag might have made our guys look like that. But the senator. That was something darker."

"Show us," said Agent Smith.

The three walked into the house and found Witch and Sheriff already photographing the bodies. Jester pulled security at the front with Agent Sunderland. The house was well appointed with dark wood finishes and the kind of elegant touch that only someone of classical taste could project.

They walked down the hall to the study, pausing briefly to examine the officer down in the hallway. Blood had pooled around the man's body, emanating from what appeared to be a knife wound to his neck. He was on his side, and the team did not turn him over to check. Colin studied Mazetti's face. There was a reverence there for his fallen colleague. He may not have known the man personally, but he was a fellow officer, and that meant something more profound to him.

Colin followed them down the hallway to the study, which was warm and filled with books and good bourbon. Before he even got two steps into the room, he could smell bleach coming from the wall. "Do you smell that?"

Agent Smith responded to Colin, "Yeah, maybe he cleaned DNA evidence of himself up before he left. It would make sense if there were a struggle."

They entered the room and saw that the fireplace gave the place an eerie glow. It became even eerier when Colin saw the senator's body on the ground. Once again, the victim looked calm and peaceful, except for the utter carnage done to her. She lay there positioned as if sleeping with her arms crossed, but her eyes, or lack thereof, stood as open, empty holes. A deep red line ran from ear to ear under her chin and looked exceedingly fresh, but no blood seeped from the wound. The hair at the rear of her head seemed matted. Colin knelt to examine it and noticed the hair was slicked with blood. He had left his gloves on and reached for her mouth to pull it open to see what the killer had left.

Mazetti began to move forward as if in protest, but Agent Smith put a hand on him to slow him down. Whether that was out of some newfound respect for him or pure curiosity at what the killer had to say, Colin wasn't sure. "What does it say?" Smith asked him. "He's taunting us."

12

17 Years Before

Susan Frost had found something. She wasn't even quite sure what it was yet; she just knew it was out of place. Her time spent working for the Assistant U.S. Attorney for D.C. so far had been productive, but it had also been grueling. It was exciting work, and she had been honored to have been given the opportunity. Her work had been more on local cases, with only a few years of law school under her belt. But the AUSA's office in D.C. was an exciting place to be. It was unique in that it was both a federal and local law enforcement arm. One day they could be handling murder, and another day they could be taking on a vast and far-ranging criminal conspiracy.

Susan, for her part, was a volunteer, having little more status than an intern, but being personally brought in by the boss did give her a certain level of freedom. She had a passion for helping missing women who were abused. Specifically, she wanted to help women who had disappeared, and foul play had been suspected. These were cases where a neighbor or friend had noticed something off, and when they called law enforcement, they found lots of evidence but no body. They couldn't prosecute without a body.

She spent her time deep within the archives in the third level basement of the old building, flipping through old yellowed pieces of paper in files that hadn't been touched in years. When she had told her boss that she wanted to help these women, he had directed her to the archives and gave her a binder that listed hundreds of cold cases divided out by category.

There were hundreds of missing women over the last forty years or so, and dozens of these cases had never been solved. At first, she had marveled at how the justice system could have failed so many, but the more she read, the more she understood. Some of these cases were so rambling, she wasn't even sure if there was a crime. It seemed to her that many of the women had just up and left their husbands, leaving all traces of their old lives behind.

Still, some of the cases were different. Violent relationship histories, abusive husbands, and condemning evidence found by investigators. All culminating in no arrest...

She had taken her time combing through the various files listed in the binder. Her hope was to choose a few and interview the people involved. Maybe uncover something investigators had missed when the cases were still new, or perhaps find that someone involved had gotten sloppy. Now she sat with her back against a filing cabinet slumped onto the floor, furiously flipping pages in an old file.

A stack of other files sat on the metal table in front of her, and with a start, she jumped off of the floor and ran over to them. She urgently rifled through the files, looking for something she had read earlier. When she found the correct folder, she pulled it out and opened it to a page in the file. She compared the two and then wrote something down on a yellow legal pad. She then placed both files in a separate, smaller pile that was growing in size slowly, day by day.

There were four files in a pile now. All of them had caught Susan's eye. She pushed a disheveled lock of blonde hair out of her view and tucked it behind her ear. Her digital watch beeped at her. *Shit,* she thought. *It's 3:30 already. Time to go pick up the boys.*

She hated to leave her work. She was onto something. A set of similarities in several disappearances too similar to ignore. She heard something behind her and turned with a start. There was nothing there. She realized she was trembling. Whether it was from exertion, excitement, or fear, she wasn't sure.

13

Present Day

Colin walked down the hall of the senator's house to the kitchen. He took a side door out of the house and out into the furiously blowing snow. There, he saw what he was looking for. A broken glass sat at the top of the trash in several paper towels. Colin closed the lid so the snow wouldn't cover the evidence and walked back inside, closing the door behind him to block the gusting snow-filled wind.

"Well?" asked Jester.

"He cleaned up the broken glass, the fucking lunatic. Put it right in the trash out there." The fact that Azrael was actually a he had been confirmed by sightings of him in the Middle East, and by the profilings they had done of the killer.

"Looks like Smith was right," said Jester. Colin stared into space, temporarily lost in thought. This scene had hit closer to home for him. He wasn't sure if it was his past, the fact that this victim was a woman, or the fact that they had arrived only just after Azrael had been here. This was the closest they had ever come to him. He had eluded them for months in a deadly dance that spun further and further out of control by the day.

Tradecraft, intelligence, and sheer cunning had kept the highly skilled Echo Team at arm's length, but the brutality and oddity of the killings had put them off balance. Colin thought it might have been seeing this done to Americans in his hometown—not strangers in some shit-hole halfway around the world—that affected him, but he knew deep down that this reminded him of his sister Susan. Her death had been similar, and though he had few details, he knew deep down that something felt the same. He needed to look this mad man in the eye, and hopefully put a bullet through each of them.

"You with me, bro?" asked Jester.

"Sorry," said Colin.

"Everything okay? You've seemed a little off your game since we got here."

Colin thought that statement might have seemed slightly laughable to anyone on the outside. Objectively speaking, he had been blown up, shot at, and jumped off a second-story roof onto a moving car all before it was lunchtime, but he saw Jester's point.

"Just a feeling I have," replied Colin. "Something is off with all of this. This guy's no spy. At least not anymore. It's too fucked up for someone in our line of work to go this far when a simple bullet in the head would suffice."

Jester looked thoughtful, or as thoughtful as he ever looked. "I agree. Clearly a fucking lunatic. But that means he's bound to make a mistake soon. I mean, we couldn't have expected to catch him watching episodes of Mind Hunter and listening to true crime podcasts. Our job's to kill the bad guys, then the guys who hired them, and then the guys who are in charge of them. Let Agent Smith be the Brainiac who finds his ass."

Jester was right. They needed to lean more heavily on the agent. She was an expert, even if she was a pain in the ass. They also needed to get ahead of Azrael for the first time. They needed to merge Smith's intelligence with their tactical know-how and slip a noose around this guy's neck, and fast. They had been playing catch-up for too long. It was time to get to work.

They walked into the study and found Agent Smith crouched

over the body, furiously recording notes into her phone. Two crime scene technicians had just arrived from the Capitol Police with strict orders from Lieutenant Mazzeti to say nothing. They had been off duty at the time but had managed to get their hands on the appropriate equipment and make it over here surprisingly quickly in the storm outside. They walked around the room, placing yellow evidence numbers around various objects in the room. *The scene is disturbing in the strangest ways,* thought Colin, stepping further into the room. He could see Senator Marks's body on the floor near the fireplace. Which was still crackling peacefully away as if nothing was the matter. She looked to be at peace with a soft smile.

Her facial expressions, now frozen for all time, showed no hint of surprise that her eyes and tongue had been removed, nor any surprise that her throat had been slit. Colin could see blood still seeping from the wound. Which looked to initially have been cleaned up, but was now soaking the red oriental carpet cradling her lifeless corpse. A slight shiver shook through Colin's body, which was saying something because the fire had made the room stiflingly warm.

"Well, did you find it?" asked Smith.

"It was in the outside trash, broken glass, and paper towels," replied Colin.

"I knew it," she said in a triumphant tone that clashed brilliantly with her somber face. Colin thought it gave her a creepy kind of Dr. Death vibe.

"So, what's your assessment?" he asked her.

"Well, it's hard to make that without all the details of the case," she began, standing up and placing her phone in her pocket. "Initially, I would say he's clearly a serial killer. He's done this before. This is a very defined murder scene. It's neat and has no mess. His trademarks are all clearly defined and don't look like an afterthought.

To do this to a person and not completely mutilate a body, outside of the carnage done, requires the immense skill of either a doctor or an experienced killer. There's also the care taken in cleaning up the broken glass, and the way the body is laid out. This took time, but not as much as the first body. I would bet he drained much of the blood out of the other senator's corpse and disposed of it to make the body seem more peaceful, maybe like some kind of offering."

Colin saw Jester shake his head at this and Colin caught his eyes silently agreeing with him. "Here, he still proceeded with great care but allowed the blood to pool beneath the corpse. Notice how he directed the pool, though." She indicated the circular pool of blood beneath the body and the marks from where some had been wiped up.

"This looks to me like he had to dispose of this in the absence of the time, so he went out of his way to make it look serene, like she was lying in a crimson pool or something. The wounds are also all cleaned and clotted. Not an easy feat, judging by the size of them. I imagine that when these bodies are tested, some kind of clotting agent will be discovered in her blood, administered sometime shortly after death or as she was dying."

Colin was slightly awestruck at the depth of her analysis in the short time she had been in the room. Jester stood next to him, his mouth slightly agape.

"Damn, that's creepy, Smith," said Jester.

Smith rolled her eyes at him. "Again, these are all just guesses based on my experience working on cases with serial killers involved. If I could get the complete picture, I might be able to tell you something more useful."

Colin thought this through for a second and knew they wouldn't get much farther if he didn't tell her the truth. He motioned for her to come with him out of the study and proceeded to tell her almost everything he knew.

14

Azrael loaded the bag into the back of the white Sprinter van and closed the rear sliding door behind it. He was in a decrepit old warehouse located near the Potomac River in a part of town that was not nearly as desirable as the place he had just left. The warehouse was owned and controlled by another Chinese shell company doing business out of Hong Kong.

He had just finished coordinating with some of the Chinese assets that were in play in the city and had set up several surprises for the team that was chasing him. He was efficient in his operations but drastically preferred to work alone. Too many questions were asked when other people saw him work, and many so-called allies had died asking those questions by his hand.

He picked up a hardcover Pelican case and loaded it into the front seat. Before he secured it with a seatbelt, he opened it and looked inside. A collection of vials and syringes lay in neatly fitted foam slots within the case. Satisfied that none were broken, he closed the case and took time to make sure it was at a neat, parallel angle to the edge of the front passenger seat.

He was meticulous to the extreme, often repeating tasks several times until he had the proper feeling about them. His obsessive-compulsive disorder was severe, especially when mixed with the tradecraft he often employed in his everyday life. In his own mind, though, the two complimented each other and made him all the more deadly. He simultaneously loved and hated this about himself. What was even more strange was his ability to snap in and out of this at will. Violence seemed to push the disorder away, while the aftermath of it brought it careening back.

The truth was that Azrael was a deadly hollowed-out shell of a man, broken from years of endless extreme violence and masked with a profession that paid him to slaughter. He was a phantom, barely in this world, but still affecting its occupants, very often sending them to the next. His long career had seen him transition from someone who killed for a country, to someone who killed out of anger, to someone who killed because the rush was all they had left. He didn't care about anyone in this world. There was only him and the ones he hunted.

His fascination with death and what happened afterward drove his mutilation of the bodies. He very often committed the bulk of his work to them while they were still alive. In his sick mind, this gave him a glimpse into what came next. Deep down, though, was the knowledge that he was often helping these people, though he despised them.

Everyone must be in as much pain as me, he reasoned. He was sending them somewhere and satisfying his own pathological need for a rush in the process.

Azrael pulled out a pad from his pocket as he walked over to the driver's side door of the van. In a messy black scrawl was written an address and a word "Sen3." Excitement welled within him. Butterflies of a different nature flew in his stomach. A baseball cap sat low over his eyes as he turned on the vehicle. He checked his rearview mirror, and a smile revealed deeply yellowed teeth.

The killer was moving again.

15

A gent Smith stood awestruck at what Colin told her in the kitchen. He had taken his time explaining to her how Azrael had first come on their radar in Afghanistan, the murder of the Taliban tribal leaders, and the subsequent push to bring them back here; he didn't share his suspicions about his sister's death. Colin had just finished the part about how the vice president and the Committee suspected the attorney general of espionage on behalf of the Chinese government, which was the reason all of this was being kept so quiet and so entirely off the books. She stood in the kitchen across from him in stunned silence. He could see the wheels turning behind her emerald green eyes.

"So, you think this Azrael was brought in from Afghanistan by the Chinese government to eliminate the investigation before we could figure out who their agent was?"

"It stands to reason," said Colin. "We've been hunting him like he's a spy, but it's become clear that he's more than that. He clearly has the training—I would say special forces at the least, but maybe even intelligence training. He's cunning and careful, but far too gruesome to his victims to be some kind of normal asset. Truthfully, I've never seen anything like it," Colin finished. He could see the wheels turning behind her eyes again.

Finally, she said, "A few years ago, I read a paper at Quantico written by a psychologist who was trying to understand why post-traumatic stress disorder turned some veterans so violent. Spousal abuse was becoming a real problem among the community that spent time deep within the wars in Afghanistan and Iraq. Their hope was to counsel these former soldiers away from violence and guide them out of their PTSD without the need for pharmaceutical drugs. They even planned to experiment with Ayahuasca to help snap soldiers out of it quickly by being deeply retrospective about their experiences through the use of hallucinogenic drugs."

Colin nodded, having heard of the drug from a local shaman on a mission in South America and about its possible effects on addiction on a popular podcast. She continued, "What was interesting was that the author hypothesized that some veterans afflicted with PTSD who also suffered from obsessive-compulsive disorder could be prone to extreme repeat violent episodes and even associate the cure for their symptoms with violence, or worse, killing again."

Colin thought about this for a second. "So you're saying a soldier with a host of mental issues combined with PTSD might lose it and start killing people to regain control?"

"I am. I interviewed the author because I started worrying that we might see a rise in serial killings occurring due to the large popula-tion of combat veterans coming home. I wanted to identify soldiers preemptively who might be at risk and make sure they got the proper treatment when they got home."

"I'm guessing that didn't go so well?"

"No, it didn't. As it turns out, accusing combat veterans of being potential serial killers would have been a bad look for the FBI. I was told to drop it, but I did file the paper with the Behavioral Sciences Division so that we could use it as a framework if a case popped up somewhere. Then, being a young agent trying to build a career, I dropped it and moved on."

Colin thought this over for a second. "A combat veteran who's been in the shit for a long time and has a high degree of training in killing and tradecraft. He's got to be either American or Russian.

Those are the only two places he could get the training required to pull off the things he's done and to have been in war all over the globe for such an extended period of time."

"I concur," said Smith. Colin leaned back against the granite countertop behind him and thought for a minute. Agent Smith interrupted him, "How do you know it's the attorney general?"

"Six operations have been compromised in Asia or against Chinese operations here in the U.S. in the last year. The common thread is that all of them had ties directly to that office. The Senate committee was able to rule out everyone else involved except the highest levels of his office. They then started digging and realized that many of the law firms he had been at before taking the job represented high-end Chinese clients and businessmen China would deem vital to the state. There's also his decidedly pro-China rhetoric, which is off given the administration's stern stance on them and the tariffs. All of this is speculation, of course. It could be someone else in his office. These are things that are so minute that most of them wouldn't even have been flagged in his vetting process, but putting them all together with these compromised operations. That's something else entirely."

Colin could tell she was completely in shock at what he had told her, and she was starting to understand why this team was operating so covertly on American soil.

"Listen," Colin said. "We need to get ahead of this guy. I'm going to lean on you to help me understand him today. For right now, I need you to tell me who this note means he's going for next so we can set a trap for him."

She nodded and took the note he was holding from him. It was simple and listed five names: Sen1, Sen2, Sen3, Sen4, and Sen5. One through three had circles around them, and Sen1 and Sen2 had been crossed out.

She studied it intensely. Colin had already sent a picture of the note to Charlie as well for analysis in an attempt to hedge his bets. "Outside of the fact that he is targeting the third senator, I'm not sure. It could be that he is targeting them in order of seniority or by some other unknown data point. The only thing I can tell you for sure is that this isn't random. He's too particular for that. I need a minute to think. Hold on." She walked down the hallway with the note and back to the study.

Just then, Colin's earpiece chimed. It was Charlie. "Boss, we have a serious problem."

16

"Hold on, Charlie; back up. What's going on?" Colin knew there was trouble as soon as Charlie's voice came through his earpiece. As it turned out, he had cracked the hacker's laptop that Sarah had retrieved from them an hour before. Having half of the hacker's password had saved Charlie much of the time it would have usually taken to break into the machine. He had just been explaining to Colin that he had also decrypted messages on the computer to what looked like two other Chinese hit teams in town. Charlie had managed to pinpoint a location on one of the units but had failed to find any position on the other. Colin thanked Charlie and turned to brief Jester and Agent Smith, who had just walked into the room.

"We've got two Chinese hit teams in town and a location on only one of them," he said.

"That's a shit situation with three senators to protect and Azrael still out there," replied Jester.

"Can't the Capital Police protect the other three?" asked Agent Smith.

Jester looked toward the hallway and said, "I doubt it."

Colin agreed with his assessment. "I have Mazetti sending more off duty guys he trusts to guard the senators, but the storm is going to wreak havoc with getting them there. I think we need to go to

Senator Rand's and see what else he can tell us. There's bound to be some other piece of intel we're missing here."

"That's a risk with those Chinese hit teams out there. They'll be ghosts in this weather," said Jester, nodding toward the near whiteout that was going on outside. "That's why we're going to split up," said Colin. "Jester, you'll join up with Witch and Agent Sunderland. He should keep you out of trouble, and go hit the Chinese hit team. I'll take Agent Smith and Sheriff to talk to Senator Rand and make sure the other senators are secure. We'll see what other intel they can provide."

"Got it," said Jester. "Witch is too ugly to meet the senators, so we go kill the bad guys."

"Affirmative," said Colin. "Your team will be Bravo, and ours will be Alpha. You got all that, Charlie?" he asked, seemingly to the air around them.

"Got it, boss," came the call from their earpieces. The team call signs of Alpha and Bravo were really for Charlie and Sarah to be able to more effectively communicate with them.

The team gathered up and briefed each other on the plan before heading out the door into the gale of wind and snow. Visibility was down to less than a hundred feet, and a full eight inches of snow was already on the ground. They began loading up into the two separate SUVs, and Colin and Jester paused to bump fists.

"Watch your six, Snowman."

"You too, Jester, I mean it—Azrael is still out there. Oh, and keep the kid out of trouble," he said, nodding to Agent Sunderland, who had jumped in the driver's seat of the rear SUV. He was scarcely three years younger than Colin.

"Will do, boss."

The SUVs split up and went in different directions. Colin's SUV proceeded down a snow-covered street toward the first senator's house. In regular weather, it would have taken ten minutes to get there; in this weather, it would be more like twenty. Agent Smith took the roads slowly with the lights on. The sun was so faint now, coming through the thick clouds, that the onslaught of white around them seemed to have shrunk to a dark gray color.

"Any more thoughts on the note?" Colin asked Agent Smith.

"No, I've got nothing, but we need to hurry. I'm still thinking about his first note, to be honest. 'Five lives must die before the last tick of the day's clock.' I'm not sure if he means the end of the day as in the night or the end of the day, like twenty-four hours. If he's sticking to a timeline, one would mean we are already too late, and the other would say we have time."

Colin thought about that, watching snow get hurled off the windshield. "I wouldn't take it too literally. Yes, he says he's going to kill five senators, but the tactical side of him wouldn't box himself into dividing out the hours per target. It would make him predictable."

"Fair enough," said Agent Smith. "But he still just called his shot in his last note. You only do that if you know you're going to sink your next basket."

Colin appreciated that she could relate something so sinister back to something as simple as basketball. "I think the same thing holds true. He may have a plan to go for one senator, but you better believe he has an alternate plan in case we pinpoint his next move."

Agent Smith nodded in agreement, trying to focus on getting them there faster in the weather and increasing her speed. Colin was still amazed at the lack of traffic. There were no cars anywhere. Admittedly, D.C. was a transient city and emptied considerably during the holidays, but it was still surprising to see. Colin knew how bad the city was at dealing with snow. The whole capital was currently shut down, and they had only a quarter of the precipitation predicted.

His thoughts drifted back to the snowy night that his sister had been slain. The similarities were haunting, but he had never been given full details on the extent of his sister's murder. He had witnessed some of it, but most of it had been blocked from his memory; the rest of the details had been spared from the ears of a young child. Being so eager to put it all behind him, he had never tried to dig any further into what happened.

Most of his personal records had been heavily obscured or entirely erased by the government upon his induction into the Echo Teams. They wanted no trace of their operatives to be readily available if anyone got curious. If he had ever wanted to look deeper, he would have found, like the NSA team that scrubbed his records from existence in the first place, that those records had disappeared years before.

17

The elevator doors opened with a ding, and Colin, Sheriff, and Agent Smith walked out into the hallway of the fifth floor. The building was upscale modern with light wood floors and sleek metal accents on the walls. Instantly, two dark-suited men who identified themselves as Capitol Police stepped in front of them and asked where they were heading. Agent Smith pulled out her FBI credentials and stepped forward to identify the team. They were expected, and the exchange was brief. They continued down the hallway toward the last condo, which was a corner unit.

When they arrived, they knocked twice, and it took a minute before the door was answered. An older looking man in tan slacks and a light gray cardigan answered the door and greeted them with a practiced but warm smile. "I take it you're Team Alien?"

"Agent Smith, FBI," said Alexandra in an official sort of way.

"Oh," said Rand inquisitively.

"That's correct, sir," said Colin, stepping in.

"I take it you're Snowman, then," Rand said with a nod of his head.

"It's nice to meet you, sir. We were hoping to ask you a few questions about the committee's investigation."

"Absolutely, come on in." The team followed him down a hallway, which opened up into a practical but well-appointed apartment. The feature that stunned them all into near silence was the beautiful floor-to-ceiling windows that looked out directly down the National Mall.

"Can I get you anything?" asked Senator Rand.

"No, thank you," said Colin. He noticed a photo album sitting on the coffee table, open to a picture of Senator Rand and a younger Senator Marks. "I've kept up to date on your progress today. You boys certainly know how to make a mess."

"With respect, sir, the situation is unprecedented. Containing it is going to be a nightmare if we can't get out ahead of it," replied Colin.

"And that's why you're here? If it is, I assure you we have the situation contained from our end."

"That's not my concern, sir. I have full confidence in your ability to keep the situation contained. My goal is to take the initiative and get out ahead of the bad guys to shut this whole thing down as quickly as possible."

"Makes sense," said Senator Rand with a slight smile. "How can I help?"

Colin heard the senator's phone vibrate and watched him pull it out to check it. A steady chime of alert notifications from his laptop positioned on a kitchen table nearby indicated that the senator was still busy working even though the whole city was shut down. Colin pulled out his own phone from his pocket and showed him a picture of the note left in Senator Carson's mouth.

"What we need to know, sir, is if there is some kind of order in which they might target the rest of your committee. If we have that information, we can set up a trap and hopefully stop this whole thing before it spirals too far out of control." The senator gave him a look that said the situation was obviously already out of control, but not in an unkind way. In fact, Colin noted his whole demeanor as friendly, from his smile to the business casual khakis and cardigan he was wearing.

The senator took the phone and stared intently at the note. "The first two here are Senator Carson and Senator Marks?" he asked.

"That's correct, sir," said Agent Smith, speaking up.

The senator kept on staring, seemingly lost in thought. They tried to be respectful and give him his time, but the team was restless. The more quickly they could put together who was next, the easier it would be to end this before any more blood was spilled. Colin tried to distract himself by staring around the room. Everything seemed to speak of practicality. This was clearly the condo of a working man.

Nothing spoke of a wife's touch or of any other inhabitants. Colin briefly wondered whether the senator had any family at all. Even the artwork around the apartment seemed to have been bought at Ikea. The only photos to speak of were of the senator with other important people.

"I'm sorry, I'm just not sure what order he would target us in. Senator Carson made sense from a starting perspective as he brought forward the initial evidence and led the committee, but why he would target Marks next is just as much of a mystery to me as it is to you. I'm the second most senior member, which is why I took over the investigation when he was killed."

"Are you sure there isn't anything?" asked Agent Smith. "No pieces of evidence you were holding individually or knowledge you were keeping segmented?"

"No, that's not really how it works," started Rand.

"When we are onto something, we mainly interview possible folks of interest as a committee and make requests to the various three-letter agencies for intelligence we think will help to back up our assumptions. We have certain back channels in place to keep from tripping any alarms suspects may have set up. We don't generally deal with much physical evidence; most of it is digital and held in a specially compartmented section of the Intelligence Community Cloud for us to access. Anything physical is held in a SCIF suite that we have permanently reserved in the basement of the capitol building. This investigation was almost all digital up to this point."

Colin knew this and had been provided access to all of the information gathered so far. "Sir, if there is no discernible pattern into which they would go after you, then let me ask you another question. Why today? Why are they choosing today to go after all of you?"

Senator Rand sat back on the couch and scratched his chin, thinking about this one. "Well," he said in a southern drawl, "there are several votes on new tariffs coming up in the new year as well as a litany of sanctions on the Chinese government for their actions on limiting democracy in Hong Kong. But none of those votes take place till after the recess that brings us into the new year. Perhaps it was a target of opportunity. As you can tell, this snowstorm has certainly inhibited our ability to respond."

The team asked a few more questions before standing to leave, but none of them led anywhere either. If there was indeed no specific order in which they would attack the senators, then their best option was to bring them all together so they could protect them properly and off the grid of traditional law enforcement. While they did this, Colin hoped that Jester's team could shake a few more trees until a new solution presented itself. The door closed behind them, and the team proceeded back down the hallway.

Rather than take the elevator down, the team decided to use the stairs, which would take them to a side entrance out of the building where their SUV was. They nodded to the Capitol Police in the hallway as they opened the door and proceeded downward. Colin got down one flight before a door from another floor two flights below them opened, and a man stepped into the staircase, turning to continue up the stairs, and then froze. Colin stopped dead, staring at him. The man's baseball cap, yellowed teeth, and smile sent a rushing flood of adrenaline-soaked fear through Colin's body. He knew without a doubt who this was, and he immediately reached for his gun.

18

17 Years Before

S usan Frost sat at the wooden kitchen table with a litany of documents spread around her and a mug of steaming coffee next to her. It was well past midnight, and the boys were already asleep, but she couldn't seem to get to bed. A coffee pot dripped steadily behind her as she sat making furious notes on a yellow legal pad. From the hundreds of case files she had pulled, she had extracted six names. All missing women, presumed dead.

The similarities in all of the cases were striking. She had a dark feeling within her that she had stumbled on something terrible. No person who was doing their job right at the law enforcement or prosecutor level could have missed this. But oddly enough, it seemed every case had been carefully spread out to different investigators and divisions. Taken individually or in a smaller group, a pattern wouldn't have been apparent, but placing all six together made an attempt to reveal what was happening even more apparent.

What made matters worse was that several of the case files had been placed in entirely wrong sections of the records room. An act which would have just seemed lazy or careless, but taken in context with the other actions here, seemed deliberate. There was also the fact that several pieces of crucial paperwork were entirely missing from the old files. Susan had to carefully piece the data back together by going to the D.C. Police Department with requests for copies of their records. Some they had, but others they did not.

She had wondered if this was deliberate as well. She looked out the dark window of the kitchen across the table from her. She couldn't see it, but she knew the last vestiges of autumn leaves would be clinging to the trees. This was a season she usually loved. A time for joy and the warmth of a home. Now she felt like the dark outside was closing in around her, with only the walls of the house holding it out.

Susan got up, a faint chill running down her spine, and walked to the front door. She got there and turned the lock again just to make sure it was locked. Peering out the small side windows of the door, she could see the dimly illuminated street outside. With a start, she stepped away from the window, scared that she had seen something move across the street. Susan took a deep breath and peered back out. It was nothing, she decided and told herself to get a grip.

She walked back to the table and looked down at her notes again. Whether it was the exhaustion of the fright she just had or the late hour, she didn't know, but she suddenly felt extremely tired. Deciding to go back over her notes one more time for good measure, she drained the last bit of coffee in the mug and picked up her pad. She scanned the notes up and down and decided something looked familiar. One of the names of the husbands stuck out at her. "Alex Tucker. She said the name over and over in her mind and puzzled over why it sounded so familiar.

His wife had disappeared approximately three years ago. According to the file, he had been suspected, but ultimately nothing was ever proven, and the police dropped him as a suspect in the end. But where had she seen him, she wondered? Then it came to her. Alex Tucker was in charge of half of the federally contracted janitorial staff in the city. She had seen his name on several maintenance reports in the office and noticed the name Tucker Janitorial on the back of several of the cleaning staff's coveralls. She wrote this down on her pad and decided to check-in and see if this was the same man tomorrow when she went back in.

This case, in particular, had puzzled her. Sarah Tucker had been a conservative, church-going woman, according to the police report. She was quiet and kept mainly to herself and her family. If it weren't for the circumstances of her disappearance, Susan wouldn't even have pulled the file. Something then clicked in Susan's mind. What if these women didn't disappear because someone was interested in them? What if they were trying to get at these women's husbands?

One of the curiously missing details out of all of the reports was personal employment details on the men the women were married to. Susan decided that it couldn't have been an error. All of these husbands had something in common, and she was going to find out what it was.

19

Present Day

Navigation is starting to become a serious issue, reflected Jester. He was in an SUV containing Witch and Agent Sunderland. They had left Senator Marks's home thirty minutes ago and were proceeding toward the suspected location of the Chinese hit team. The nine inches of snow covering the ground wasn't giving the SUV much trouble, but many drivers who had chosen to brave the weather were now stuck in the middle of various streets, presenting constant hazards in the whiteout all around them.

The highest speed it seemed they could ever make it to was thirty miles an hour, and that was at deadly peril to the occupants of their vehicle and any civilians brave enough to be outside in this weather. Visibility was scarcely one hundred feet, and the wind whipping between the buildings made for random snow drifts that seemed to pile in ever more dangerous places.

The SUV finally pulled onto U Street and made its way slowly down toward the suspected location of the Chinese hit team. The navigation program they used had identified the place as a local hole-in-the-wall Chinese restaurant hidden on a small side street off of the main avenue. According to the FBI database and the Metropolitan

Police's Major Crimes Unit, this was a suspected front for Chinese mob activity.

"Ain't nothing coming out of China the government doesn't get a piece of," Jester had remarked on being handed the information from Agent Sunderland. He closed the tablet and rechecked the GPS. "Should be about two streets up on your right. Park on the corner out of sight, and we'll scout the situation out." Agent Sunderland, who hadn't said much the whole day, nodded and pulled the SUV up to the recommended point. The only sound apart from the engine and the truck's heater was the whipping of the wind lazily moving the vehicle back and forth.

"Place is a fucking ghost town," said Witch from the back, staring out the window at their surroundings.

"This area's full of college students, but most of them have probably already gone home for the holidays. Everyone else is holed up inside, and visibility sucks, so they can probably barely see the street anyway," said Agent Sunderland.

Jester took another look outside. It didn't look like any of the businesses he saw were open, and he didn't see any civilians out. "Witch, you circle around to the back and wait for my signal. Sunderland, you stay with the ride and be ready to chase any squeakers. I'll take the front."

Witch took off, and Jester moved swiftly off with him, splitting off after a hundred feet toward the front of the Chinese restaurant. He stuck to the wall and tried his best to appear like a casual walker just trying to stay out of the snow and to take in the colorful storefronts and bars. His Sig Sauer P226 was in a concealed holster at his front, and he was ready to grab it at a moment's notice.

The snow was well past his ankles, and it made his movement slower than he would have liked, but it was a light snow, not the thick, wet kind he was used to from his childhood ski trips in New England. Snow clung to his beard as he made his way closer to the objective, and he took controlled breaths to ensure that his elevated heart rate didn't make his aim inaccurate if he had to fire his weapon quickly. When he got one storefront away, he pulled his gun and screwed a suppressor onto the front of it. The last thing he wanted was to wake the whole neighborhood up in a running gun battle with a Chinese hit team, but it served another purpose as well. The suppressed fire would help alert Witch to his teammate's position in a potential firefight as well.

Witch's voice came over his earpiece. "Jester, this place is empty."

"I thought we were breaching on my go?" said Jester, a bit bemused.

"Come around back and check this shit out," replied Witch.

It took Jester a few minutes to get through a trash strewn alley that wreaked of old food, but he managed to get around the back of the restaurant, and he immediately saw what Jester was talking about. The door to the back of the Chinese restaurant hung half off its hinges. Blood droplets stood out brilliantly in the freshly fallen snow, and tire tracks that couldn't have been twenty minutes old, judging by the depth of the snowfall refilling them, led out of the alley. The lights through the back door of the restaurant were still on. The back alley reeked of old Chinese food, and Jester strongly suspected the overflowing dumpster in the corner hadn't been picked up because of the storm.

Witch had his weapon trained through the door and said, "I think it's empty, but let's clear it."

They went slowly and methodically, checking for booby traps, explosives, and surveillance gear that would alert the Chinese that they were hot on their heels. After searching for ten minutes and finding nothing, they came back to the kitchen. Blood pooled in globs on the stainless steel table in the center of the room. Rags soaked with blood littered the floor and surrounding tables. Someone had clearly bled a lot in this room, and judging by the shade of the blood, it had been recently. "I thought that kid must have gotten hit," said Jester.

"I was surprised they opened up on us so carelessly. Not exactly a hostage rescue team," replied Witch. "Probably a kill capture type of situation. Let's see if we can find anything they left behind."

It took several more minutes, but finally, Witch called out, "Got something over here."

Jester walked out back of the kitchen he was rummaging in to see Witch holding a bloody cell phone he had dug out of the dumpster. "Jackpot! Let's see what Charlie can shake out of it."

20

"Do you really need another one?" asked Sarah Gonzalez as she handed Charlie his fifth Red Bull of the day. They stood in a towering aircraft hangar surrounded by folding tables, computers, monitors, and pelican cases filled with equipment. Charlie hesitated briefly before taking the drink, catching Sarah's fiery gaze.

She had been helping him try to lose weight for months now with little success, but giving up was not something Sarah did. Charlie reasoned that the team needed him operating at maximum mental capacity and popped the top to the drink. He turned back to his station, which looked more like a professional gaming rig than something that would be in a tactical command center, and began banging away on his extremely clicky mechanical keyboard. Sarah found the sound annoying but had learned to tune it out over the course of the past year.

She turned back to the standing height table that was behind her and began swiping through documents on a 12.9-inch iPad, looking for anything that would help tell them why this was happening now. So far, she had been stumped. She had a Master's Degree in Political Science from Georgetown, and she was completely stumped. She nervously clicked the top of a pen over and over again as she read.

She was currently digging through classified Senate Intelligence

Committee briefings and looking for conclusions drawn by U.S. Pacific Command on enemy intentions. More specifically, she was looking for anything that would cause rapid policy shifts overnight that the Chinese needed to stop.

Charlie, on the other hand, was busy remotely downloading the cellphone that Witch and Jester had found in the dumpster. He had the file now but was having a significant amount of trouble trying to hack into the information. Lockpick could have done this in seconds, but Charlie was back to doing it the old-fashioned way. Even though it was near freezing in the hangar with the doors closed, the fans on Charlie's massive gaming-style computing rig were blowing full blast, trying to cool the hardware inside. Brute force lines of code flew against the locked contents of the cellphone, attempting to find back doors in the technically unbreakable AES 256-bit encryption.

Just as China had long been suspected of placing back doors in commonly used software and hardware, the NSA had been hard at work placing their own in everything from cell phones to smart locks. Another copy of the cellphone had been cloned and placed in a secret partitioned NSA server, which was now running on a virtual machine on Charlie's computer. This machine was the extremely classified big brother to Lockpick, which also leveraged the power of quantum computing to melt through modern encryption methods.

The trouble was that the system took time to spin up. In addition to using an incredible amount of energy, the system also required cooling from liquid nitrogen to keep from being overheated immediately. At the moment, it was the equivalent of what the original room-sized computers had been to calculators; undoubtedly more effective at certain tasks but limited in functionality. This machine's, affectionately named The Battering Ram by its makers, sole purpose was to smash through the cyber defenses of foreign governments in the event of a cyberwar, thus paving the way for more conventional cyber-attacks.

Charlie was one of the few people in the entire world who knew about its existence and had access to it. Technically, even he was supposed to ask permission to use it, but he dubbed this a national security emergency and figured it was better to ask forgiveness than permission. A status bar at the bottom of the window indicated that Battering Ram's startup status was at 98 percent. He took another sip of Red Bull and cracked his knuckles. A soft chime let him know it was ready, and he typed the key command to execute, and within seconds, the encryption was shattered like thin glass protecting the phone's contents.

He took a deep breath and hoped he could find something for the team to go on. It wasn't always easy for Charlie to sit back while the team was in danger. He felt a sense of urgency to get results that he judged was the equivalent of a soldier trying to get to a wounded comrade on the battlefield. Except his battlefield played out in ones and zeros rather than bullets and blood.

He opened the cell phone's file directory and instantly knew something was wrong. The fans were the first thing that gave it away. His computer rig was water-cooled, and in the icy hangar, he shouldn't have heard his computer's fans redline so quickly. Visual indicators of trouble followed. A red dragon skull popped up over the files, and the rest of his screen grayed out. He furiously tapped his keyboard and moved his mouse, but nothing happened.

He slapped the tower of his rig, knowing it would do nothing, but felt better about it all the same. Anxiety welled up inside him, and he began to sweat even more than he already was. He reached for his mouse again but accidentally knocked over his Red Bull in the process, spilling its contents onto the table. "Shit!" he cursed.

"What is it?" Sarah asked.

His face said it all as he stared back at her in horror. They had been hacked.

21

Colin only froze for a split second, but to him, it felt like an eternity. A rush of emotions shot through him the second he saw the familiar face.

A face he had seen once before as a child and countless times in nightmares since that terrible night.

In that moment, the truth was finally revealed to him. Everything was connected. He had suspected that, of course, but seeing truly was believing. Colin's hand shot immediately to his weapon. He drew it in the blink of an eye and had it up and ready to go, but Azrael had taken off back down the stairs. Colin bounded after him, the team following moments behind him. He took the steps three at a time, descending the stairs at perilous speed. A burst of light at the bottom of the stairwell told Colin that Azrael had made it out into the side alley. He pushed himself harder, accelerating to the exit, the concrete walls moving by in a blur before he slammed through the door into a burst of freezing air, light, and snow.

The second his foot hit the slick pavement, Colin lost his footing, and his momentum carried him into a group of metal trashcans standing against a snow coated brick wall. He scrambled to his feet and took off down the alley just as Agent Smith and Sheriff came out of the exit. Colin ran as fast as he could in the snow, doing his best to keep his footing. Azrael turned the corner at the end of the alley, and Colin momentarily lost sight of him.

"Charlie, I need a twenty on Azrael from the drone," Colin yelled over the sound of the wind and snow rushing past him. He got nothing in reply. "Charlie, do you copy?" He tried again.

Nothing.

He pushed his pace faster. Azrael was in the distance, turning another corner. "Sheriff, do you copy?!" Colin yelled, but got nothing in response.

Sheriff was a mere twenty feet behind him, but the loss of comms was worrying. Snow blew into Colin's eyes, and he tried to ignore the freezing temperatures as he ran. Azrael turned again up ahead, clearly trying to lose Colin in the maze of back alleys, and Colin raced after him. He reached the turn in twenty paces and slipped hard on a patch of ice, sending his boots up over his head as he crashed down on the ground. He felt two projectiles race over him, missing the top of his head by an inch, and heard the gunshots a split second later.

He had no time to reflect on this and scrambled to his feet to chase the now fleeing Azrael. A hot, aggravating pain welled from his knee as he went, telling him that his tactical pants were now rubbing against newly split open flesh. Sheriff and Smith had caught up to him now, and they ran in unison toward the end of the alley.

Gunshots from around a corner slowed their pace, and they stopped in time to move more tactically through the situation. Operators in the special forces community always heard that slow was smooth and smooth was fast, but the only thing on Colin's mind at the moment was a white-hot rage. It had grown with every step he took, culminating in a fast is fast and slow is dead type of attitude. His singular goal was the capture of Azrael. Alive or dead didn't matter, but Colin preferred the latter. They cleared the corner in time to see Azrael kick in a door to the back of a warehouse and run inside. They chased after, Smith surprising both Colin and Sheriff with her speed.

Colin saw her fly through the door to the warehouse first and knew instantly that she had made a mistake. He dove through a split second after tackling her to the ground as a torrent of gunfire rained down on them from a small catwalk above. The shots ricocheted off the concrete floor around them except for one, which caught Colin in the back of his liquid body armor vest. Sheriff came through the door behind them and poured rounds onto the catwalk above them, giving Agent Smith just enough time to pull the now scrambling Colin behind a large crate. Smith began to search Colin for wounds while Sheriff covered them.

"I'm fine!" yelled Colin over the hail of gunfire all around them. The rounds punched into a wooden box near Colin, sending splinters like small wooden darts into his face. He was only half lying. The pain of getting hit in the new liquid armor vest was significantly less than in a traditional vest, but it still felt like getting hit with a sledgehammer.

The vest was a prototype that was being given to tier-one teams in the U.S. military and intelligence community. It replaced the ceramic plate usually in Kevlar vests with Kevlar layers coated with shear-thickening fluid, which added incredible tensile strength and cut down on the number of overall layers needed for effective ballistic protection. It was also far lighter, more comfortable, and more flexible than traditional vests. The team who had developed it at the Army Research Laboratory had named it Mithril after the armor in *Lord of the Rings*, which was as light as silk but as hard as diamonds.

It took Colin a second to catch his breath. He and Agent Smith crouched back to back behind the crate she had dragged him behind. His ears were ringing from the gunfire in the warehouse. "Thanks for saving me," she said to him. Before he could say anything, she pivoted and fired a series of rounds in the direction of Azrael.

"He's moving!" shouted Sheriff from behind him. Colin rolled out from behind the crate and began to chase after Azrael again, a stinging sensation ringing through his upper back. He ran up a set of rusting metal stairs that creaked in protest with every step to the catwalk above. He got there just in time to see Azrael jump through a plate glass window onto the roof outside and slide down it before he disappeared from sight. Colin turned on his heel, thinking better of jumping onto a metal roof covered with ice and snow.

"Alley North Side!" Colin yelled. They ran to the other side of the warehouse, dodging crates and slipping on spent brass before shouldered through the door out into the cold, guns up, looking for signs of Azrael, but he had vanished like a ghost in the whiteout.

22

"Shit, grab me the silver hard drive out of the black pelican case!" Charlie yelled to Sarah. He was running back and forth between his computer and a laptop connected to it via a thunderbolt four cable, frantically inputting commands. Sweat dripped from his brow, and his breath came out in puffs of mist in the freezing hangar.

"Charlie, what's going on?" demanded Sarah for the third time.

"Trojan horse... infecting everything," he sputtered.

"Charlie, speak English," she ordered in a heavy Latino accent that tended to flare up when she was angry.

He looked at her with wide eyes. "Cyber-attack!"

She handed him the hard drive from the pelican case, and he slotted it into the USB-C connection after his shaking hands missed the port several times. He seemed to be vibrating as he moved, barely able to contain his excitement and extreme anxiety. Whoever had tricked him had been one hell of a hacker. Charlie was busy furiously spinning up virtual cloud computers to try and fight the intrusion and was using them to launch simultaneous attacks of his own on the now multiplying virus.

These instances existed to help companies use virtual computers that were not their own to run complex operations in the cloud without having to buy costly servers of their own. These specific models were reserved for the U.S. government and were extremely powerful. Without them, Charlie would have never been able to battle the virus sweeping through his system.

Sarah watched with a look that was a mixture of bewilderment and helplessness. They had lost contact with the team at a critical juncture in the operation. The answers they obtained could be instrumental in finding out why all of these things were happening today. He knew she was growing frustrated at the simple lack of comms that they had with their team a mere two miles away.

Charlie finally opened the program that had been on the silver hard drive and dropped it into three hundred simultaneous cloud computers that were waiting for his command. He took a deep breath and entered the command to execute. The program he had ordered the computers to run was extremely complex and of his own making. It essentially used a backup from his primary computer and loaded it into the cloud. It then told the computers to behave similar to a blockchain, but in reality it was a state-of-the-art data storage virtualization technology, that provided top tier data security, by introducing peer-to-peer data parity checks to ensure data wasn't compromised or corrupted.

Which, in essence, linked all of the machines together and told them that they were all the same. If anything read differently than the majority of the machines, it was considered a security intrusion and was corrected using the joint power of all 301 machines to correct anything that was not the original computer backup. It was simpler in essence than Charlie guessing what systems were infected and trying to kill the virus. This same technology was used by the financial world to keep transactions extremely secure. Charlie had merely corrupted the technology for his own needs. He just hoped that it worked. If it didn't, they had likely lost control of all of their data and compromised the team's entire mission.

"Well, did you fix it?" Sarah asked, as he had finally stopped moving after entering the execute command. Charlie took a deep breath. The cyberworld could be rather anticlimactic at times, he reflected. "No, it hasn't even started yet. It'll take some time for the system to initialize.

"Can't you make it go faster?" she asked. "No, I can't. This is one of the most advanced systems in the world, running on hundreds of servers across the country simultaneously. We're on the bleeding edge of computing here, limited only by how fast data can fly back and forth to all of those computers to self-correct the problem. Unless you've got another quantum computer lying around that we didn't blow up, this is going to take some time," he said exasperated. "Okay, Charlie, I'm sorry. I'm just worried about our guys. They're depending on us. I know you can handle this," she said, patting him on the shoulder. He nodded back reassuringly and internally hoped she was right.

23

The LEDs in the stained drop ceiling of the twenty-four hour convenience store flickered with the gusting wind outside. The owner of the store had been more than a little apprehensive about letting the burly-looking man with the gun use his landline but gave in when the man flashed FBI credentials stating he was Special Agent John Doe. The owner also found it a little suspicious that the agent had such a fake-sounding name, but the Afghan eased up a little when Jester had said, "Everything will be fine, my friend," in Pashtun to him. It had been a long time since anyone had spoken to him in his native language, and it had the effect of instantly putting him at ease.

Jester wasn't exactly sure what his plan was, but he had lost all communication with Charlie and Colin's team only thirty minutes before. None of the Echo Team carried personal cellphones with them on missions as a matter of operational security. That no one had seriously considered an echo team might lose all of its sophisticated communications was, in his opinion, a major oversight.

He placed a call to the private aviation terminal adjacent to the new 35X replacement terminal and waited for someone to answer. When no one did, he was greeted with a menu of options asking if he wished to contact a specific hangar. He thought back to when they had exited the plane and remembered seeing the number four painted on one of the doors and entered that menu option. The phone rang for a tense minute before a female Latino accent came over the line. "Hello," they said apprehensively.

"Shit, Sarah, it's Jester. What are you doing answering the phones?"

"We're the only ones here," she said. "When I heard the landline ring, I just hoped it was one of you. What's going on?" she asked.

"Nothing here. We can't get in contact with Snowman and his team, and we've been waiting for next steps from you. What's going on over there? Why did we lose coms?" Jester said, looking over his shoulder to ensure the tall Afghan wasn't listening in. He wasn't, and Jester swept his gaze to the rear of the store over the thousands of multi-colored products to ensure he had given them some space. He had.

"That phone was a booby trap. As soon as Charlie broke it, it infected all of our gear with a virus. He's getting things back under control, but it's going to take some time before communications are back again."

She sounded grave, and Jester decided it was better to keep moving with the conversation rather than reassure her. Sarah wasn't one to be coddled. "Copy. What should we do in the meantime? Do you have a twenty on Snowman's team?"

Before she could answer, Witch spoke from near the bodega's window. He was peering out from underneath a sign for cigarettes. "Agent Doe, I've got a Chinese F.A.M. with eyes on us across the street," he said, referring to Jester's alias and using the acronym for fighting age male.

"Copy, keep an eye—"

"Ah shit, Jester," said Witch, cutting him off. "I've got five more F.A.M.s armed to the teeth heading our way," he said, dropping the guise that they were FBI agents.

Agent Sunderland spoke up from near the beverage refrigerators on the opposite side of the store. "Sir, get yourself into the bathroom in back and stay down," he finished as he pulled his Glock. The man who had wandered out to see what the commotion was all about, didn't need to be told twice. He ran into the back room without another word.

"Ah, Sarah, I think we found one of the Chinese hit teams."

"Where?" she asked, bewildered.

"Well, they're about to breach the door of this bodega. Call you back in a few."

Jester pulled his Sig Sauer P226 and moved at a crouch to the windows at the front of the convenience store. Witch crouched on the other side of the door with Agent Sunderland. "They see you, Witch?" asked Jester.

"I don't think so, but they must have watched us come in. I doubt they think we know they're out there."

"All right, let's wait till they get in close, then open up on them," said Jester, sneaking closer to the glass front door and peering out of the bottom. They were approximately twenty yards out and starting to slowly move in their direction.

"I doubt they can see much—there's a tint on the glass and it's snowing like hell out. I'm gonna see if there's a rear entrance," said Agent Sunderland, scurrying back through the aisles at a low crouch. He returned a minute later. "Well, that's a violation of fire code— there's shelves filled with shit blocking the rear entrance. It would take at least twenty minutes to clear it."

"Roger that. Only one way out," said Jester. He stole another glance out the bottom of the glass door. "Ten yards. Let me take the first shot, then you two open up on the guys outside."

The next few seconds felt like an eternity. Made worse by the fact that Jester could literally see the seconds tick by on a lottery clock behind the counter. They seemed to slow with his breathing as he tried to lower his heart rate to keep his aim accurate and his weapon from swaying. His palms were sweating, and he wiped them on his pants to keep his weapon from slipping during the fight. He supposed leaving their assault rifles in their SUV outside might have been the wrong move, but he pushed the thought from his head to focus on the present. It was game time.

Jester slowed his breathing again and steadied himself. The front door of the convenience store began to slowly creep open, and Jester saw a hand pushing the door toward his side of the opening. Witch and Agent Sunderland were far enough away that the man opening the door couldn't see them yet. As soon as Jester saw the man's head follow his assault rifle into view of the top pane of glass, he popped up and shot him clean through the face. His brains exploded out of the back of his head, spraying all over the second breacher's face, momentarily blinding him.

He let loose a spray of automatic weapons fire through the glass where Jester had been only seconds before. The other members of the hit team took a step back, surprised by the sudden and violent death of the man in front of them. They pivoted, leaving their dead comrade lying in the entranceway and blocking the door from closing, and fired through the same window as their other comrade was. Broken glass careened down on Jester's head and the rounds shredded packages of dried goods and smashed glass refrigerator doors in the back, spraying milk, soda, and energy drinks all over the floor.

Just as the hit team began firing through one set of windows, Witch and Sunderland stood and fired through the other window, catching one attacker in the neck and another in the upper shoulder, shattering his collarbone as it tore through the right of the strap of the vest protecting the rest of his body. They both fell to the ground, and the other attackers dove behind the cover of the armored suburban that Witch, Jester, and Sunderland had driven there in.

Jester stood again, having placed the half-spent magazine in his pocket and with a fresh one loaded and fired several shots toward the other side of the SUV, while Agent Sunderland, slightly slower on the uptake, followed Witch out the front door to engage the attackers in the street. Jester followed shortly after, as Witch and Sunderland provided covering fire.

The change in temperature was staggering, from the inside of the convenience store to the blizzard conditions outside. Jester's eyes watered as he bounded to the cover of what he assumed was the bodega's owner's snow-covered Honda Civic in the small parking lot in front of the store. He slid in behind it and brushed snow that had fallen from the roof off of his head. He crept to the rear of the vehicle and pivoted around the taillight, firing three shots toward the attackers. One of the bullets skipped off of the frozen concrete and shredded the Achilles heel of one of the men behind the SUV. There were now two attackers left who weren't dead or wounded.

This changed rapidly as the man who had been shot in the collar bone and was lying on the ground reached for his weapon with his good arm. Witch, who had been moving to the left, promptly shot him through his right eye and proceeded to the extremely dangerous position of behind the front wheel on the opposite side of the SUV as the hit team. Jester stood up, fired more rounds to cover him, and started moving toward the SUV, firing as he went.

This had the effect of keeping the attackers' heads down. When his weapon went dry and he reached the SUV Agent Sunderland covered him from behind the Civic. Jester used this opportunity to pivot around the rear of the vehicle. A shot not aimed at Jester, Sunderland, or Witch told Jester that they had executed their wounded comrade to keep him from being taken alive.

The attackers were caught unprepared, thinking the attack was coming only from one side, and Jester shot one of them in the head. The other tried to get around the other side of the vehicle, but Witch took him from a distance of five yards, firing two shots in rapid succession, one hitting him in the head and the other in the neck. "Clear," said Jester. "Clear, called Witch. They waited, but heard nothing from Agent Sunderland. They both looked at each other concerned, with snow falling between them, but Jester thought that he might not know to say the words.

"Sunderland, you good?!" Witch shouted. There was no reply.

Jester repeated his query. "You all good, Sunderland?" He heard nothing and looked at Witch with concern, knowing something was wrong. They both bounded around the vehicle, weapons raised.

Sunderland came into view moments later with his hands up and a gun to the back of his head.

24

C olin stood doubled over panting with his hands on his knees when the rest of the team finally caught up with him. He wasn't sure how far behind they'd been, but he was just starting to catch his breath when they rounded the corner and made their way to him. Azrael was gone, and worse yet, the team had no idea where he had gone.

They spent the next twenty minutes searching around the dark alley, but the snow had fallen in drifts here, and the tracks were inconsistent and disappeared in parts before they lost the trail entirely. It seemed like the killer had vanished into thin air.

"He can't just have disappeared," Smith said in exasperation. Placing her hands on her hips. She had come over to join Colin and Sheriff after her own look around the alley.

"You don't know this guy like we do," said Sheriff, still panting.

"We've tracked him over three continents—he's always a step ahead. This is the closest we've ever come to catching him, and he still gave us the slip," Colin chimed in. He was crouched over one of the last sets of footprints and was surprised to see a drop of blood in the snow by it.

"Did either of you hit him?" asked Colin.

"Nah, I didn't hit shit," said Sheriff.

"I don't think I hit him either," said Alexandra. "Why?" she asked.

Colin waved her over. "I think he's bleeding," he said, pointing out the blood droplet in the snow. Smith reached into the cargo pocket of her pants and pulled out a small kit. She opened it and pulled a small plastic vial with a stopper on top. She uncorked it and scooped up the small patch of red snow, quickly putting the stopper back on. She then returned the vial to the kit and put it back in her pocket.

"We've run this guy's DNA before," said Colin. "He's a ghost."

"You do things your way, I do them mine, Snowman," she said somewhat condescendingly, as if the team's use of code names was somewhat ridiculous. Colin thought he had caught a hint of playfulness in the comment, though, mainly due to the way she subtly batted her eyelashes as she said it. Colin gave her a slightly bemused look, prodding her to explain. "A wound from our chase might not be the only reason he's bleeding," she said.

"What other reasons would there be?" asked Colin. "Self-mutilation comes to mind," she responded. "Some serial murderers have a tendency toward it, among other things. Just as some have a tendency toward sexual despondency or violence. This one doesn't strike me as having any of the traditional sexual tendencies made famous by your traditional serial killer. He strikes me more as a sociopath."

"This going back to your sociopathic PTSD veteran theory?" asked Colin.

"Yes, in a manner of speaking. There are two things at odds with each other here. One, the clean nature of the actual death stroke in the kill. He's a real pro, which makes me think he is a high-end operator. Two, the violence and trophy-taking involved, as in removing the eyes and tongues of his victims. My guess is that the violent first act used to exist as a cover-up of the professional nature of his hits. The question is, why does he continue to do it? I imagine he has dozens of victims, and judging by the fact that he's a complete ghost, it doesn't matter if he covers up the professional nature of the hits. I think he's lying to himself about what he really is at this point. I would bet he disposes of the eyes and tongues but keeps another trophy. It's an internal compromise that allows his sociopathic side to cover up the monster he really is from his more sensible half. My guess is that's why he is so high-functioning. I've never really seen anything like it. Only read theories that I'm stringing together." She once again sounded like Doctor Death to Colin, helped by the graphic hand motions that accompanied her speech. Still, Colin couldn't help but find her a contradiction. The way the snow had settled onto her blonde hair as she spoke was both peaceful and beautiful. It was calming in a way he couldn't explain.

Colin stood silent for a moment, and Sheriff caught his eye. They were both thinking through her statement and internally comparing it to what they had seen. "So he's a sociopath, a serial killer, and a highly trained operative? It sounds like he's got multiple personality disorder," said Colin.

"Maybe in a sense," she began, "but I think he's too high functioning to be schizophrenic. I would think of it more like this. All spooks are basically sociopaths. Or at least they have to be really good at lying to do their job well. Imagine if one had really bad PTSD and felt like he couldn't control the world around him. Every day, the condition affects him more and more, until one day he realizes the only time he can control the world around him is when he's lying. Now imagine that guy gets a job whacking guys for the government or some other contractor. He discovers the ultimate way to control the world around him is to literally play god to the people he has to kill."

The shocking thing to Colin was how quickly that clicked in his mind. He knew guys on the teams who enjoyed what they did for a living. He also knew that the guys who really enjoyed the killing part of their job generally didn't last long on the teams. He thought to some of the spooks he met on missions. It was eerie to think of how short the road could be to this possibility. The silence in the alley, which was blocking them from some of the heavy wind, left Colin nearly alone with these thoughts, and they echoed from his head to the bricks surrounding them in an uncomfortable sort of way.

They began the long walk back to their SUV in relative silence. The whistling wind picked up through the building's alley as they went, but the alley itself did provide them some cover from the snow. This changed when they exited the alley back onto the side street that they had run down before. Colin was once again struck by the amount of snow that had fallen in such a short period of time. Fire hydrants were starting to get buried in high drifts, and Colin still. hadn't seen a single plow. Their ability to respond to developments and get around the city was quickly eroding.

Colin only saw one vehicle out on the road. It was an old Jeep Wrangler with giant mud tires driving up and over snowbanks and drifting around a corner. It appeared to Colin that the driver was just out and having fun. It struck him again that this operation, which was as black as they came, was happening in the middle of the capital. People a mere hundred feet away had no idea that an assault on their way of life was taking place so close. But these people were inside, if they were here at all. Likely watching Christmas movies so close to the holidays and enjoying what would likely be a nice few days of working from home.

"I think we need to get to the other senators and consolidate them in one place as quickly as possible," said Colin. "Having them all in one place should afford them more protection and make protecting them easier. I know it seems counterintuitive, but I'm not sure they'll be expecting the break in protocol. And there's safety in numbers." Colin finished. He was referring to typical protocol, which would have been to separate the targets to make them harder to get to. But Colin was sure the opposite might be true in this case.

"I agree—now that he feels like he's knocked us off balance, he will likely go for his next victim," said Alexandra.

"The question is, which senator do we secure first?" asked Sheriff.

Colin thought about this for a second, trying to make up his mind. Time wasn't on his side.

25

The killer moved swiftly and silently, like the predator he was. Snow blew in peaceful flurries past him as he ran in the shadows through a series of alleys mere blocks away from where he had just escaped. The killer's gambit had worked, though he would have very much enjoyed killing the people chasing him. Their time would come. For now, he had thrown them off and hopefully confused them as to where he was heading next.

The killer could feel the cloth of his jacket scraping the scab of his newly cauterized wound. Blood dripped down his arm and into his hand. The warm, wet sensation was infuriating to him—a clumsy result of underestimating his enemies' ability to respond. The woman was new to him. He had seen the men before endlessly chasing him about the world, but she was something new, something interesting, something he could use.

The killer's pension for murdering women was not something that was new. Life had never been exactly kind to him. But it didn't come from the more typical places that inspired white middle-aged men to hack women to bits and leave their own calling cards. Those impulses usually came from childhood traumas or feelings of inadequacy. The killer was an outlier in these senses, having suffered no childhood trauma to speak of and being on the far side of middle-age.

His trauma had come as an adult. The result of thousands of violent actions and the deaths of hundreds. The result of being forced from honor to disgrace. The result of understanding that no one could ever comprehend that he had done the right thing to protect them.

From there, the killer's fall from grace was similar to that of Lucifer from heaven. That was, a fall to a world of his own making. A hellish evil from which there was no escape but to embrace that which he had become. This made him smile—not because he had fallen from grace, but because he had embraced his fall. And because he knew what he was doing was, in a way, righteous and for himself. The truth was that women needed to be taken primarily because men cherished them so much. If half of his soul had been taken, then perhaps the taking of others would serve to humble those who thought themselves invincible.

Of course, his usual targets these days were men. A product of their disproportionate participation in the world in which the killer made his career. Which was part of the reason today was so invigorating to him. A chance to mix work and pleasure was somewhat rare. On top of the other female senators, this new woman chasing him presented an opportunity that was too sweet to pass up. A chance to turn the tables. A chance to allow the hunter to become the hunted.

26

"It's working." Charlie sighed. He leaned back in the custom red and black leather gaming chair he brought with him on every mission that looked more like the seat of a high end sports car. His arms were shaking as if he had just finished an intense workout. Some combination of stress, caffeine, nerves, and now hope were serving to make him feel as if he'd just won some kind of sick race where the winner stayed alive and the loser died.

Charlie knew this wasn't table stakes for himself, but merely his teammates in the field, which ramped the pressure up infinitely for him. He moved his fingers back toward his keyboard to check something, but with his hands shaking, he merely knocked over the orange soda he was now drinking. The orange liquid spilled off of the beige folding table and pooled on the concrete floor below him.

"Dammit, Charlie. You need to calm down," scolded Sarah. She had just returned from answering a ringing phone in the other room, and went immediately to grab a towel from one of the gear bags the team had brought with them. She swished as she went, having donned a black Gore-Tex waterproof jacket and gloves. *She never was very good in the cold,* thought Charlie. He was still in merely a sweatshirt and pants, although he had to admit it was cold in the hangar even with the expansive heating on. He was actually slightly surprised that the orange soda hadn't frozen on the ground already. But he enjoyed the cold, so he ignored it.

"Sorry Sarah. I've got too much on my mind."

She squinted her eyes at him as she returned. "It's all this crap you're drinking. Coffee would do the job fine and help with your weight loss." He sighed again, knowing their next workout together would be brutal. Sarah had taken his health as her personal mission, and though he appreciated the sentiment, he couldn't help but be a bit scared of her at times. He returned his attention to his screen, but suddenly snapped his eyes away as he remembered the ringing phone. "Wait, who was calling?" he asked, justly realizing the phone call had been odd.

"It was Jester. Apparently, one of the hit teams found them, so he said he would call me back," she said matter of factory.

"Well, are they okay?" he asked.

"They seemed fine to me. A little perturbed about the loss of comms but I told him we're working on it." Charlie got the distinct impression she was downplaying things to keep him focused, but he was also sure Jester could handle himself.

"Any word from the boss?" he asked. "Nothing," she replied. He nodded and returned his attention to his work, and Sarah went back to where the ringing had come from—he assumed to wait for another call.

Charlie couldn't be sure how long it would take, but the blockchain system running in the cloud was slowly but surely rooting out the virus from every file in their systems. The beautiful part about being an independent entity, at least in theory, from the official U.S. government was that Charlie was free to do things his way, free from levels of bureaucracy and red tape. This worked both ways, though. Whereas at the NSA, he would have had a team of dozens of cyber warriors at his disposal, here he had himself and an army of artificial bots to do his bidding. Bots were great, but they couldn't quite think the way humans did. He found himself losing himself in the cyberworld. In a way, it seemed to make sense to him, which the physical world just never did.

Sarah had run into the other room what seemed like ages ago to wait for another call. She couldn't exactly help Charlie with what he was doing, but his nervous personality made it such that he wished she was standing here with him. She had a kind of motherly personality—well, maybe more of a big sister, he reflected—that made him feel comfortable no matter the situation. This typically came in handy in some of the more dangerous places in the world that they operated out of.

Charlie opened the terminal application again and queried the cloud system to check the progress of the system cleanse. The system had gone through about 40 percent of the files and was having trouble estimating the remaining time to completion. Charlie could have, of course, cleansed the system more quickly, but much of the signals intelligence the team gathered was intentionally sequestered on their system and kept separate from the larger government systems. This was because of the frightful state of cybersecurity within the federal government at this point. A very small portion of the government outside of the intelligence community had migrated their systems to the far more secure Gov-Cloud system.

Worse yet, a large portion of government technology had very obscure sourcing protocols. Meaning that components in a server could be made by Chinese, Russian, or other unfriendly countries looking to install back doors in U.S. systems. The government was, of course, looking to fix this, with the next phase being the massive multi-billion-dollar JEDI cloud contract to migrate the entire DOD's infrastructure to the more secure system. But in the meantime, Charlie intended to stick with his more secure, and more advanced, he judged, system.

The system progress bar made another small jump. Charlie took another big chug of the orange soda that hadn't spilled and was nervously bouncing about in his free hand. The team had been out of contact for over an hour now. Charlie knew that small operational teams without the support of ISR and, more often, close air support were almost always overmatched by superior forces. The same two things that made small teams so lethal against larger forces could quickly become their undoing if they were lost. Charlie had seen it before on numerous missions prior to working with Team Alien. He had to get the team's advantage back before it was too late.

27

Senator Walker tapped the refresh button on the browser of the iMac for the third time and cursed under his breath. "Fucking Internet."

He was attempting to search Google for any news of dead senators leaking, but the internet didn't seem to be cooperating. With a low electronic jolt, the power shut off throughout the small office in the rented house in Northwest D.C. The senator nearly jumped out of his skin. The man was on edge with the news of the deaths of now two of his colleagues. Something was coming for them one by one, and the fear was building in the back of his mind like a deer catching a whiff of a hunter on the morning breeze.

The front door to the house opened, and the senator sat up in alarm. "Who's there?" he demanded in the dark. The only light in the room came from an evergreen Christmas candle burning at the edge of his tidy desk.

"It's me, Senator," came the call of his new lead security officer coming down the hallway. "I saw the power go out, and I wanted to check on you, sir."

The senator didn't respond for a moment. The quiet that had enveloped the house was remarkably discomforting. The only sound was the wind outside and the quietly crackling wooden flame of the candle burning next to him. "Ah… Yes, thank you, Riggs," the senator said, recovering. "Where's Marquette?" he continued inquiring after his other Capitol Police guard. The senator prided himself on knowing everything about the people who worked with him, from full names to birthdays to children's names.

"Doing a perimeter check of the rear of the house, sir. I just spoke with him a second ago."

"Good… good," said the senator. "There's a generator in the shed. I'm not sure it's ever been used, but let's try and get it running," said the senator, standing to leave the room. "Sir, I think you should stay in the house. I can go get the generator started."

The senator gave Riggs the same withering look that had cowed countless other politicians and reporters. He hated not leading from the front and rolling his sleeves up to get things done—a remnant from his days as an army officer decades before in another part of the world. "Riggs, you can either stay here or follow me out that door; either way, I'm going."

Riggs thought about challenging him, but decided it wasn't worth it. "Please follow me, Senator," he said, stepping out into the hall-way. They proceeded toward the rear door of the house but froze dead in their tracks when they heard a noise upstairs.

The senator, who was considered by most to be a brave man, was more fearful than he chose to admit. He found that he was actually sweating and wiped a drip from his brow. He looked back at Riggs. "J-Just the wind. There's a bit of loose siding on the side of the house." He hadn't heard himself stutter since he was a child and told himself internally to get a grip.

"Would you like me to check it out, sir? We secured the upstairs of the house when we arrived earlier," said Riggs.

"No, it's nothing. Let's get this generator on. The temperature is already dropping in here."

28

C olin could feel water dripping down his back beneath the protective vest he wore. It had only been thirty minutes since he had been shot. The snow he had balled up and placed over the rapidly forming bruise from the bullet impact to his vest was already starting to melt. The cold provided some relief, but the pain killers he had popped when they got back to the SUV would take a while to really kick in.

Sheriff, Colin, and Agent Smith were gathered around the open trunk of the SUV, looking at the tablet, which displayed a map of D.C. and the locations of the remaining senators. Due to their communications troubles, they couldn't communicate with home base or Jester's team to get any kind of update, so they were operating partially blind.

"We have no way of telling which senator is going to be targeted next and no way of communicating with Bravo team, which leaves us with a big problem," said Smith to the group.

"We're going to have to split up. We can't risk the senators' safety by picking and choosing which ones we go to first," said Colin.

"That's a risky business, brother. We are seriously outgunned right now," interjected Sheriff.

"We're all operating blind in this storm. Splitting gives us the advantage. We'll be able to move like ghosts in this storm. You take Agent Smith and the vehicle with you and head to Senator Miller's house. I'll use the storm as cover and move the five blocks to Senator Walkers. Once you have the senator secure, exfil to my location. We'll take both senators to Senator Rand's and make that our Alamo while we go hunting," said Colin.

"Copy that," replied Sheriff. Colin reached into one of the bags in the back and pulled out an MP7 submachine gun and several additional magazines, which he stored in his pockets. The weapon he tucked under his jacket.

Colin set off at a light run a few minutes later, doing his best to maintain speed in the ever-deepening snow. Visibility had shrunk to less than a hundred feet, and Colin had to be careful to keep track of street signs and landmarks as he went to ensure he didn't miss his objective. It was remarkable how much more difficult snow made things in any operation. Especially when the team didn't have adequate cold-weather gear and had to stay low profile.

Colin didn't see a soul out in the blizzard, and even more strangely, he didn't see a single light on in any of the houses he could make out from the street. He decided the power must have gone off and wondered, judging by the day's events, if it was due to the weather or something more malicious.

He passed the second street, indicating he had three blocks left to run. Colin was barely even panting yet due to his excellent conditioning, but the bruise forming on his chest was a source of significant discomfort to him every time he took a deep breath. He was just thankful the experimental vest had taken the round, and he reflected that it had hurt much less than traditional style armor.

Colin had been shot three times in his career, not including today. Twice in the vest in Afghanistan, and once in the leg on a kill mission in Africa. The latter still bothered him when it was cold, meaning it was bothering him now. He put the pain out of his mind and pushed himself to run more quickly. The senator's life depended on Colin reaching him in time.

He passed two more streets and slowed slightly as he approached his target's location. When he stepped onto the objective's block, he had returned to a casual walk. Colin looked around now, taking in his surroundings and looking for anything out of the ordinary. It was an older, more established neighborhood with brick style houses that wouldn't have looked all that out of place in colonial America. All of the houses were dark on this street as well. Colin saw the half-built remnants of a snowman in a small front yard across the street, but judging by the significant coat of fresh powder on it, he could only assume its builders had gone inside several hours ago.

He passed two more houses before cautiously approaching the front steps of the house he was looking for. They were made of handsome blue stone and had clearly been shoveled meticulously throughout the day. It was clear that likely an hour had passed before they had last been cleared of precipitation, which added to Colin's feeling of unease.

He looked up at the house. It was a brick style colonial as well, with green shutters and white trim. The kind of house that old money might buy you in a traditional southern city. Instantly, Colin could tell something was wrong. The front door stood slightly ajar, and Colin didn't see either of the two protective officers.

He pulled the MP7 from beneath his jacket and moved slowly up the snow-covered stone steps toward the house. He decided to do a quick look around the perimeter of the house to make sure neither of the agents was in the rear. He didn't want to get shot by anyone who didn't know who he was. He transited the house slowly and quietly, being sure to stay low beneath the sight of any of the house's windows. When he reached the rear, he nearly tripped over something beneath the snow.

He recovered his balance and kneeled down, keeping his weapon up. He dusted off what he tripped over and was unsurprised to see that it was the body of one of the agents. He had a half-frozen exit wound out of the front of his forehead, but the body was still relatively warmer than the snow around it. Colin estimated he hadn't been dead for more than an hour. In fact, on further examination, it looked to Colin like snow had been intentionally pushed over the man. His alert level instantly ratcheted up.

When he finished his perimeter check, he came back to the front door and slowly pushed it open, pivoting into the house behind it, weapon up, scanning for targets. The house had a central wooden staircase next to a hallway and two rooms off of the front entrance. A gold chandelier wreathed in darkness hung above him, and a plush green runner carpet cushioned his footfalls. The house was painfully silent. Colin decided not to break the silence for the time being. The first room appeared to be the senator's office, which was empty apart from a candle burning on the desk. Its wooden wick crackled in the darkness, spreading an evergreen scent through the room.

Colin then pushed into the other room, which was a lightly furnished living room, the way a beach house might be. With only stock items, and not many of the personal momentos found in one's permanent residence. From this room, he followed cautiously into a dining room, which was blatantly over the top, with carved wooden furniture and silver candlesticks adorning a twelve-foot-long dining table. Colin could picture the senator wining and dining his colleagues here in an effort to keep the wheels of congressional power turning.

He moved slowly, checking underneath the dining room table before coming to an open doorway that led to the kitchen. He methodically moved into this room, seeing a woman face down on the table with a gaping hole in the back of her head and a shattered coffee mug beneath her skull. It appeared that the force of the bullet's impact had slammed her face into the table, crushing the ceramic mug beneath her. A mixture of coffee and blood dripped from the table to the floor and echoed in the silence like water in a cave. Colin felt the skin of her neck with the small part of the top of his wrist exposed above his gloves. She was still partially warm.

Colin searched the rest of the house, nearly shooting a cat that jumped out of a closet and knocked over a vase on its way to hide from him.

The house was empty. This puzzled Colin. There were definite signs of a struggle, with various objects knocked about the upstairs and a door that was splintered in its frame, but the senator was gone. Whether he had escaped or been taken by someone, Colin wasn't sure, but the dead police officers outside did not bode well.

29

J ester couldn't decide if it was by dumb luck or sheer stupidity that the hacker Kong had, for some reason, decided to accompany one of the Chinese hit teams to try and kill his squad. He held a pistol to the back of Agent Sunderland's head with one arm, and his other was in a makeshift sling. Fury emanated out of his one eye that was still open. The other was swollen shut from the shot Colin had given him when they fought outside of the warehouse. His cheeks were rosy red from the cold, and it looked like the weather may have been causing him to shake slightly as well. Jester took this information in processing it as he went trying to calculate out some kind of internal decision about how to handle this situation. He decided to try and talk with him for a moment while he decided what to do.

"You want to put that gun down before you get hurt, kid?" asked Jester. He and Witch stood about twenty feet from where he was holding Sunderland, guns up and trained on the hacker's head.

"Fuck you!" Kong screamed back. "I take the agent and don't kill him if you let us leave in peace," he said in a heavy Chinese accent.

"Whoa, he is not in a friendly mood today, Jester," said Witch.

Jester couldn't see Witch, only hear his deep voice from somewhere on his left. His eyes were sighted down the barrel of his Sig.

Jester wasn't sure he saw a way out of this that didn't end in violence, and he needed to communicate that to Witch. He thought of ways to do this but, in the end, decided to do it verbally. This kid was too amped up to deal with sudden movements, and Jester didn't want him to shoot Sunderland accidentally. He found himself breathing deeply, steadying his aim in the split second before he spoke. The snowflakes traced lazy patterns downward as they cascaded between the men down to the ground below.

"How about you drop the gun, and we don't kill you immediately?" said Jester. He then heard Witch mutter "Yup" beneath his breath in nearly silent agreement.

"Fuck you! I kill him if..." Kong never finished the sentence. Bullets from both Witch and Jester entered his eye sockets at nearly the same time, blowing his brains out of the back of his head and sending him toppling over the hood of the car behind him. Even the suppressed shots echoed slightly off of the surrounding buildings, giving a momentary pause to the world around them.

"Holy shit!" yelled Sunderland, breaking the peace. "You could have fucking killed me."

"How about 'thanks for saving my life'?" said Witch sarcastically. Jester looked over at Witch, finding his comment amusing. He saw beads of water dripping from his bald head and down his face. He recognized it as melting snow on his head. Witch wouldn't have sweated from the stress in a situation like this. *He is as cool as a cucumber,* thought Jester.

"You couldn't have talked him down! It's not like he had anywhere to go!" yelled Sunderland, still completely shocked.

"We don't negotiate with terrorists," said Jester, walking over and kicking the weapon from Kong's limp hand.

"Or assholes," said Witch, walking over and examining Kong's lifeless form.

Sunderland took a deep breath, trying to calm down. Jester could see in the wide look in Sunderland's eyes that he was thinking he was in way over his head. This was spy shit, not law enforcement, and he hadn't been trained for anything like it. He was breathing deep now, and the shaking in Sunderland's hands seemed to be calming down. "I'm sorry," he said, bending down and picking up his Glock. "I was not expecting that."

"No problem," said Jester.

"We tend to deal with the unexpected," chimed in Witch.

"We need to unass this place now and check back in with Sarah before the real cops show up," said Jester. But he couldn't hear any sirens in the distance. *This is eerie,* he thought. *What the fuck could be happening that the police aren't responding to hails of gunfire in the middle of the city?* But then he took in his surroundings. And something clicked into place that hadn't before. There were no lights anywhere.

Where are the lights? Judging by the sudden silence that overcame everyone at the same time, they were all thinking the same thing. The adrenaline was wearing off, and their senses were properly returning. It was shocking how dark it had become. The late afternoon, obscured by the thick snow clouds, had transformed light gray into dark gray in a timeframe Jester couldn't believe. The sun must have been setting somewhere behind the clouds, and Jester was shocked by just how dark the world had become.

30

Weather Operations Report Immediate Traffic OBS to NORAD
Source- KH-12 Designation Athena 32, Geosynchronous Orbit

1. Large scale power outage reported in vicinity of and affecting Nation's Capital.
2. Outage is believed to be caused by Winter Storm Douglas and is NOT due to suspected foul play at this time.
3. Tier One National infrastructure in the area is fully functional at this time.
4. Local infrastructure is likely inadequate to deal with reported precipitation levels.

Recommend message declassification and dissemination to partner federal agencies, including FBI, FEMA, Commander National Guard (Virginia, and Maryland), Secret Service.

End Traffic.

31

17 Years Before

Susan walked down the brick Georgetown sidewalk, taking in the crisp fall air and changing colors of the leaves. It was a cloudy day, and the dark clouds threatened rain any minute. A gust of wind blew her hair back and penetrated the outer layers of her clothing. She pulled her coat tighter around her and pushed on up the side street toward Alex Tucker's house.

The file she had uncovered with his name on it as a suspect in his wife's murder was neatly tucked into a messenger bag over her shoulder. She continued up the side street, heading uphill away from the Potomac River, before finally coming to the street she was looking for.

She was immediately taken aback by the small armada of police cars, caution tape, and flashing lights that she saw closing the small block off. Her blood froze. She had no way of knowing if Alex Tucker was the victim in this chaos, but she had a strong gut feeling. She parted a strand of hair that had blown into her eye away from her face and approached an officer standing guard over the cordon blocking off the street.

"Sorry, ma'am, this street's closed. You'll have to go around," the officer said to her. His name tag read Carr.

"Officer Carr, I'm with the District Attorney's office—what's going on here?" she said, handing him a thin paper business card.

He examined the card and looked back at her before pocketing it. "Hello, Ms. Frost. It looks like a suicide. Some guy jumped off of his brownstone headfirst into the sidewalk."

"What's his name?" she asked.

"Hang on," he said, walking away to ask another officer. He came back over and, in a low voice, told her, "ID in the man's wallet said Alex Tucker."

Susan didn't say anything. She stared at the ground, lost in thought for a moment. Chills ran down her neck, and the wind suddenly seemed very loud. She had pulled his information less than a week ago, and now he was dead. This was not a coincidence, and she felt like she was in imminent danger. Her head shot up, and she began scanning the faces of bystanders all around the crime scene. She didn't see anyone who looked familiar or even suspicious, but in truth, she had no idea what she was really looking for.

"Are you all right, Ms. Frost?" asked the officer.

She took another second to respond. Her mind was racing, and fear was growing in the pit of her stomach. She swallowed before she said, "Um, I'm fine, thanks. Were there any signs of foul play?" she asked the officer.

"No, ma'am, it looks like a suicide. No signs of a struggle, and the body is clear of the usual signs of confrontation."

Susan didn't respond again. Her inner dialogue rotated from "maybe he couldn't deal with life without his wife" to "maybe it was guilt over killing her" to "why now?" It was too much of a coincidence. Susan knew something was very wrong here. What she didn't know was how someone had found out that she had pulled his file. She had been very careful to cover her tracks.

"Ma'am, are you sure you're okay?" the officer asked.

"Yes, thank you," she responded, still partially lost in thought.

"Were you here to see Alex Tucker?" he asked, being a cop and naturally suspicious.

"No," she lied. "Will you be on duty here until tonight?" she asked.

"I will be," Carr responded.

"Do you have a card, officer?"

Officer Carr reached into the pocket behind his name tag and handed Susan a card.

"Thank you. I or someone from my office may be in touch with you about this," she said, turning and walking away before he could respond. She felt his eyes on her all the way down the street, knowing he was suspicious, but she didn't care. Her mind was moving more quickly than she could effectively process. She was unquestionably onto something dark, and now the only link she had identified had been murdered. It could be suicide, she reasoned internally, trying to calm herself down. But she knew she was lying to herself.

She didn't even register the man sitting outside at the cafe across the street with the baseball cap low over his eyes.

32

"Snowman, you here?" Colin heard as he examined the body of the dead woman in the kitchen. He instantly recognized the voice as Sheriff's.

"In the kitchen," Colin called back. A moment later, they joined him in the kitchen, where he had been examining the body of the fallen officer face down on the table. Smith looked shocked by the scene in the kitchen, but Sheriff barely looked fazed. "Senator Walker isn't here. I found him and his partner, who was facedown out back like this when I got here," said Colin.

"Signs of a struggle?" asked Agent Smith.

"The upstairs is trashed, and there's a splintered door. Outside of that, I wasn't able to find any blood or traces of where the senator may have gone. I'm not sure if he escaped or was taken, but my bet's on the latter."

"That doesn't sound like Azrael," said Sheriff, who was reaching into one of his pockets.

"More likely one of the Chinese hit teams," replied Agent Smith.

"I think so as well. Were you able to secure Senator Miller?" asked Colin.

"We opted to bring him right to Senator Rand's as the two locations were close. Less time for something to go wrong," said Sheriff.

Colin noted with dark amusement that Sheriff had pulled a protein bar out and was preparing to eat it. Colin felt hunger ache within his own stomach and remembered that he hadn't eaten in nearly twelve hours. Normally, this wouldn't have bothered him, as he fasted regularly, but with the level of physical exertion today, he was ravenous. He put the thought out of his mind. It wasn't the time.

"Good call," replied Colin.

"I'm going to take a look around," said Smith, looking at Sheriff disgusted that anyone could eat at a time like this and heading off toward the upstairs.

When she left the room, Sheriff turned to Colin, finishing his first bite. "A hostage throws a serious wrench into this situation."

"It tells us one of two things. Either we are gaining ground on them and the Chinese teams want leverage, or there is a deeper plan at play here," said Colin.

"Public execution?" asked Sheriff, his eyes widening.

"Negative. They're too smart to draw that much attention to what they're doing. The plan is to provoke fear that a serial killer is on the loose offing important political figures. Internally, the political elite will hear rumors of who's really behind it, but if the media gets wind of too much, then conspiracy theories will start to abound. The Chinese don't want a witch hunt. They want to scare American politicians from the shadows."

"I don't know, Snowman, this whole thing seems totally fucking crazy to me," lamented Sheriff, taking another bite.

"I don't disagree, but the pattern holds. In Afghanistan, they did the same thing, only they disguised it behind terrorists and jihad. Here, they are hiding it behind a serial killer. In both situations, they are using a proxy to get what they want, which is control or information in all cases," finished Colin, crossing his arms.

"So what's the next move, then, boss man?"

"Consolidate so we can go on the offensive. We need comms back up and to rendezvous with Bravo to figure out what their status is. Once we have those pieces in place, we can start clearing the board."

Agent Smith walked into the room as he finished and held up a wrapper in her hand with Chinese characters on it. "Well, it was definitely one of the Chinese teams that took the senator. I found this in the trashed master upstairs. Unless the senator enjoys Chinese candy, I would say one of the attackers dropped this in the struggle."

33

Robert F. Kennedy Department of Justice Building, 950 Pennsylvania Avenue, NW

A ttorney General Mark Poole set his coffee mug down too hard, splashing some of its contents onto the desk he was sitting at. "What do you mean we don't know what's going on? Are you telling me there's been an explosion and several shootouts across the city, and you can't tell me what's happening? It's the storm of the century out there—people are supposed to be inside watching TV, not rioting," he said to his frazzled-looking aid.

He could tell she thought she should have had the day off. Everyone else did, after all. He despised this laziness in her. Mark Poole made most type A personality types look downright relaxed next to his borderline obsessive work tendencies. "Perhaps you think you should have had the day off, Karen. Is that what you want?" he demanded of her.

"No, sir. I just mean, it seems awfully dangerous out there, and law enforcement hasn't been able to get to the scenes quickly enough to provide answers. The power outage isn't helping, sir," she said, nearly quivering.

"Did I ask about the fucking power, Karen? Crime clearly doesn't take any days off, so neither do we. For fuck's sake, you told me you wanted to work when you took this job," he said indignantly.

She stuttered, trying to find the words to say. Working here was generally a hostile environment, but she was one of the only people in the office today, making her job especially difficult. She was determined to be attorney general herself one day, so she knew she had no choice but to take the abuse.

"I don't want any excuses—just get out there and get me the answers, Karen, and find Matt Coughlin while you're at it. If you aren't capable, then you can spend all the time at home that you like," he said, cutting her off.

"Y-Yes sir," she said, turning and walking out the door of his office.

Mark Poole stood and walked to the windows of his expansive office at the Department of Justice. It was an old school type of room with dark wood, vaulted ceilings, and an ornately patterned blue carpet. There were bookshelves filled with ponderous tomes on federal statutes, and a fireplace that was never lit in the corner. The lights flickered slightly as he went due to the power being generated by the diesel generators in the basement of the building.

He could feel the cold air emanating through the old glass of the windows of his office. Snow flurries hit the window and sidled off in one direction or another, but outside of that, he couldn't see more than a hundred feet from the glass. Mark Poole was angry, but more than anything else, he was nervous. There were so many things in motion at the moment that he wasn't sure any of them could possibly succeed. The snow made matters worse.

Why the fuck did a random freak snowstorm of the century decide to hit now of all weeks, he thought.

Worse yet, if any of them were discovered, he would likely have to resign in disgrace and more likely spend the rest of his life in prison. He was playing a dangerous game, and he knew it. But he knew that a dangerous game had to be played to accomplish his ultimate mission and rise to the ultimate position of power in the world.

34

A zrael stood in the dark corner of the warehouse, watching the white Sprinter van enter from the blizzard outside. Several Chinese men exited the vehicle, dragging a bound and hooded man behind them. One of them closed the garage door to the warehouse and locked it from the inside. The one the men called Commander Chen approached Azrael. The man was a specimen of physical fitness and looked more like a boy scout than the tier one operator and member of China's PLA special forces unit, Oriental Sword.

Much like the U.S. Army's Green Berets, select Oriental Sword commandos were often inserted into guerrilla forces, or in this case, gangs to lend support and help prop up forces against foreign governments. In this particular instance, a local sect of the Triads.

"We have the senator. Where would you like him?" he asked Azrael.

It had been nearly forty minutes since they had taken him and killed his protectors. Azrael nodded toward the back office of the warehouse, and commander Chen motioned his men to take the senator there. He watched as they dragged him along the cold concrete floor, the black hood lightly illuminated by the fluorescent pod lights far above. Azrael despised the arrogant special forces commander assigned to this mission. It was a sign of the lack of trust of his employer that he could get the mission done.

He decided he would likely kill the man when the day was over and blame it on the American team hunting him. Azrael walked over to a table in the corner and looked at the feed from a Dragon Two stealth drone that was orbiting the house of the senator they had just kidnapped. It appeared that more of the American team had consolidated at the house. He tapped his hand on the table, thinking. He always tapped his hand in sets of even numbers. Never odd numbers, except for sets of five.

He felt the Chinese commando behind him more than heard him. A result of his highly tuned predator instincts. Instantly, he became embarrassed and annoyed that Commander Chen had seen his hand-tapping ritual.

"Where do you want my team next?" the commando asked him in a bored tone.

Azrael turned on his heel and shot him a predatory death stare that raised the hair on the back of his neck. Commander Chen knew perfectly well where his team was supposed to be next. He just had no faith in Azrael's ability to plan that far ahead within an operation.

Azrael took secret pleasure in the knowledge that the commander's insolent other team had been massacred minutes ago by one of the American teams. It was their stupidity in not listening to Azrael that had led them to this point. The commander turned and led his team back to the van. Azrael turned back to the drone feed and smiled, showing his yellow teeth. Everything was going according to plan, but he had yet to pull the final string, and when he did, there was nothing they could do to save themselves.

35

The pen top clicked in and out once, then twice, then three times, before a rapid machine gun like clicking ensued. "Charlie!" Sarah yelled, her voice echoing off the hangar. "Sorry," he replied. "Just nervous."

"Is it working?" she shot back like an annoyed older sister, placing her hands on her hips. "Well, yeah," he replied. "Then stop clicking the damn pen before I click your head."

He placed the pen down beside the keyboard on his desk, not wanting to encourage any more of her wrath. She was nervous like he was; she just showed it in different ways. He took a sip of the bottled water that was now next to him. She had flat out refused to bring him any more sodas or energy drinks.

Charlie keyed in an API that began reassembling several applications whose source code had been scrambled by the brutal cyberwar taking place over his system. The system was now 98 percent clear of malicious code, and Charlie had all but won this battle. His blockchain net of powerful cloud computers had almost completed their task.

Charlie was currently in the process of recompiling the encrypted control net that the drone they had used to communicate navigation and video data to him had sent. As soon as the drone had lost connection with the net, it had gone into idle mode and was tracing lazy loops across the snow-filled sky. It took Charlie another five minutes to complete this, and when he tested the net, he was happy to see the live video feed from the drone begin to stream into the app.

A chime from the speakers on his computer indicated that the last of the malicious code had been eliminated. Better yet, the neural net that the code was modeled on, which had been programmed like the body's immune system, had learned from the code and developed effective internal defenses which would make future attacks by code like this nearly impossible. Charlie ran another API, which recompiled the team's communication system, and within moments, messages from the team began to stream into the application.

"Sarah! I've got communications back up!"

She came running back to her station and put on a headset sitting near her iPad. "Snowman, do you copy?"

Nothing. He repeated his query. "Snowman do you copy?"

A static buzz came through the speakers, and Charlie typed a few commands into the application to adjust some settings. He could feel his heart beating as he finished and tried his query one more time. If this didn't work, he was at a loss for why. "Snowman, do you copy?" he said rather more forcefully than he usually spoke.

"Overlord, is that you?" They heard Colin's voice come through the speaker using her and Charlie's technical code name. Charlie shot Sarah a thumbs-up.

"You got it, Snowman. Here and ready to assist. ISR is getting back overhead now," she said. The drone was now able to use the team's location and move back into orbit above them.

"Where the hell have you guys been?" asked Colin.

"The phone Jester secured had a Trojan horse virus in its system. As soon as we broke it it infected our entire system. We only just managed to clear it," chimed in Charlie.

"How compromised is our Infosec? Is this a secure channel?" asked Colin, referring to the team's information security.

"Rock solid," said Charlie. "It doesn't look like they got any of our information—the virus was only able to disable our systems. This channel is definitely secure."

"Roger that. Jester, you getting this?" asked Colin.

"I've gotcha, Snowman," replied Jester.

"SITREP?" asked Colin.

"One Chinese hit team KIA, including the Chinese hacker," said Jester.

"Copy. Rally at Senator Walker's house ASAP."

36

S carcely twenty minutes had passed since the arrival of Senator
Miller. A time that, in Rand's view, had been marked by point-
less conversation and a whole lot of security double checks of the
premises. He was sure his own guards had done a fine job, but then
again, one could never be too careful. Senator Rand brought in the
two mugs of coffee and placed them on a small table between two
armchairs.

He walked back across the small office to a desk and retrieved a
bottle of private label whiskey from his family's distillery in the
Deep South. The amber liquid caught the glow of the small gas fireplace insert and reflected the dancing flames onto the clean white
ceiling. The power was out in the apartment, but the gas still worked,
allowing the senator to boil water for his French press coffee maker
filled with his favorite District Joe ground beans and to keep the
small gas fireplace going in the office off the living room of his D.C.
apartment.

"I find the whiskey helps with two things up here," said the
senator in his thick southern drawl. "One, to keep you warm, and
two, to cut through the stress of a long day," he finished, pouring a
good measure into each steaming mug of coffee.

Senator Miller looked around the office of his more senior counterpart. The office seemed very clean except for several black framed photographs hanging at neat intervals across the office of him and several presidents, among other important figures that he could see in the dim light. The only other light in the room came from the floor to ceiling windows, but it was so dark and the visibility was so poor outside now that one could effectively argue it was nighttime. In truth, it was only late afternoon, but the deep blues and dark grays of the outside world were working hard to disprove this belief.

Both senators took sips from their mugs and sat quietly for a moment. Senator Miller kept fidgeting, but Senator Rand seemed calm, as if he had done this a thousand times before. "I don't like this. We should have just gone to the FBI," said Miller.

Senator Rand just stared into the fire, the flames casting intermittent shadows on his face. Finally, he turned back to the other senator. "We both know that would have been a poor idea."

"Rand, I don't like that this lunatic is mowing down our security like grass, and for all we know, we're the only two left. That means we're next. And we're sitting ducks here!" said Miller.

"Perhaps if you hadn't fought so hard to restrict personal gun rights, you would have felt a little more safe in your own house," said Rand matter-of-factly. He was toying with the senator now. Of the committee, he was one of the most junior and still one of the most idealistic of the whole bunch. Rand rotated in and out of finding it inspiring and incredibly annoying. The man wanted to be out there, fighting the maniac chasing him, but that wasn't his job anymore. He needed to learn how things worked at this level of power. And the smug look on his face let the man know it.

"Really, that's what you're going to bring up at a time like this?" Miller asked. Looking quite surprised.

"My point is, Senator, you made your bed, and now you need to lie in it. You're not a navy man anymore; you're a politician. Politicians make policy. We make the hard choices so that society doesn't fall apart. That means when there's a crisis, you don't get to fall off the wagon and play hero anymore. You simply sit back, enjoy some of the best whiskey in the world, and let the nightmares you employ wreak havoc on your enemies' lives," said Rand swirling the contents of his mug.

"I'm not seeing any way that this works out as a win anymore, Senator. Two of us dead, a third missing, A black ops team shooting their way around the capital like it's the Wild West. We'll be lucky if we don't wind up spending the holidays unemployed or, at this rate, dead," said Miller, picking up the coffee and draining a large, hot, whiskey-infused gulp.

"Perhaps you need to learn something about the power of positivity, Miller. We're at the core of unraveling a Chinese-backed terrorist plot to frighten high-level U.S. government officials into submission and espionage. Two of our committee is dead, but when we come through the other side of this, we'll be fucking heroes, with enough political capital to do whatever we want forever. No one will care about ways and means. They will care about the Chinese and the senators that dared to defy them and their lunatic killer to ensure the hallowed halls of democracy are safe. Monuments will be built to our dead and empires by our sacrifice," finished Rand, sitting back in his chair.

Miller didn't say anything for a time. He was clearly deep in thought. And with some satisfaction, Rand could see that he looked seriously worried about what might happen today. Of course, Rand wasn't necessarily sure what was going to happen today. He took another sip of whiskey coffee and wondered how they were ever going to get out of this.

37

I've got *too many layers on to be inside*, he thought, wiping sweat from the back of his neck. Colin was crouched over a splintered door in the hallway upstairs when he heard a commotion downstairs. "Honey, I'm home," called Jester. The team had been spread out around the house looking for signs of where the senator had been taken but immediately collapsed downstairs to the sound of Jester's voice. It had been nearly an hour since they had established communications again, and Colin found himself thundering down the stairs in a hurry to check in with his lost teammates.

"Where the fuck have you been?" asked Colin, arriving at the bottom of the stairs to greet the other half of his team. Jester wasted no time recounting the attempted attack and subsequent elimination of the Chinese hit team and the hacker Kong.

"Are you all right?" Colin asked Agent Sunderland.

"I'm fine, thanks," he said.

"Any intel from any of them?" Colin asked, turning to Jester.

"Negative, boss. We got nothing. What happened to you guys?" Jester asked, looking at Colin with a look that dared him to one-up their experience.

When Colin was done recounting their visit to Senator Rand, their subsequent chase of Azrael and their decision to split the team, which had ultimately lead them to this grisly scene, Jester sighed. "Damn, we got close again."

"Super fucking close, bro," Colin replied.

"Everyone whole?" asked Jester.

"We're good," replied Colin.

Agent Smith came out of the office to Colin's right and said, "Hate to interrupt the reunion, but I've got something." She looked over at Sunderland. "You okay?" she asked.

"Fine," he said with the look of a child being embarrassed by his mother. She had always acted kind of like a big sister to him, even though she was barely a year older. Agent Smith held up a black leather-bound Moleskin notebook. She flipped it open to the first page. "Look at the name here." The team gathered around her to read.

On the first page of the notebook, it said property of Anthony Carson. "You're saying the senator who was killed first gave Senator Walker his notebook?" asked Jester.

"Or he stole it from him," interjected Agent Sunderland.

"I don't think so," said Agent Smith. "Check this out." She flipped a few more pages, which were scrawled with messy notes to the last page of the notebook with any markings. On it was an address near Navy Yard that was circled with an arrow pointing to it and a note scrawled beneath it.

Walker,

I entrust this to you. I think our investigation is finally yielding some interesting results. I'm having this delivered to you in the event anything goes awry. Bring it to the committee next week if I do not. I think he knows we're on to him.

—A

"I think Carson may have found something before he was killed," said Agent Smith. The team silently nodded in agreement, and there was a silence in the air as they all took in the latest development.

"It seems like it," replied Colin. "I think we head to this address. We have nothing else to go on at the moment, and it seems important enough to have killed a senator over. If it's big enough, it may finally give us the initiative," Colin finished. He bit his lip for a second and continued to stare at the paper as if lost in thought. It was almost like he was trying to see through the paper to see what was behind it. After a moment, Jester broke his concentration.

"Roger that boss," he said, already heading toward the door. The team nodded in agreement, and everyone began to grab their things.

"If they knew the senator was aware of this location, it may be a trap," said Agent Smith when they were alone in the hallway. It was a thoughtful comment, and the fact that she waited until they were alone made the hallway seem like a safe space where their thoughts could echo back and forth between each other and morph into ideas. He looked back at her, taking in her cheeks, which were rosy with the cold. He liked that.

Colin stared into her eyes and nodded with a smile. "I'm counting on it."

38

Snow whipped off the windshield of the forward-most SUV in the small convoy of two vehicles. Heat blasted in the two vehicles, keeping Colin and his team warm and somewhat comfortable for their ride to the address listed in the senator's notebook. Team Alien had a tendency to pop ibuprofen pills like candy throughout the course of most missions, as they all usually sported numerous bruises, cuts, and other injuries due to the amount of time they spent in the field.

It was ironic that they were finally back in civilization, and they were unable to enjoy any of the comforts of the capital of the most powerful country in the world. It had been nearly twenty minutes since they had left the senator's house, and Colin was shocked at how much snow had fallen since he had first arrived there.

Agent Smith sat in the back of the first SUV, speed-reading her way through the contents of the senator's notebook. She had finally acquiesced and let Sheriff drive the SUV to the new target location. She didn't enjoy driving in the snow, and Sheriff had grown up in New England. He was guiding the SUV through the whiteout conditions with controlled but slow precision. A drive that would have normally taken twenty minutes with traffic was now taking forty with no traffic.

Colin was in the front passenger seat, flipping through various camera feeds from the drone orbiting their position on an iPad. The standard visual spectrum was ineffective due to the whiteout conditions, so he settled on the thermal feed and was carefully tracking the convoy's progress through the streets of D.C.

Colin looked up to try and catch a view of the street signs at an intersection they were coming through to confirm their location. He got the first three letters of the sign but couldn't make out the rest. They matched, and he knew they were on track. Colin knew D.C. was, for an old city, laid out in an extremely organized fashion. The Capitol Building was the nexus, with streets lettered alphabetically proceeding outward from that point both north and south, and numbered streets starting at one and counting up proceeding both east and west. Apart from that, the city was broken up neatly into four quadrants—northwest, northeast, southwest, and southeast. Once you got the hang of this, the city was incredibly easy to navigate. Living here as a child was certainly an advantage, but the city had changed a lot in recent years.

Colin, being a student of history and having read more than a few books on the subject, knew the framework like the back of his hand. The city always seemed like home to him—changing, but home. Every year, a line of gentrification moved further out from the nexus of the Capitol Building, making D.C. a major hub of both government and industry. For all of this, though, the city's small bones were having trouble keeping up with the hyper-growth of its industry, population, and bureaucracy.

Sheriff took a turn, and Colin saw they were now on a numbered street proceeding east. Cars lay buried beneath a foot of snow on either side of the road. The SUV seemed to slide every twenty yards on patches of black ice beneath the snow. The rear vehicle maintained twenty yards of distance from the vehicle in front of it to keep from colliding if the first SUV stopped short. Colin looked up from the tablet and took in the scene in front of him. It was dark gray, buried under mountains of brilliant white snow—mountains that boxed them in.

"Get us off this fucking street," Colin said to Sheriff. "Alien, be advised. We are getting off this street. We're too boxed in here," said Sheriff into his earpiece.

"Are you really worried about someone hitting us on the move in this weather?" asked Agent Smith from the back seat.

Colin looked back down at the tablet and zoomed the feed out. His acute sense of danger told him this was a bad spot. Sure enough, less than fifty yards ahead, he started to see glowing red and orange dots emerge surrounding the street in what looked like a pincer ambush.

Sarah came through his earpiece. "Snowman, are you seeing this?"

39

17 Years Before

Susan had briefly met with Officer Carr again. In fact, she had cornered him outside of the police station the next evening and asked him if they could get a drink together and talk about what had happened the other day. He had taken her to a pub called Murphy's in Old Town Alexandria, where he lived. It was a known cop bar, and it was out of the way enough that Susan was confident she wouldn't be followed. Which she was sure was happening at this point.

Underneath the litany of police patches, he told Susan she had not been the only woman to visit the crime scene the day before. In fact, he had given Susan the name of Alex Tucker's longtime secretary. She had shown up to the crime scene and been more than just hysterical at her longtime boss' apparent suicide. Apparently, she had been screaming between exasperated sobs that he hadn't killed himself and that he had been murdered.

This had led Susan to where she was now—sitting at a small table in the back of a cafe that Alex Tucker's longtime secretary, Cindy, had said she would be willing to meet Susan at. The woman was ten minutes late, which had Susan worried that they might have gotten to her as well. But finally, she saw her walking toward the rear of the restaurant in a tan overcoat, headscarf, and sunglasses still on.

"Susan?" she asked quietly before she sat down.

"Yes," said Susan.

The woman sat down and stared at Susan for a moment before exhaling a breath that reeked of gin and removing her sunglasses. Her eyes were red and puffy, like she had been crying.

"I'm so sorry for your loss," said Susan. Cindy pulled out a handkerchief and wiped a fresh tear from her eye. She then pulled out a flask, took a long pull from it, and subsequently offered some to Susan. She refused and was about to start questioning the woman when she began on her own.

"Alex Tucker didn't kill himself, and he didn't kill his wife either," she began matter-of-factly. "They tried to frame him for his wife's murder to make him cooperate," she finished.

"Who's 'they,' Cindy?" Susan asked.

"I don't know, I don't know," the woman said somewhat hysterically.

"How do you know they tried to frame him?" Susan pried.

It took her a moment and another gulp of gin to respond. "Mr. Tucker always liked to work late. He always told me to go home and be with my family, but I didn't like the idea of him having to run things all by himself. You see, when he first started, it was just him and I," she paused, waiting for acknowledgment. Susan nodded in reply.

"When he finally landed the local government janitorial contract, it was a huge deal. Suddenly, we were handling most of the government buildings in the city and had a lot of people working for the company. One night, I left my scarf at the office and came back to get it, and I heard someone arguing with Mr. Tucker. He was refusing to give them something they wanted, and they said they would kill his wife if he told anyone and didn't do what they wanted. I thought he had just gotten in too deep at the tracks again. He liked to go and bet on the ponies, you see. I got out of there in a hurry because I was scared. The next day, when I got up the courage to ask him if he needed help, he said no and not to worry about it." She started crying again. Susan put a hand on hers comfortingly and nudged her along in rapt interest.

Cindy took another gulp of gin and continued, "A week later, his wife turned up dead, and the police thought he had killed her. He couldn't have hurt a fly, he was such a kind man."

She was nearing hysteria again. Susan decided to keep pushing her while the floodgates were open, her curiosity driving her deeper. "Cindy, I don't get it. If they wanted something from him, wouldn't killing his wife eliminate the only leverage they had?" Cindy stared back wide-eyed.

"His children," she muttered in barely a whisper, as if she didn't want to be heard.

"His wife was a message of what would happen to them. Was that why it was so brutal?" Susan asked. Cindy nodded, seeming too fearful to speak, and took another sip of gin from the flask. "Then why didn't they just kill him?" Susan asked. "Clearly, he gave them what they wanted if he's been around this long."

Cindy took another minute to respond. Her eyes were becoming unfocused from the booze and the crying. "A few days ago, I heard voices again from his office. They sounded angry, and he sounded scared. He kept swearing he didn't say anything, and then he left work in a hurry," she said, her voice breaking down completely as she began sobbing. "I hadn't seen him again since he... since he... since he..."

Susan comforted her, half lost in thought, trying to get her to not cause a scene. A thought had entered her head that was weighing heavily on her soul. Had she been the reason for Alex Tucker's murder, and if so, would she be next if she kept digging? It was something almost too terrible to contemplate. Because if it was true, then it wasn't just her at risk. Images of Colin and James floated into her head, and she instantly tried to fan them away, as if whatever darkness was hunting her could sense her thoughts. Her stomach dropped as fear flooded her brain, making her skin chill and her pupils dilate. She tried desperately to fill her mind with something else, but in the back of her head, she knew that her little brothers could be in grave danger.

40

"Charlie, are we emitting any signals we shouldn't be?" asked Colin.

"Hang on," responded Charlie. He flipped the drone's feed over to a radio detector mode that made signals show up like waves emanating from their source. Each vehicle was stopped at the intersection before the block the ambush was set on. Charlie studied each vehicle. Each emitted four signals. A GPS transmitter and the communication feed of each individual operator on the Echo Team, and what Charlie guessed was the cell phone signals for Agents Smith and Sunderland's FBI-issued phones. He adjusted the image and zoomed in on a slight distortion on the tailing vehicle's wheel well.

"Snowman, I'm not sure about this, but there's a weird distortion coming off the back left wheel well of the tail vehicle."

"Standby," said Colin. He hopped out of the SUV into the blustery wind and snow directly into a drift that came up to his knees. Trudging his way back to the rear SUV, he crouched down at the spot

Charlie had indicated. It took his eyes a second to adjust to the darkness under the wheel well, but when they did, he saw what he was looking for. A small magnetic, flattened sphere was attached to the inside of the well. "Got a tracker here," said Colin.

"Want me to block the signal?" asked Charlie.

"Sorry, boss, the Chinese team must've put it on when we mixed it up with them at the bodega," chimed Jester.

A faint rumbling in the distance gave Colin an idea. "Sit tight," he said to the team. He took off toward the one-way street that intersected their block with the one where the ambush was set up. Sure enough, Colin saw a very undersized plow making its way toward him.

The driver waved as he passed Colin, clearly having no way of knowing what he was in the middle of. Colin waited till he was just past him, tossed the tracker into the salt bed on the back of the truck, and ran back toward their SUV.

"Charlie, keep the drone zeroed on that signal, and let me know if they follow." Colin jumped back into the SUV and slammed the door behind him. "Go," he commanded. Sheriff put the Suburban in gear and took off toward the intersection. "Left," Colin said. Sheriff didn't hesitate, turning the wrong way on the one-way street. He used the reprieve of the freshly plowed ground, which was already turning white with snow again, to accelerate faster than he had been able to in hours.

Five minutes passed before Charlie came back over their earpieces again. "Looks like they followed the decoy, Snowman. You're good to proceed to the target address."

"Roger that," replied Colin.

"You were counting on that?" asked Agent Smith.

"I thought they might know we were coming, but I didn't want to fight them on their terms. This buys us the initiative and forces them to react to us."

"What happens when they catch the plow?" Smith asked.

"They won't. The salt dispenser will spit it out a couple miles down the road, and they'll realize we tricked them."

"What happens when they come looking for us again?" she asked.

"We'll see them coming."

41

The team arrived at the new townhouse in Navy Yard twenty-minutes after getting rid of the tracker. The house was in the same style as nearly all of the new developments in the area. A four-level brick townhouse with black window inserts and two Juliet balconies on the third level. A garage was located in the rear of the house, and the neighbors appeared to be home, judging by the flickering of a candle in the upstairs window.

Colin, Jester, Witch, and Agent Smith proceeded to the front door while Sheriff and Agent Sunderland pulled the two Suburban's around to the rear of the house. They got to the front door, which was a dark chestnut color, and Colin gave Witch the signal to pick the lock while he and Jester kept an eye on the street. It was almost unnecessary. There were no cars in sight, and they could see scarcely fifty feet in the swirling snow.

It took time to complete the picking process. The freezing cold was taking its toll on the metal tools and lock. Colin closed his eyes briefly against the cold, willing his tired mind to recharge itself by breathing deeply. He knew that his decision making ability would be key to keeping his team in one piece today, and the fatigue he now felt was threatening that. Colin, like many soldiers, prided himself on his ability to fall asleep nearly anywhere, anytime, when there was a lull in the action. This skill, however, was more attuned to his military life than his newer spy one.

There were no real lulls in missions like this, only slight downtimes between dangerous activities. More importantly, their team was so small they never really had a safe place to fall asleep at. In this sense, Colin did slightly miss the broader military. There, they had resources to fall back on. Here, all of them were always on watch. Colin pushed the thoughts out of his head, knowing he was being dramatic. Fatigue had a way of making hard men soft. And Colin couldn't afford to be soft.

Witch took a step back, and Jester stepped forward to open the door. They all pulled weapons from beneath their coats, and the Echo Team members attached suppressors to their MP7s.

Colin turned to Smith. "Hang here and watch the street for a second. If we get into a gunfight, your weapon will wake the neighbors," he said, nodding to the house next door. FBI agents were typically not issued suppressors, especially if they were not in a tactical job setting. And the truth was that silencers didn't really silence a gunshot—they simply dampened the sound down to a more tolerable level, leaving the FBI brass conflicted on typical agent use of the weapon accessory.

Smith nodded, lingering on his eyes perhaps a second longer than she should have, and Colin followed Jester into the house. His first thought was that it smelled new, like drywall and hardwood floor polish. It took Colin a second to realize this, as even the low heat in the house burned his cheeks and nostrils. He blinked excess water from his eyes as they adjusted to the new temperature. It was dark inside and sparsely decorated. They proceeded up the stairs to the first level, moving slowly and making as little noise as possible.

They couldn't hear any movement in the house, but they were being cautious nonetheless. The second floor of the house consisted of a kitchen, family room, and dining room. It was sparsely decorated with only a table, a few chairs, and a sofa, all of them mismatched and old. They proceeded through an archway into the dining room. A wooden table took up most of the room and was covered with military-grade assault weapons, ammunition, flashbang grenades, night-vision goggles, and various other bits of tactical equipment. Colin paused for a moment, unsure if he had just walked into a dining room or an armory, but his training kicked in and he kept moving.

The team proceeded upstairs and cleared bedrooms, bathrooms, and closets, all of which were empty. When they were satisfied, the house was secure, they proceeded back downstairs to the dining room, which was filled with military hardware.

"Sheriff, the house is secure. We found a big cache of weapons up here. Pull perimeter security with Sunderland and let me know if anyone is creeping on us," said Colin to his earpiece.

"Copy, Snowman. Coast is clear. Will advise if anything changes."

Colin walked over to the table and joined the rest of the team, who were picking up and inspecting weapons and equipment. There were M4s with a mixture of red dot and ACOG optics, Glocks of various makes, M9 Barretta's, M84 flashbang grenades, and various caliber ammunition in various makes, including hollow point and subsonic rounds, littered everywhere.

"This is some serious equipment," said Agent Smith.

"This doesn't make sense," said Colin. Witch and Jester nodded in agreement while inspecting different weapons.

"What do you mean?" she asked.

"This equipment is, well, generic." She looked at Colin, puzzled. Colin took a second to respond, weighing his words. As a Green Beret, Colin had been trained to fire nearly every weapon on the planet, from machine guns to bows and arrows. Working with guerillas all over the planet demanded the use of often ancient indigenous weapons. Colin had made sure the rest of his team had received the same training upon their induction into the Echo Teams.

"Law enforcement would carry this stuff. No custom mods, looks brand-new, everything made in the U.S., and check this out." Colin flipped the Colt M4 over to show her the serial number above the magazine. "The serial numbers are still here. Doesn't seem very covert to me," he said.

"What does that mean?" she asked, puzzled. These looked like a lot of the weapons she had been trained to carry at Quantico. In fact, she knew herself to be qualified for almost every weapon on the table.

Colin put the gun down. "I think these are U.S. government weapons."

42

Department of Justice

Attorney General Mark Poole was not happy. His district attorney for Washington D.C. was MIA. The District of Columbia was not a state and therefore fell under the direct jurisdiction of Congress and the Department of Justice. This meant that the district attorney in Washington D.C. not only handled federal law enforcement but high-level local crimes as well. No one had heard from Matt Coughlin, the district attorney, in over six hours, and the reports of violence and civil distress were growing by the hour. Poole's temper was flaring, and the very hardwood and tightly bound leather of his sitting chairs seemed to pulse with his anger.

The Metropolitan Police Department, which was the sixth-largest in the country, had been caught completely off guard by the sudden onset of the storm. The power outage had severely slowed their ability to communicate, and the roads were so bad that only a small portion of their vehicles were able to be used. On top of that, most officers were not able to make it to work due to impassable roads and the metro being offline from the power outage.

At least the backup generators are working here, Poole reflected. Their direct inability to handle a simple snowstorm in the capital of the most powerful country in the world reflected extremely poorly on the Department of Justice's leadership, though, which in turn reflected poorly on him.

Mark Poole knew this wasn't his fault. Congress was sympathetic to the District of Columbia's local government and had granted them more autonomy and more freedom over the Metropolitan Police's budget. They had squandered the dollars on nonsense, and now disaster had struck. Making matters worse, the man in charge of this disaster was now missing. Poole would have his ass for this. Poole had personally chewed the man out for over an hour the last time the department had failed to adequately respond to a snowstorm.

The department has a budget of over five hundred million dollars a year, and yet somehow they couldn't find the money for four-wheel-drive vehicles, Pool thought. Not to mention the Metropolitan Police was the only police force in the country that could be federalized in an emergency, which it now seemed clear wouldn't matter at all if a simple snowstorm hit.

Poole seethed with anger at the incompetence of the man in charge. A white-hot flash of rage at the ineptitude sent his third mug of coffee of the day flying across the room into a wall. The rage was nothing compared to the ball of anxiety in his stomach, though. His team had now gone quiet as well. His operation seemed to have stalled out of nowhere, and if it failed, he would likely go with it. He looked at a shelf that held various trophies from his career in public service. He had clawed his way from being a public defender to a district attorney, turned down a judgeship, and ultimately pushed his way to this office. Much had to be sacrificed in the pursuit of power, but everything hung on a knife's edge now. The only question on his mind was... would he fall?

43

The plow driver was having a very strange day. As a snow removal worker for the District of Columbia, Alex Loughlin rarely got the opportunity to work as it was, but the snow wasn't even the strange part. The strange part was when a group of deranged-looking Asian men had cut his plow off and searched his vehicle at gunpoint for "the Americans," as they kept describing them.

Shortly after this encounter, they had simply driven away. The even weirder part was that the Metropolitan Police had responded to none of his radio calls for help. Alex assumed this was because of the power outage, which he also assumed explained the lack of light and traffic signals in the city. The good news was that his cellular-based GPS routing system was still telling him which routes needed to be plowed by central dispatch. So in the absence of other directions, he intended to keep going until his shift was over, and maybe even after that to collect the generous government overtime pay.

The day had receded from dark gray to dark navy blue as the early onset of night typical of winter approached through the thick snowfall. Alex took a right and adjusted the angle of his plow blade to better fit the narrow street. He buried several cars as he passed in the process that had clearly not gotten the message about no parking on a snow emergency route. *Where are the damn police,* he wondered. His route had taken him from Southeast D.C. to Northeast D.C., and he was on a direct course toward the outer borders of the district in Maryland.

This wasn't the route he remembered being assigned, but he assumed the geniuses at central dispatch had probably figured out a better way to do things than the experienced plow drivers. He shook his head, annoyed that some twenty-two-year-old civil engineer who had seen snow once in his life was trying to tell him what to do.

Alex reached for his now-cold coffee and promptly dropped it on the floor of his truck when he hit a bump in the road. Without thinking, he reached down to grab it. He had no way of knowing the malware that had shut the power off in D.C. had now penetrated all the way to the servers of the Office of D.C. Snow Removal's central dispatch system. It was not only sending all of the plows to random, out of the way parts of the city but also trying to cause collisions between plows that came close to each other.

He never saw the other plow emerge from the one-way street until the blade of the plow t-boned his and slammed his head, which was still down looking for his coffee, into the plastic steering wheel. The plow blade colliding with his truck snapped instantly as it drove his vehicle into a group of parked cars buried in snow behind him. He looked up, bleeding and dazed, at what had just happened. The smell of gasoline penetrated the quickly cooling air of the truck's cabin like a knife through butter. He frantically unbuttoned his seatbelt and jumped from the door of the plow onto one of the parked sedans he had just crashed into as fire began to dance from the hood of his plow truck.

He jumped from the roof and ran around the side of his plow to check on the other driver. Yellow light reflected eerily off of the falling snow from the other plow's headlights. Alex saw the other plow driver unconscious with his head on the wheel.

"Hey!" he shouted. The driver was nonresponsive. Alex jumped up onto the running board of the plow and pulled on the door handle. It was either locked or jammed shut. He banged on the window.

"Hey, wake up! You've got to get out of there!" he screamed. The man didn't stir. Alex coughed. A thick black smoke was beginning to pour from his truck. Alex banged harder on the window, trying frantically to wake the man. "Hey! Get up!" he yelled. The man's head rolled to the side. It took him a second, and he started to look up at Alex, dazed. Alex continued banging on the window as the smoke thickened from his truck. The man suddenly snapped to, and seeing the smoke from the burning plow he had hit, he began to panic. He started frantically pulling at the door handle, trying to get the door open before both vehicles were engulfed in flames.

44

"Charlie, I'm sending you some pictures of weapon serial numbers. Can you run them through the government firearms inventory database and see if there's a match?" Colin said, finishing taking the last picture with his tablet. It had taken only ten minutes to explain his theory to Agent Smith before he contacted Charlie.

"Sure thing, Snowman," came Charlie's voice through the team's earpieces. "It'll just take a minute." It took another five minutes before Charlie responded, "Ah, Snowman, we may have a problem here."

"What is it, Charlie?" asked Colin.

"These weapons have been washed, and I'm getting flag for level-nine clearance to see by who," Charlie responded. Washed referred to a process where the serial numbers and manufacturing records of a federally purchased weapon were erased so they could be used untraceably in black operations. This, in and of itself, was bizarre to Colin. He had never seen a washed weapon inside the U.S.

"You have level-nine clearance, Charlie. What's the holdup?" asked Colin. Echo Team leaders and extreme technical experts like Charlie were some of the few within the government who had such clearances. They gave one access to programs so black, one could be forgiven for thinking they weren't actually there if they were standing right in front of them. Echo Teams needed it to use advanced experimental weaponry and equipment and to gain access to sensitive information and programs that their missions might involve. Charlie had earned his way in on pure merit before the Echo Teams even technically existed.

"The holdup is that someone will know that I'm requesting access to the information, which could compromise operational security," said Charlie.

Colin thought about this for a second, weighing the pros and cons. He judged it to be of minimal risk, as most people who had the clearances to access level-nine classified information logs only existed within the defense and intelligence community outside the typical bounds of the Department of Justice. "Do it," said Colin.

"Okay, hang on," replied Charlie. "Whoa," he said a second later.

"What?" asked Colin.

"Have you ever heard of a facility called Lowercase?" asked Charlie.

"That place is a rumor," said Colin, somewhat in disbelief that Charlie had just mentioned the name.

"What's Lowercase?" asked Agent Smith.

"It's a myth in the special ops and intelligence community," Jester chimed in. "It's a black facility supposedly located in the Capital. It's supposedly a secure place for high-level intelligence types to meet the worst of the worst bad guys and interrogate them, among other things."

"What's with the name?" asked Smith.

"What's the opposite of a capital letter?" asked Colin in return.

"A lowercase one," replied Smith.

Colin nodded. "That, and it's the opposite of all of the above-board activities the government carries out in the capital. Hence the name."

"Sounds fake," said Smith.

"It is," interjected Sheriff.

"Actually, it looks like it's real," said Charlie in their earpieces.

"You're not serious," said Colin, a little bewildered. Colin's level-nine security clearance gave him access to information on all manner of black programs. His close relationship with Charlie guaranteed that he knew about a litany of others he would never have even looked at. Colin knew Lowercase was a myth, or at least he had known. As someone with a proverbial license to kill from the government and a high level of access, Colin was surprised by very little when it came to conspiracy theories. But he had thought this one was too good to be true, and the fact that Charlie had thought so too really said something.

"What is a Chinese hit team doing with weapons from a highly classified government facility?" asked Smith.

"Well, as you know, someone in the attorney general's office or even the attorney general himself is suspected of espionage for the Chinese. It's possible that he secured the weapons for them. It would reduce the risk of getting caught buying weapons off the street, provided he was careful," said Colin.

"Well, if the weapons were washed as you said, it would also make them untraceable to regular law enforcement if they were discovered," replied Smith. "Charlie, can you get into the facility records and see if there is some kind of trace of the weapons being removed, surveillance video, or something? I'm sure he used some kind of middleman, but at least it will give us a lead."

"I'd love to, but those systems are air-gapped from the rest of the world," replied Charlie.

"Air-gapped?" asked Smith.

"All of the electronics in the facility have no capability of connecting to the internet or any external signals," replied Colin. "You guys need to get in there if you want to see what happened," said Charlie.

"How are we supposed to get into a government facility that doesn't exist?" asked Smith.

Colin smiled. "I'm going to make a call."

45

Senator Rand's Apartment

"I know it's irregular. Just give them access," Rand said into the cellphone. The director of the Special Activities Division at Langley was in charge of the facility. Rand waited for his response, sitting next to Senator Miller in a leather armchair. He took a sip of his alcohol-infused coffee and watched the flames' yellow light from the fireplace flicker off of his colleague's confused face.

"I'd love to, sir, but Lowercase is a myth—it doesn't exist. I really can't help you," he responded through the phone.

"Art, would you have your current job if it weren't for me? Do you remember when you were in hot shit with the Intelligence Committee over Morocco? Who pulled your ass out of that fire, Art?" demanded Rand to the man on the phone.

"Sir, respectfully, you would need level-eight clearance and a presidential order to get you into this facility if it even existed," replied the man, sounding a bit alarmed by the level of anger he had provoked from the senator.

"Level nine, actually, and check your encrypted email. You should see the presidential order any second now," said Rand coolly.

"Level-nine clearance is a myth too, Senator."

There was a brief pause before the senator spoke. "Art, do I seem like I'm in a joking mood right now?" asked Rand.

"No, sir. I have the email here," said the director. He paused for another moment. "Send them to the address I'm forwarding to your secure email. They'll be let into the garage, and the facilities manager will take it from there."

"Thank you, Art. As always, it's a pleasure," said Rand in his signature southern drawl, hanging up before the man could reply. How the hell the Echo Team had linked stolen weapons to a government facility that technically didn't exist, and how that factored into everything, Rand wasn't sure. He just hoped that they would complete their mission soon before everything he and the committee had worked for was lost forever.

46

Northwest D.C.

The office building was medium height with tinted gold windows. It came in at one story short of the height limit imposed on all buildings within the nation's capital. This was intentional so as to make the building unremarkable from the air. Team Alien had proceeded from Navy Yard all the way over to the unremarkable building off of E Street and waited patiently by the garage that led to the basement of the building.

Colin looked around while they waited for the door to be opened and remarked at how unremarkable the building was in front of them. Snow fell softly onto the truck's windshield before being swatted away by the car's wipers. Finally, the garage door began to open, and Colin saw a steep descent in front of them where nothing but the ramp going down was visible. The SUVs proceeded orderly down the dimly lit ramp, and Colin heard the garage door closing behind them.

The two trucks emerged into a brightly lit and expansive garage with a small lobby in the middle that contained the elevators. Brightly colored red and blue pipes ran the length of the concrete garage in various directions. Colin saw a man who had the distinct look of a private security contractor waving them over to park in front of the lobby. The two vehicles parked, and the team disembarked.

"Welcome to Lowercase. Please follow me into the lobby. We'll need you to surrender your weapons and submit to a search to enter," said the man. He had long, dark, unkempt hair beneath a tactical-style baseball hat with Velcro where a patch should have been and a beard that covered much of his lower facial features. Colin saw a Sig pistol on his hip and was sure the man was proficient in using it.

"Not happening," said Colin matter-of-factly.

"Sorry, guy, it's protocol. No one gets in without a proper search."

"We've got an all-access pass," said Colin. As if in answer to his statement, a frazzled-looking man in a poorly fitting blue suit came through the sliding doors to the lobby.

"Snowman?" he asked.

"That's me," replied Colin.

The security contractor gave Colin a stupid look. He ignored it. The man extended his hand. "I'm Rick Baker. I'm the director of this facility." Colin shook the man's hand.

"Must be hard to put on your resume, seeing as this place doesn't exist," said Colin.

"I imagine you have the same problem," he returned.

"Plenty of private-sector opportunities for FBI agents," said Colin.

"I'm sure," the man replied sarcastically. "I've been told to grant you full access. They can keep their weapons," he said to the security contractor.

"Thank you," said Colin. "We'll need access to all of your facility's electronic surveillance. Video, audio, visitor logs, cyber data, everything," finished Colin.

The man looked hesitant. "This goes against my better judgment," he said.

"That's fine," replied Colin, staring him straight in the eye. The man continued his objections, trying to dissuade them. "Everything is air-gapped, and for obvious security reasons, our logs only go back a month. Everything else is destroyed."

"That will do fine. We'll download all the data we need for analysis and destroy it once we're done." The man stood staring at Colin as if trying to figure out whether to trust him. "Lead the way," said Colin forcefully, having no patience for the bureaucracy. He seemed to decide that Colin was not a man to be argued with and turned on his heel toward the elevators.

They followed him into a clean, white tiled lobby with two elevators. The man hit the button to call it, and one of the doors slid open. The team followed him inside and watched him hit the only button on the inside. It turned red, and the man bent over and placed his eye on a small sensor. It must have confirmed his identity because Colin saw the button turn green and felt the elevator lurch downward. Colin was more than a little surprised at how long the elevator felt like it was going down for. When it finally stopped and the doors opened, Colin was greeted with a receptionist desk in another small lobby that one could have mistaken for a dentist's office. The man walked forward and spoke for a minute with a rather plain-looking blonde woman sitting behind the desk.

Jester turned to Colin. "Boss, as cool as this is, we're wasting a lot of time down here while Azrael is on the loose up there."

"I know," said Colin, "but this is our only lead, and we need to follow it."

A door clicked open behind the receptionist, and they followed the man through a plain white hallway with many blue doors on either side. When they arrived at the tenth door on the right side, the man stopped again and unlocked it with his fingerprint. The door swung open to reveal a twenty-foot by twenty-foot server room with a small desk near the door.

"The server room's in here. This terminal here will grant you access to the records. You will need to use this access card," he said, handing a plain white swipe card to Colin.

Colin turned to Sheriff and handed it to him. "Download everything and send it to Charlie for parsing."

Sheriff proceeded to the terminal and started pulling out a tablet and a cord that would allow him to connect with the servers. Sheriff was the most technically proficient member of the team outside of Charlie, and Colin often relied on him to handle situations like this.

"If you'll follow me down the hall, there's a kitchen with coffee you can wait in while he grabs the data," said the man.

They followed him down the hallway, drawn by the smell of freshly brewed coffee. When they arrived, the team helped themselves to coffee and a few bags of chips and protein bars that were laid out on the counter.

"Can I have a quick word?" Rick asked Colin.

"Sure," replied Colin. He followed him outside of the kitchen and a short way down the hallway. Rick looked slightly nervous. "What's up?" asked Colin.

"I shouldn't be asking you this, but did your man say Azrael?" he asked. Colin normally would have deflected the question to keep others out of the team's business, but something in the man's eyes made him want to answer.

"He did," said Colin.

"Would I be correct in saying you're after him?" asked Rick.

Colin paused a moment before answering, trying to further read the man. "Possibly."

"Well, if you are, there's someone here you may want to talk to."

"Someone who works here knows who Azrael is?" asked Colin.

"No. But someone who is detained here does."

47

"Charlie, are you getting this?" asked Sheriff sitting up in his chair inside the IT closet, as he had started calling it.

"I'm receiving the data now. Give me a second to begin parsing and categorizing it. Crazy that this facility actually exists. I thought it was a total rumor," said Charlie. He had a tendency to talk a lot when he was excited.

"Pretty crazy," said Sheriff with a yawn. He took a sip out of the plain paper cup Jester had brought him a few minutes ago, filled with some truly terrible coffee, and sat back in the incredibly stiff pleather office chair that looked straight out of the nineteen nineties.

"Wow, this is crazy. People who work here are here on three-month deployments," said Charlie.

"Like they actually stay underground for three months at a time? How big is the staff?" asked Sheriff.

"It looks like ten to twenty full-time staff members depending on the time of year, and anywhere from fifteen to twenty inmates at any one time," said Charlie excitedly.

"Damn, that's one black hole. Anyone we've heard of?" asked Sheriff.

"A few high-level terrorists, two hackers, a couple of foreign agents, and a few I've never heard of," replied Charlie.

There was a brief pause. "Wow, this place is seriously extensive," exclaimed Charlie.

"What do you mean?" asked Sheriff.

"Lowercase is a small part of the overall facility, and it's deep underground. Like, if there was a nuclear strike, you'd probably be okay. But the rest of the facility is in the building above you and is full of government labs looking into things that would make DARPA hot and bothered. The whole building is basically a giant, specially compartmented information facility. The outside of the building is basically nothing, and the main facility is held within the core of the building. I doubt anyone who works on any of the projects realizes the entire facility is a lab and a black site," buzzed Charlie excitedly.

"How do they pull that off?" asked Sheriff skeptically.

"Well, outside of the usual compartment facility protocols, it looks like the elevators are coded to only take certain individuals to certain floors based on their biometrics. But the only way into Lowercase is through the garage, and it looks like no one who works upstairs has access to that. It even looks like there's totally separate elevators," said Charlie. Sheriff had been in his fair share of classified government facilities, but this was by far the most impressive.

"Is there an armory?" asked Sheriff.

"A big one," said Charlie. "I'm working on narrowing the data parsing to that, but it's going to take some time. The facility and its security are extensive."

Sheriff sighed again, his feeling of stress and unease growing. "Time is one thing we don't have, Charlie."

"I know, I know, hang on," said Charlie. It took him another few minutes before he spoke again. "Wait, hang on, this can't be right," he said suddenly. Sheriff could hear the sense of bemusement in Charlie's voice that was usually reserved for cool new pieces of tech.

"What is it?" he asked, knowing something bad was coming. Sheriff knew Charlie was one to sugarcoat things. Which was why he knew if Charlie said something wasn't right, then something was probably seriously wrong.

There was another brief pause as Charlie seemed to process what he was seeing. "Sheriff, I think we have a problem here."

48

Colin hadn't received any additional context before being placed in a ten-by-ten concrete room with two metal chairs facing each other.

A bright LED light sat overhead the middle of the two chairs, and a two-way mirror sat on the wall to Colin's right. In front of him was a man in a bright orange jumpsuit, handcuffed around his ankles to the floor and around his back to the chair. He was pale white in a Gaelic sort of way, with a bald head and gaunt brown eyes. His sleeves were rolled up, and Colin saw many tattoos covering his muscled arms. Colin placed the man in his late fifties and noticed the dagger with wings tattooed on his arm, signifying he was likely a former British SAS commando. What one of those was doing in a black site, and in U.S. custody, Colin wasn't sure.

He stared impassibly at the man for another moment, trying to read what was behind his eyes. They were cold in the way that men's eyes often were when they killed for a living. However, the usual flare of life common in the eyes of special operators was totally absent. They almost had a sad tinge to them, as if the life had been sucked out of them by his captors. Colin supposed that it likely had.

"I'm told I should talk to you," opened Colin.

The man stared blankly back before asking in a British accent, "Why?"

"I've been hunting for someone you may know. Have any idea who I'm talking about?" Colin asked.

The man's eyes revealed nothing. "If you're going to speak in riddles, then fuck off. I'm tired of American games," he returned bluntly.

Colin nodded. "Ever heard of someone called Azrael?"

The man looked up at him in an intrigued but guarded sort of way. "Possibly. Why do you ask?"

Colin continued, "He's killed a lot of people, and now he's engaged in a plot to assassinate high-ranking politicians in the U.S. I need to stop him."

The man laughed. "So now that some fancy politicians are getting whacked, people are finally going to do something about this?"

"What do you mean, 'finally going to do something about this'?" Colin asked, genuinely curious.

"You really don't know?" the man asked with a cynical laugh. Colin saw a small amount of life flicker into the man's eyes. He didn't wait for Colin to answer. "The man you're talking about. Him and I used to work together. Ever heard of something called a Dagger Team?" he asked.

Colin thought he had heard that name a while back from an old spook when he was deployed at a forward operating base in Kandahar as a Green Beret. "It was a fast-response team, wasn't it?" Colin asked.

The man nodded, the light glinting off his bald head. "A NATO fast-response team made up of the best operators from all NATO members. The idea was that in an Article Five emergency, the team could be the tip of the spear. Counterterrorism, assassinations, decapitation strikes, nuclear interdiction—you name it, we were trained for it. We were blacker than black, very little red tape, near-constant operational tempo. We became the go-to instrument of NATO leading up to 9/11. Before the Americans stopped caring about public perception and started whacking everyone they could get their hands on with special forces and drones," the man said, smiling and remembering his old life.

"Sounds like NATO leadership read Tom Clancy's Rainbow Six," said Colin.

The man laughed. "You got that right. Half our missions read like the pages of a novel. That was, until the incident," the man said, stopping abruptly and staring off into space at the concrete walls.

"What incident?" Colin asked.

"Leading up to nine-eleven, there was increasing terrorist chatter. NATO was working to target and eliminate cells before they could get up and running. Airstrikes were out. The terrorists were too smart and started keeping innocents with them everywhere they went. Women, children, you name it. The multinational leadership at NATO had no stomach for collateral damage. They started wielding us like a kitchen knife, cutting up everything in sight. The men were burnt out and dead tired. The intel on the missions we got started to degrade the faster we moved. An assassination op we went on went wrong, and we got pinned down and surrounded by hundreds of them. The jihadists used women and children as human shields as they rushed our position. Most of the men couldn't or wouldn't take shots to defend themselves and were killed. Myself and our commander defended ourselves."

Colin knew what the man was getting at, but he pushed him. "Defended yourselves?" he asked, goading him on with a sense of urgency.

"Fifty women and children dead. We were the only two who made it out. After that, leadership burned the team. I was captured a few years later, fleeing from them. The man you know as Azrael escaped and was no longer the man I knew," he finished.

"What do you mean by that?"

"John was unhinged. The man I knew was careful to the point of obsession, but clear and a damn strong leader. After that, he could barely look you in the eye. Before, he was empathetic and even kind at times. After that, he could have shot up a room of children and felt nothing. There was nothing left in him after that. I think the last remnants of his soul left him the day he had to repeatedly pump rounds into children to protect himself. I'm not sure if he just couldn't forgive himself, or if he just had nothing left." The words hung in the dark room like a thick fog.

Colin had been in some bad situations before. Children with suicide vests and humans using others as shields to protect themselves. But this situation was nearly unimaginable. He had no sympathy for the man in front of him, only understanding for some of the horror that had put him in this position. He wasn't sure what he would have done. Protecting himself and his team or risking killing women and children. This intensely bothered him about himself, and he was thankful that he hadn't been placed in the other man's shoes. Colin didn't feel guilt over killing his country's enemies, but he did feel an intense drive to protect those who could not protect themselves.

"I've met men like you before," the man continued, unsolicited. "I was a man like you before. I can see it in your eyes. I'm sorry for what I've done, but I wouldn't have done a thing differently when it came to protecting my men or being slaughtered by animals. The only thing you can't protect when you step over the line to kill for your country is yourself. My only advice for you is to save yourself while you still can. While there's still some of you left."

Colin looked him dead in the eye with the most serious expression he had ever given anyone in his life. "I'm nothing like you." But even as he said it, he found himself doubting the words. How could he be nothing like a man with such a similar background? His thoughts were interrupted by Sheriff's voice in his ear. "Boss, we need you. Now."

49

"Boss, you there?" Charlie asked through Colin's earpiece for the third time. Colin shook his head to clear the remnants of the conversation he had just had. The man's words had rung in his head all the way back to the small kitchen, where the team sat eating power bars and drinking coffee. He had briefed them on what the man had said about Azrael but had left out the man's parting words.

The truth was, Colin knew they were different. Sure, they had more leeway when it came to kinetic action in all forms, but Colin prided himself and his team's use of restraint and intellect in as many situations as possible. Colin also knew that his sense of right and wrong was far more developed than that of the man he had spoken to. That was something Susan had taught him more than anyone else. But he also couldn't say that sleep always came easy.

"Sorry, Charlie. What do you got?" responded Colin. Sheriff walked into the kitchen as Charlie began talking, and Colin knew something was up by the look on his face.

"The weapons were signed out by an FBI team for an off-the-books investigation," said Charlie. "

Wait, what?" said Jester, immediately turning to Agent Smith.

"I thought those weapons were being used by the Chinese hit team," said Witch.

"Hang on, how did you put this together, Charlie?" asked Colin.

"The agents were part of an FBI counter-espionage team with the clearance to make it into the facility. Although I doubt they just knew about it. Someone higher up must have gotten them in here. The weapons were signed out of the armory, and they listed a bogus case file number as a reason why. I ran the agents' faces from the video surveillance in the facility through facial recognition and matched them to their federal IDs. They're for sure FBI. What the hell they were doing here, signing weapons out, I have no idea."

"So either our worst fears have been realized and elements of the FBI and Justice Department are totally compromised, or they know something and are running their own counter-espionage investigation," said Colin.

"Maybe we should ask our FBI friends what's really going on here. They've clearly known something was going on the whole time," said Jester, continuing to lock eyes with Agent Smith and stepping toward her.

"Hey, back off!" exclaimed Agent Sunderland, stepping in front of Agent Smith and pushing Jester. He sidestepped the push in the blink of an eye, using Agent Sunderland's momentum against him and throwing him up face-first against the wall.

"Whoa, whoa, calm down!" shouted Agent Smith. "We had no idea that there was FBI involved in this."

"No offense, Agent Smith, but how do we have any idea you're not involved in this? We've certainly walked into one buzzsaw after another today?" asked Colin. He seriously doubted these two had anything to do with everything today. In fact, he had Charlie vet both of them on the flight over, but he wanted to see what she would say to defend herself and her partner.

"We were brought into this case from the outside. We work serial killers, not espionage. I think you know that, 'Snowman,' or we would have never been brought into this," replied Smith sharply. She was smart enough to know that Colin would have had her vetted before bringing her into this case, especially with the allegations on the table toward the Department of Justice.

"Jester, let him go," said Colin. Agent Sunderland looked like he was on the verge of passing out when Jester finally let him go.

"You're right," said Colin, "but we need to figure out what the hell is going on here, so you're going to make a call and set a meeting, and we're going to get some answers."

Colin began walking out of the room as if the matter were settled, internally thinking, if only it would be that easy.

50

The team had to leave the facility in order to make the call. Before they left, they had restocked on ammunition from the central armory and confirmed the missing weapons. The SUVs headed back out into the snow before proceeding down an empty alleyway and parking. Agent Smith searched the FBI personnel database and located the contact information for the agent who was supposedly in charge of the FBI counter-espionage team. Colin waited in the passenger seat, watching snow dance in front of the SUVs bright yellow lights as Agent Smith connected the call.

"Agent Savarese speaking," said a gruff-sounding man through the speakers on the phone.

"Ah, hello Agent Savarese, this is Special Agent Alexandra Smith out of the C.I.D.," said Alexandra, referring to the FBI's Criminal Investigative Division.

There was a brief pause on the other end of the line. "This wouldn't happen to be the Agent Smith who broke open the Potomac Nights–man case, would it?" he asked, sounding impressed.

"That's correct, sir," she responded.

"Wow, can't believe you caught that son of a bitch. Fifteen women dead, and you somehow kept your cool and didn't shoot the bastard when you caught him. Can't say I would have been able to do the same. How can I help you, Agent Smith?" he asked.

Colin had read about that case, and it was one of the reasons he had Charlie request her. Smith had somehow managed to profile the fact that the killer couldn't stand the smell of the women he murdered when he revisited their corpses. She caught him buying Vicks to rub under his nose before he committed the act by triangulating a pharmacy at the center of all of his killings.

"Well, Agent Savarese, I think we can actually help each other," she said.

"Oh, really, and how's that?" he asked.

"Well, I'm hunting a serial killer who I think is related to your current counter-espionage investigation," she answered, waiting for his response. Colin understood what she was doing. Giving him just enough information to keep him talking but also being cryptic enough that he might reveal things she didn't know through his answers.

"What counter-espionage investigation?" he asked, sounding suspicious.

"The one you just signed a whole boatload of weapons out from Lowercase to support," she said, dropping the hammer.

"I don't know what you're talking about," he replied.

"Listen, I don't want to play games with you. I'm not sure if you're investigating or somehow involved, but either way, I think you need to meet me and hear what I have to say."

"Really, and why's that?" he asked.

"Because I'm either going to catch you red-handed or break your case wide open," Smith said.

She had to wait a minute for him to respond, "Fine. Where and when?"

"In front of The Queens English Pub by the National Mall, thirty minutes. Know where it is?"

"Yeah, I'll be there."

Colin watched Agent Smith put the car in gear and set off toward the other end of the alley. The expression on her face spoke to an unsure fear percolating beneath her skin. "We'll figure this out," Colin said reassuringly. She took a second to respond, and he could tell she was considering something. "I guess I'm just hoping that your team is wrong and that the bad guys aren't actually who I thought the good guys were all along."

51

17 Years Before

Susan wasn't entirely sure where to turn next. She knew what it was that she needed in order to prove everything that she had discovered, but she had no idea how to obtain it. Her research had told her that only one person had the comprehensive authority to assign and sweep away the cases of the missing women. The man she had trusted most and had given her a second chance at life when her parents had passed—her boss, the assistant U.S. attorney for the District of Columbia.

It was clear to her now that the only way she was going to prove what had happened to these poor women was that she had to catch him in the act or prove that he had somehow been involved in these heinous killings. Luckily, she did have an idea of how to obtain a critical piece of evidence. Her boss was extremely thorough with his notes and logs and where and when he was. He also loved to embrace technology to help him be more thorough. Susan knew for a fact that the man kept all of these logs on the desktop computer in his office. She knew because, in his attempts to mentor her, he had shown her his note-taking system on his computer.

Of course, there were paper copies of these as well, but Susan judged them to be much more difficult to steal. Most of them were located in filing cabinets in his office, and Susan would have to sneak in, remove stacks of files, go and copy them, then return them all without being seen. Her plan to steal the digital copies would hopefully only involve a compact disc, her purse, and only one trip to his office.

For all of this, though, Susan had not come up with a probable excuse to get into his office yet. The door was often kept locked when he wasn't there, and his secretary was an older, incredibly nosey woman who loved her boss with all of her heart. She needed a good excuse to get into the office, or she needed to steal the keys and go back when no one was there. Either presented an incredible amount of risk. If she was caught, she would likely be fired and possibly even charged with evidence tampering, among other things. Susan couldn't let down all of the women who were killed by him and his associates. But more than anything else, she couldn't let down herself and her brothers.

She also knew that if she was caught, they would likely have all of the reasons they needed to eliminate her. Susan knew that they were as close as it was. More strange things had begun happening to her. Apart from the near-constant feeling of the hairs standing up on the back of her neck from someone she was sure was watching her at all times, things had gotten worse at home.

Several times now, she had come home to see her trash cans clearly gone through, and objects repeatedly seemed to be misplaced around the Frost house as if someone had been there when they weren't. Worse yet, there were the glimpses she got of what she had started referring to as "the man" internally. She never saw him more than once, and when she did, it was only a glance out of the corner of her eye. Every time she tried to get a better look, he had disappeared.

She was tired now. The dark circles under her eyes grew more pronounced every day, and sleep was something she barely even knew anymore. She was jumpy and irritated, becoming paranoid to the point of obsession. It was all she could do to put on a good front for Colin and James to not alarm them at the shell of their former sister. For all of this, though, her resolve had not lessened. She was close now, like a match in the hand of someone about to light a candle. All she had to do was move toward the igniter and strike.

52

Present Day

The Queens English Pub sat on the left side of the National Mall if you were facing the Capitol Building. The small street had a concrete wall on its left side that had an elevated government building on top of it and a series of small bars on the right side, which, if you were sitting outside, afforded you a beautiful view of the concrete wall.

The Queen's English Pub was possibly the most British place in all of D.C. except for the British Embassy. It and the bars adjacent to it were a frequent haunt of many lobbyists and staffers on the hill due to their close proximity to the Capitol Building. Whereas usually it was full of lively conversations and many meetings, it was now empty, with the lights off and a foot of snow piled in front of its entrance.

Agent Smith had chosen the spot due to its seclusion in the current weather, the lack of entrances and exits in case they needed to arrest Agent Savarese, and her familiarity with the bar as a somewhat regular patron. The team was currently several blocks away from the small street off of the National Mall, battling the buffeting wind, gusting snow, and terrible road conditions to get there. It was nearly completely dark now. The roads were nearly completely empty, and the city was almost entirely without power except for the few buildings with backup generators. The traffic lights weren't working, and neither were the streetlights. All of these things worked for and against them as they proceeded to the street the pub was on.

Colin and Sheriff were walking through the tactical situation with the team via their earpieces, trying to decide on the best way to handle the situation. They settled on parking each SUV at an exit and having Colin and Agent Smith meet with Agent Savarese. It had only been ten minutes since Agent Smith had set the meeting, meaning they needed to arrive in the next five to get set before Savarese arrived. Charlie had looked up Agent Savarese's place of residence in the FBI database and calculated that it would take him twenty-five minutes to get there with the current weather and driving conditions. That was if he was home. Charlie had not been able to trace his phone and could not get a GPS fix on him, which was rare in this day and age. Charlie had to settle for watching the target location through a fuzzy infrared picture on the team's drone orbiting overhead.

"You there, Smith?" Colin asked her from the front seat. She had been lost in thought at everything going on. The situation before her was absolutely unprecedented, but if there was anything she had learned in hunting serial killers, it was to go with the flow—it very often led you right to a solution. Her main issue was trying to peg down whether Agent Savarese and his team really were somehow working with the bad actors who had orchestrated all of this.

The thought that a fellow FBI agent, especially one tasked with stopping things like this, could have betrayed the Bureau and everything it stood for was sickening to her. How many good agents needed to be lost in the pursuit of justice to satisfy their own selfish needs? That was to say nothing of the extreme corruption occurring at the highest level of the supposedly fairest and most just system of laws and governance ever created. Her institutional faith had been somewhat shaken, she had to admit, but she was trying not to let it cloud her judgment of the situation.

"Yeah, I'm here, sorry," she said.

"Listen, if things go south and bullets start flying, I want you to shoot first and ask questions later. There's no cover, and we can't very well get to the bottom of this if we're dead," Colin said.

"But he's the strongest lead we've had in this investigation!" exclaimed Smith.

"I know, and we're going to try and take him alive if it comes to that. I just want you to be prepared if Uncle Murphy comes to visit," he finished.

"Uncle Murphy?" she inquired.

"Murphy's law," spoke up Sheriff from the back. "As you've likely noticed today, anything that can go wrong will go wrong if you're not prepared."

"Seeing as we don't have a lot of time to prepare for this, I just want you to keep in mind that things could, in fact, go wrong," said Colin.

"In law enforcement, you can't just shoot your way out of every situation. We don't even know if he's even doing anything wrong," she said, sounding angry at the team's attitude toward her fellow agent.

"We're not law enforcement, and we don't have that luxury, but you know as well as I that I want to hear this guy out," said Colin.

"I'm more worried that he is an asshole and he brings backup," said Jester, having heard their conversation via his earpiece.

Colin spoke up, "Well, we're going to have to cross that bridge when we get to it. For now, we need to talk to this guy, and if things go south, try and take him and anyone else with him alive so they can answer questions."

53

Gloria Maxwell was not sure what to do anymore. As mayor of Washington D.C., she was tasked with the leadership and protection of the city's some six-hundred thousand citizens. Her role was murky in these types of disaster situations. It was becoming clear that she needed to declare a state of emergency, but she wasn't sure how it was going to help right now.

The public would most likely receive the information through their mobile phones, but there were reports that the towers were overloaded due to the internet being down with the power. She reflected on this as the last gasps of light peaked from the clouded gray horizon through her window. Snow and wind beat the thin windows of her office like a drum, causing them to rattle every so often. A sound that made her jump.

The question was, how could she most effectively render aid to the people who might be freezing in their own houses? By all accounts, there was near chaos taking place outside. There had been several shootings, a bombing of the old Spy Museum, their dispatch network for plows, and now possibly law enforcement communication looked to be hacked, and no one could explain why the power was off. Their current best guess was that this was a cyber-attack as well, because such a complete outage was not likely due to the weather.

She was past the point of pride now that the local government could handle themselves and needed help. The question was to which level she needed to request aid. She shivered slightly and wished her aid would hurry with the cup of steaming mint green tea she was bringing her. Cold was not her thing. The Metropolitan Police reported at some level to the mayor, but in truth, they reported far more to federal authorities than her, and she wasn't sure requesting they be federalized would do anything. There was, of course, the D.C. National Guard, but she could only request them—she had no actual command authority over them like the governor of a state. In fact, it was not overly clear who had command over the D.C. Army and Air National Guard administration-to-administration. The president technically had command authority, but he passed the roll typically to the Secretary of Defense, who in turn usually passed it to the Army and Air Force secretaries and, in some cases, so on.

She cursed the bureaucracy, knowing it was a complete product of can kicking and non-caring for everyday Americans. But she knew it was disingenuous in her heart. Scarcely anyone knew how things truly worked in D.C., and that went double when federal authorities were involved. Her assistant arrived, shuttling a cup of steaming tea. The minty aroma wafted from the mug into her nostrils, filling her with a renewed sense of strength.

She decided the National Guard would likely be her best bet for restoring order. The D.C. National Guard was unique in the fact that they could be used for law enforcement in unique situations. They could also respond the most quickly and effectively to what looked to be a unilateral threat and humanitarian crisis due to a lack of basic services and unrest. D.C. had struggled for years to regain some semblance of its own independence and power. It was technically the only spot in the nation that had no federal representation in the republic. This crisis would rob them of more of their independence.

But Gloria knew it was the right thing to do. She couldn't help the fact that a freak storm, cyber-attack, and civil unrest all occurred at the same time. She would do her duty and put forward the state of emergency to request the National Guard. She sighed and picked up her phone, hoping she was making the right call.

54

I t was shocking how dark it was in the city. The only dim light
came from the few windows with lights on in the federal building
that sat on top of the twenty-foot concrete wall next to them. The
snow had intensified, and they stood in over a foot of unplowed
white powder. Visibility due to the thick mist of falling snow and
darkness of night was under fifty feet, and that was only once their
eyes had adjusted. The snow blanketed all sound except for the
howling of the wind blowing through the concrete like wind tunnel
they were standing in. Large flakes bit Colin's face, and at times, he
had to shield his eyes from the intense wind-driven snow gusts that
blew.

They had been waiting for ten minutes in the cold now for Agent
Savarese to arrive. The drone was temporarily down, having landed
at Jester's vehicle to get its battery pack changed so it could continue
orbiting. They were temporarily blind at the worst possible moment.
But nothing had happened yet, and Agent Savarese was late. Another
biting gust of wind whipped through the narrowly enclosed street,
and Colin thought he saw someone approaching like a ghost through
the white precipitation. "He's coming," said Colin.

"Where? I don't see him," replied Smith, craning her neck and
putting her hand over her eyes to get a better look.

Agent Savarese came into clear view a few moments later. He was a shorter skinnier man with bushy eyebrows that stuck out from underneath his gray knit beanie hat. He wore a black jacket with a fur hood and a Canada Goose patch on the sleeve. He was pale white even in the dim light, and his other features were hard to distinguish from the snow that kept sticking to his face. Agent Savarese walked up to them and stood before them at a distance of only five feet. It was just close enough to hear him speak with only a raised voice, and just far enough away, Colin judged, that he felt like he could get his gun out in a hurry. Colin judged that this was why his hands were still in his jacket pockets.

"I'm guessing you're Agent Smith?" said the man.

"That's me," she said.

"And who's your friend?" he asked, looking at Colin.

"I'm Agent Doe," said Colin, staring back at the man, his hand close to his own weapon tucked in the pocket of his jacket.

Agent Savarese's bullshit detector was clearly finely tuned. "Sure you are," said Savarese.

"Agent Doe is working with me on my serial murder investigation," interjected Smith.

"Sure. So what do you and your Special Activities Division friend have that I need to know about?" asked Savarese, referring to the CIA's arm that conducted paramilitary operations. It was a good guess, Colin thought. This guy was clearly sharp, which only made Colin warier of him.

"What were you and your team doing at Lowercase?" asked Colin.

"What's Lowercase?" Savarese returned.

"The facility you and your team pulled a whole boatload of guns out of," replied Smith, having to speak up slightly to be heard over the wind.

"Yeah, I have no idea what you're talking about," Savarese stated, playing dumb.

"Well, if you want to play stupid, I can just arrest you for conspiracy to commit treason," said Smith, sounding frustrated.

"Or I could arrest you for obstruction of justice, if you'd prefer," retorted Savarese.

"You're not in a position to make threats here," said Colin, growing annoyed with the games that were being played.

Charlie came over Colin's earpiece. "Boss, overwatch is back up, and you've got five unidentifieds creeping up on you."

Colin had thought he had caught a brief glance of someone moving near the bar to his left, but he wasn't sure until Charlie had said something. Colin pulled his gun from his pocket and brought it to a low ready. Savarese saw him and went for his, but before Savarese could even blink, Colin had his gun up and aimed at his head.

The tension was white-hot, even in the freezing weather. Agent Smith went for her gun, but instead of aiming it at Savarese, she pointed it at a newly emerged figure out of the snow at their left. Colin judged this to be a worst-possible scenario. Either Savarese and his now emerging team thought they had been discovered in the act of committing treason, or they thought Colin and Smith were part of some yet unknown treason and were here to kill them. Either way, this was likely to end in a gunfight.

Two more figures emerged from the snow on Savarese's side, bringing the total number of bad guys to four. All had their weapons raised and pointed at Colin and Smith.

"I think both of you should drop your weapons," said Savarese.

"Nah, we're good. Plus, we have the high ground," replied Colin smoothly. As he said that, Jester, Sheriff, Witch, and Agent Sunderland emerged over the top of the concrete wall, their MP7s and Glocks pointed down at Agent Savarese and his team. Colin spoke again, "Now I'm going to ask you nicely one more time: What were you and your team doing at Lowercase? Or we can always do this the hard way."

55

"Looks like we got ourselves a Mexican standoff here," yelled Jester over the wall.

"Listen, we know you took the guns from Lowercase. What we don't know is why," said Smith.

"What I don't know is what this has to do with a serial killer," yelled Savarese over the now-roaring wind. Colin sensed this was going nowhere. He could not let it devolve into a gunfight. These guys were their only lead, and whether they were good or bad didn't really matter. What mattered was getting answers, and Colin decided the most rapid way to get them was honesty.

"Listen, me and my team have been tracking a serial assassin across three continents suspected of working for the Chinese government, and now he's in D.C. He's offed two senators, and a third is missing, all within the last twenty-four hours. We suspect he's doing this at the behest of the Chinese government, and we need to find him," said Colin.

Savarese paused slightly, stunned at what Colin had just said, and asked, "Why is he offing senators? That's a direct act of war; the Chinese aren't that stupid."

"The senators are involved in an off-the-books investigation looking into corruption and espionage at the highest levels of government. A few weeks ago, they discovered a possible deep cover plant at the very top of the DOJ. We suspect the Chinese are using this guy and his brutal methods to try and intimidate anyone who may know about this from ever looking into it again," replied Colin.

Savarese seemed to relax slightly for a second as he processed. Then he tensed slightly, as if remembering something. The slight twitch nearly caused Colin to shoot him, but he restrained himself in light of the current situation.

"If that's true, then who do you really work for?" Savarese asked.

"I told you we're with the FBI CID. We were brought in off the books from another division to figure this thing out," Smith responded, butting back into the conversation.

"That's impossible," Savarese said, his voice sounding increasingly confused.

"Why?" Colin asked.

Savarese responded, "Because we were brought in to investigate the same thing."

56

Department of Justice

The email had flashed across AG Mark Poole's desktop computer screen more than a minute ago. An emergency request of this magnitude was concerning to him, to say the least. The valuable resources it would draw away from an already tense situation were even more concerning. The last thing he wanted was more eyes on this. As attorney general of the United States, it was his responsibility to vet emergency requests like this to decide how legal they were and if they could be approved. A job that was usually fairly cut and dry. Congressional oversight and investigations didn't typically look too deeply into helping Americans in disaster zones, as they didn't typically help congressmen at the ballot box.

The truth was he wasn't going to approve this order. Not because it was illegal, but because it would be his ass on the line if things went too far. He knew that non-elected officials were the ones who always seemed to get chopped when everything went wrong. And he fancied himself smarter than the average government drone.

Emergency requests were by nature tricky situations, and the opportunities for legal deniability of them were numerous as they usually lived in some legal gray area, hence why they were considered emergencies. The nervous feeling that had plagued him all day continued unabated and had only grown as darkness fell on the capital.

He was being quieter than usual. Whether or not anyone noticed was questionable, as the few who had made it into the office were probably too relieved that he wasn't yelling at them to care. He knew this but reasoned that he was just being a good guy, giving them a break, even though he only cared for the quality of their work, not their well-being as a people, even if he sometimes put on a different face to the public. He knew some would think of him as a sociopath; he just considered himself a pragmatist.

Poole wasn't nervous by nature—at least he hadn't been since he was a little boy. He had long since learned to drown out the negative voices inside of him with a relentless flow of work and physical exercise. Today was very different, however. Things were now in motion, and they could not be stopped, even if his feet were beginning to get slightly cold.

There were multiple powers in the ring, and the only way out of this was to win. He hated himself for the weakness that he felt at the moment. He had not gotten to his position by showing a hint of infallibility, and he would not get to the next position by starting now. Dropping to the floor, he did a few pushups in rapid succession, feeling his heart rate increase past its current quick nervous rhythm. When he stood up, his mind cleared up slightly, he took a few deep breaths.

His path forward was now clear. Protect the operation at all costs, or be dragged down with it.

He hit reply and typed his response.

Emergency Request Denied.

57

Colin was somewhat skeptical because this had to have been one of the most twisted situations he had ever been involved in. "Prove it," he said. He took another scan around the concrete walled road, making sure no other threats had entered the picture. Apart from the gusting snow and near complete dark all he saw were the few agents with Savarese and Team Alien covering them from the top of the wall. He took this all in in a fraction of a second, darting his eyes back to Savarese, knowing only seconds had passed since the FBI agent's shocking revelation.

Savarese shot a look back that said the same thing, but he seemed to decide that since they had been honest with him, he would be honest with them to try and buy some goodwill. "A few months back, we were approached by the assistant director of the Counterintelligence Directorate. He told us that there was reason to believe that someone at the top of the Department of Justice was spying for a foreign power. Numerous operations had been blown, and after an extensive investigation, they had determined that the leak was not internal, and the only other group that was privy was the leadership of the DOJ. He told us that due to the nature of the situation, he was starting up an off the books investigation of his own to look into who the fuck was leaking information.

"Our team was selected as we usually run operations on the West Coast, and we were considered not likely to be involved. We'd been quietly investigating until this week, when we started to hear chatter about some kind of operation. Truthfully, I thought you and your team were brought in to clean house and eliminate any loose ends before we got to the truth of it all. It looks like I was wrong," finished Savarese.

"Apology not accepted," yelled Jester over the wall.

"Well, that's good, because I didn't apologize," replied Savarese. The wind whipped up again, and Colin had to momentarily shield his eyes from the snow. He took the opportunity to lower his weapon in another show of good faith. It took a moment, but slowly everyone else did as well.

"Who gave you the order?" Smith asked, stepping closer so she could be heard over the weather.

"Deputy Director Mullins," replied Savarese.

"Where'd you get access to Lowercase and the intel that we were in town to clean house?" inquired Colin.

"That came from Mullins. I'm not sure where he got it, but truthfully, we were written a blank check and told to be as independent as possible. So we didn't ask questions and kept our heads down."

"That's why you drew the weapons out of Lowercase?" Smith questioned.

"That was Mullins's idea. He said that we needed to have the firepower to protect ourselves from the threat, but he feared drawing the weapons through conventional means could tip someone off to the investigation."

Colin saw Smith frown, and he felt the same way. If this was true, then their worst fears would have been realized. The highest levels of the FBI were, at some level, compromised as well. They had been right to go in under the radar. The question was, who was pulling Deputy Director Mullins's strings, and why had he turned traitor? The other question on Colin's mind was how Deputy Director Mullins had known Colin's team would be in town? Echo Teams were a secret, but there was a small handful of people at the highest echelons of government who knew they existed.

It was how they technically had real credentials for every government agency. Colin wasn't sure who all of these people were, but he guessed that it was at least possible that the attorney general could have been one of them. If that was the case, it would have easily been possible for him to suspect that this kind of resource might be brought to bear in this situation. The rest was a simple matter of using the vast resources at his disposal to watch the airports for their arrival.

"Did you have a line on us as soon as we arrived?" Colin asked.

"Not immediately, but the trail of chaos you were leaving behind was a fairly big indicator and made it relatively easy to guess who it was. Our only problem with interdicting you was that all of the traditional digital methods we would have used to track you kept conveniently going dead whenever we got close. The weather did the rest," Savarese stated. Colin made a mental note to thank Charlie more often, even though he was sure he was listening in on the conversation and likely smiling to himself.

"Have you had any trouble with the Chinese hit teams in town?" Smith asked.

"Chinese hit teams? I didn't even know they were involved until you told us a minute ago. Mullins told us this was most likely Russian, and given all of their interference in American politics lately, we didn't think it would be anything else."

"I've met Mullins before. He was a real crusader, from everything I remember. I have a hard time believing that he could have done something like this," said Smith.

"I know what you mean. But given everything you guys have said, something's definitely up here. I get keeping investigative teams segmented, but having one actively target another can only mean one thing. Someone is trying to cover something up." Savarese said.

"Agreed. I think it's time we paid the deputy director a visit," said Colin.

Savarese nodded. "He doesn't live far from here. Why don't you guys grab your trucks and follow us? We'll lead the way there, and we can ask him our questions together."

58

Sheriff had the heat blasting by the time Colin got back into the Suburban. He dusted snow out of his hair and felt his cheeks instantly start to burn at the sudden blast of warm air. Usually, Colin was far more partial to cold weather and rarely, if ever, had the heat on anywhere, but he was thankful for it now. His Oakley tactical gloves were not waterproof—an oversight by the manufacturer, he thought. He also wished, at the moment, that they were insulated, but the padding would have inevitably slowed down his trigger speeds, so the cold was here to stay.

"Well, that was interesting," said Sheriff.

"More like alarming," replied Smith curtly.

Colin didn't answer. He was once again lost in thought. He absentmindedly watched Sheriff put the vehicle in drive and pull away after two dark Dodge Durango's that held Agent Savarese and his team. A second later, Colin saw the headlights of Jester's vehicle in the passenger-side mirror of their car.

This situation was becoming more complicated by the minute, and they couldn't afford any missteps at this point. The problem was that everything that was now happening was totally unprecedented, even in Colin's book. A deputy director of the FBI had lied to a team of agents and given them access to a highly classified facility to pull nearly untraceable weapons to use against another U.S. government asset. They were off the map here.

It was possible that Deputy Director Mullins was the sole conspirator, but Colin deemed it highly unlikely. The Senate committee's intelligence said it was a higher-up in the DOJ. Mullins was high, but not that high. He also wouldn't likely have had access on his own to information about the movements of Colin's team. That would have been director level or higher. Still, though, Colin knew it was useless to speculate under current circumstances. Any guesses he had about how this day would have gone were completely wrong at this point. A deeper desire had unquestionably been awakened within him, though. A thirst for justice for who he was sure was his sister's killer. He wasn't sure how he was tangled up in all of this or how the two were related, but he knew who Azrael was now. Charlie was combing through old DOD and NATO records to try and learn more about the man, but he was coming up empty at the moment. Colin wanted the truth about who had killed his sister more badly than he could ever recall wanting anything.

The truth burned inside of him like some kind of white-hot fire. But what truth was that exactly? Yes, they knew more than they did before, and it was somehow wedged into this massive conspiracy, but it didn't really change who Azrael was to them. Well, it did change who Azrael was to him, Colin thought. He remembered what the prisoner had said to him in Lowercase, how the man had just snapped from too many missions and too much combat stress. Colin's team had been running flat out for nearly half a year now, with little to no break. Colin wondered internally what that line was and what truly pushed someone past it.

He pushed this from his mind, realizing he was thinking in circles. He knew who he was, and second-guessing himself wouldn't do anyone any good and would likely get one of his people killed. "Charlie, anything?" Colin asked.

"I've plotted the deputy director's address, and it looks like you're right on track to be there in about twenty minutes. I'm also monitoring their conversations via Agent Savarese's cellphone. Apart from thinking Jester is a dick, everything seems above board," replied Charlie.

Agent Smith couldn't hear what Charlie was saying as it was over Colin's earpiece, but she had heard enough. "You still don't trust them?"

"I do. But in the event that I'm wrong, I'd rather know it than get shot thinking I'm right," Colin replied.

"They're FBI agents, not spies," said Agent Smith.

"After everything that's happened today, are you really willing to give them your total unflinching trust? I thought cops were supposed to be natural skeptics," questioned Colin.

She didn't immediately respond to this. When she did, her tone seemed slightly more reasoned. "I guess I am skeptical, but I want to trust them. I'm not used to this counter-espionage stuff. In my world, there's the good guys who are the FBI and the bad guys who are deranged serial killers. This world is, well, muddier. It must be hard to know what to do and who to trust."

Colin felt no joy in being right in this argument. In fact, he was growing to like Smith a great deal in the short time that he had known her. She clearly had a more straightforward view of the world, and Colin missed having that himself.

"You have no idea. Most of the time, we can't even drive straight. If it weren't for the weather, we'd have done about a hundred SDR's today and pretty much gotten to everywhere in the same amount of time. And remember, without your work on Azrael, we'd be nowhere so far," said Colin, referring to a surveillance detection run and trying to make her feel like this wasn't all totally over her head.

In truth, the team was in way over their heads when it came to hunting a killer, so he was shooting straight with her. Colin looked in the rearview mirror at her, and she caught his gaze and returned it, smiling back at him as if to say, "Thanks, that was sweet." Colin held it for perhaps a second longer than he should have, but she didn't seem to mind.

He returned his gaze to the street outside, which was blanketed in over a foot of snow, and hoped that the deputy director would be the key to unraveling everything.

59

17 years Before

It was late in the office, and the only lights were coming from the few desk lamps that had been left on by long since departed staff. Susan sat at her desk, her head down in a file that she hadn't actually been reading for over an hour now. Her foot nervously tapped the ground, and her fingers continuously fidgeted with a pencil. The office, in typical government fashion, was in a beautiful old building filled with furniture that did everything possible to detract from the ornateness of the architecture.

Susan didn't notice this, though. In fact, she barely noticed anything except the sounds around her, which seemed to continuously make her jump. Time seemed to be moving painfully slowly. The last few hours had felt like days, if not weeks, to her.

The boys were at home with a babysitter. Susan had lied, saying she needed to work late. She was at the office, but she had no plans to work. In fact, her plan had been a few weeks in the making. Tonight was the night she would finally break into her boss' office and steal the piece of evidence she knew must be on his computer. She had a new compact disc she had purchased at an office supply store in her purse to ensure the files would copy without incident—

the ones around the office tended to be reused, which often resulted in data loss.

It was nearly Christmas Eve, and Susan had judged that this would be the ideal time to make her move. Everyone was leaving the office earlier and earlier, and when they were here, they were either heads down trying to finish up the last of their work for the year or so distracted by the fact it was almost Christmas they were paying no attention at all.

Her boss, who usually worked late, seemed to be in the spirit as well and had actually left at five o'clock this evening. Well, Susan thought, his reasons for leaving were likely more sinister than the Christmas spirit. Susan looked up from her desk in time to see the last other person left in the office packing her things up and putting on her coat. A few moments later, the petite brunette named Betsy, who worked a few desks over from her, waved on her way out. "Have a good night, Susan. See you tomorrow," she said as she walked out the front door to the office. Susan was now completely alone, and it was so quiet she could hear her heart beating in her ears. The only sound came from the occasional creaking of the white-painted radiators that were trying to keep up with the inadequate windows of the old building.

Susan waited another few moments to ensure that Betsy hadn't forgotten anything. Those moments felt like hours to her. When she was confident that Betsy wouldn't come back, she got up and did a lap around the office to ensure that it was truly empty. Every dark shadow made the hair on the back of her neck stand up. Susan caught a glimpse of herself in one of the dark windows as she passed by. Outside, the lights of other D.C. office buildings shone yellow in the winter night, but inside she saw her own reflection painted on the glass.

She was tired, and her appearance advertised this. Her usually neat blonde hair seemed slightly disheveled, which was saying some-thing for her, and her eyes had dark circles under them. She was paler than usual, paler than she usually got in winter, and even she thought she looked thin. She stood there for a moment before whipping around with a start at the sudden creak of a radiator across the room.

Susan thought for a moment she had seen something, but then noticed she could see her reflection across the office in the window opposite her. She took a deep breath to steady herself. This wasn't the first time she had thought someone was watching her. Over the past few weeks, she had felt that way constantly. The only feeling of respite from her nervousness was sleep, which came rarely and was filled with the kind of desperate nightmares one just wanted to wake up from. Susan walked back to her desk and retrieved her purse. It was time.

She walked down the hallway to the left of her desk, which led past a break room, a bathroom, and a few small offices. She arrived at the end of the dark-paneled hallway, which housed a door that went to the assistant U.S. attorney's office and a desk that his secretary usually sat at. She had rushed out a scant five minutes after he had, eager to take the early night off of work as these opportunities were so few.

Susan walked to her desk and pulled on the long, flat drawer that sat above the chair. It was locked. Susan reached into her purse and fished out the master key she had stolen from the building maintenance office a few days earlier. Every desk in the building that had a lock had to open to one master key. This ensured that an employee's desk could always be opened if they were terminated and not allowed back. The government achieved this by ordering massive numbers of the same type of cheap generic desks and dictating the requirement to the manufacturer.

The drawer unlocked with a metallic click, and the desk drawer slid open. It was immaculately neat and housed many different colors of sticky notes and pens. Susan saw the keys and grabbed them. She closed the desk drawer and walked to the door behind her, which she proceeded to open and walk inside, then closed it behind her, locking it for good measure. The office was empty and dark, and she couldn't shake the feeling that she was somehow in the lion's den.

She walked to the desk and powered on the computer. It took

several minutes to boot up. Susan could hear the clock ticking above the door to the office, the sounds coming in what sounded like slow motion. The fans spun up on the computer as it booted up, and when it finally did, Susan saw a login screen. She clicked his username and froze for a second, trying to remember the password she had seen him type in the first time he had shown her his note-taking system.

She typed it in, and the computer said it was incorrect. Her stomach dropped. Was her whole plan going to be derailed because she couldn't remember a fucking password? She became nearly hysterical inside her head and started breathing heavily before she could calm herself down again. She tried the password again, carefully pecking on the keys to make sure she got everything right. Thankfully, the computer unlocked. It took her another few minutes to search through the file architecture to find what she was looking for.

She clicked another button, and it began copying the files to the compact disc. Susan thought she heard a footstep outside the door. She shot up, craning her neck to listen more carefully. She heard nothing. Creeping to the door as silently as possible, she discreetly peered out the small part of the glass that wasn't frosted next to the wooden door. She saw nothing. *Get a hold of yourself,* she said in her head.

A soft chime emanated from the computer, indicating the copy was complete. Shit, Susan thought—she had forgotten to turn off the sound. She went back to the desk and double-checked that the files had in fact been copied. Then she closed the files and removed the compact disc, powering down the computer and making sure to set everything just as it had been. Silently, she crept out of the office, locking it and returning the key to its proper place.

Moving down the hallway and back to her desk to gather her things, she couldn't help feeling triumphant, albeit mixed with a bit of nervous dread about what she had just done. She slipped the disk into a small cutout she had made in the lining of her purse, put on her jacket, and walked out the door, never even noticing the silhouette of the man standing in the dark shadows of the nearby office.

60

Colin sniffled slightly from the cold as the SUVs slid to a stop. Whether the building they arrived at was newer or older was nearly impossible to tell in the dark. The FBI and Echo Team moved to the glass door in a decidedly un-tactical manner. This wasn't a breach-and-clear; this was a knock-and-talk with the boss of several of the people there. Inside the glass was a mostly dark lobby that only had emergency lighting on and an empty desk where a doorman would usually have sat.

"This cold sucks," said Savarese.

"Not quite the same as sunny California, eh?" asked Jester. They tried the front door, but it was locked.

"Let's look for a side entrance," said Smith.

"Hang on," replied Colin. He took a cellphone from his pocket that only Charlie could communicate with. He opened an app on the screen and walked up to the glowing red light of a FOB scanner. Holding the device there, he watched numbers zip by on the screen while it zeroed in on the correct NFC frequency. Then he saw the light turn green on the scanner and heard a beep. He pulled the door open for the teams. "After you," he said. They proceeded into the lobby, Savarese moving in last, right before Colin.

"FBI my ass," he said, walking past.

They proceeded through the gray tile floor of the lobby and past the dim yellow emergency lights emanating from an exit sign. One of the FBI team members pushed open the door to a stairwell, and the team filed in and began climbing up after him. It was nearly black from the lack of lights in the stairwell, the emergency lighting clearly not working in this section of the building at all. A few of the FBI agents pulled out their cellphones and ignited the flashlights on them with a few taps of their touch screens. This gave them some light they could follow and made the trip a bit less dangerous.

One of the FBI agents remarked, "Well, this is definitely a fire hazard."

"I'll let the deputy director know," said Savarese sarcastically. They proceeded up seven flights of stairs before finally arriving at the floor the condo was on. Nearly everyone, with the exception of Team Alien, was breathing hard. They walked through the door and proceeded down the hallway to unit seven sixty-eight. It was dim and dark here too, with emergency lights every fifty feet or so, which helped to distract from the fact that this was not a very nice building. *Government salaries certainly don't buy you much in D.C. anymore, which makes a lot of sense considering this is where the federal government operates,* thought Colin.

They arrived at the unit, and Savarese knocked. There was no answer. He knocked again. "Deputy Director Mullins, it's Agent Savarese. I need to talk to you." There was no answer again. Savarese waited another second before pounding on the door this time.

Colin didn't like this. It was dark out, and there was almost a foot and a half of snow on the ground. There was no way this guy was out and about. He walked up next to Agent Savarese and tried the door handle. It was unlocked, and the white-painted door creaked open. Colin instantly drew his weapon, feeling something was very wrong.

"What are you doing?" said an exasperated Savarese.

Colin ignored him, moving into the condo weapon up. It was dark, but Colin could tell it was tidy and well kept. He heard foot-steps behind him as the others began to follow him into the apartment. Colin came through a hallway and into a family room and kitchen area and was greeted by a scene of gruesome carnage.

Deputy Director Mullins, Colin assumed, was sitting in a computer chair in front of a small desk in the corner. He was slumped backward, his right hand hanging down and holding a silver .38 special revolver. Half of the top of his head was blown off, splattered all over the ceiling and surrounding area. Colin didn't smell him yet, and blood still dripped in rapidly coagulating drops from his head and off of objects around him. This had happened recently.

"Jesus," said Agent Smith, walking into the room. Colin walked closer to the body as a few of the team members spread out into the rest of the apartment to clear it. He saw a note on the desk with a few droplets of blood on it and a pencil next to it. Colin pulled a flashlight from his pocket and turned it on, shining it over the note.

I cannot live with myself anymore. I am living a lie. I have been spying for a foreign government. I was not alone. My accomplice, AG Mark Poole, brought me into the fold. He knew I needed money. I was desperate. I couldn't afford to send my kids to college and keep my house. I am a failure as a man. My only hope is that this note will help him meet justice. I'm sorry for the people I've hurt.
-Mullins

Colin stared at the note for what felt to him like a little while, reading and rereading until he heard Jester's voice near him. "Place is clear, boss."

Savarese walked toward them from the other room. "We need to call this in."

Colin frowned at him. "Not yet. We need to investigate this more thoroughly first. If Poole was the mole, there may be others involved. We could seriously shoot ourselves in the foot by trying to bring others in on this before we get a handle on the situation."

"He's the deputy director of the FBI—we can't just do nothing!" Savarese exclaimed.

"I'm not saying we do nothing. We just need to poke around for a few minutes and understand what's happening here," replied Colin, trying to cajole him.

"Trust him. With everything that's happened today, being a bit more cautious is the right call," Smith chimed in.

Savarese put up his hands in mock surrender. "All right, since it seems like my career's already down the toilet, we'll do it your way. Let's have a look around."

61

Everything was falling into place for Azrael. He drove the white Sprinter van casually but determinedly away from the deputy director of the FBI's downtown condo. He almost felt happy at what he had just done, as one might feel after completing a long day's work. The man had pleaded with him at first, crying that he could still be useful and that the best was yet to come. When that had failed, Mullins had resorted to threats and attempted violence.

That was until the syringe filled with tetrodotoxin, a paralyzing nerve agent commonly found in venomous fish, had entered his neck in the struggle. The poison pumped its way through his veins before immobilizing him completely. The only thing left for the man to do as he was maneuvered into position was to watch as Azrael placed his own gun into his immobilized hand, brought the barrel to his temple, and pulled the trigger.

This wasn't the way Azrael would have chosen to do it if he had time. However, Mullins was anything but his typical victim. Although Azrael sold his skills to the highest bidder, there was still a certain amount of, well, pleasure he liked to gain from the experience. He had enjoyed the paralyzed but knowing fear in the man's eyes when he knew it was all over, but what truly made him angry was the determined look of defiance in the man's eyes to the very last.

This was why Azrael preferred to kill with a knife. He enjoyed the determination in his victims to escape him, but he enjoyed the look of defeat in their eyes far more when the pain caused by their wounds drove all defiance from them more. There was nothing so sweet as defeat. Of course, he utilized tetrodotoxin in his kills quite often as well. It not only helped keep his victims still, but it also inspired a certain sense of helplessness and calm serenity in situations that needed to be quicker. That, mixed with a clotting agent, helped to keep the victims from bleeding too much on the artwork; that was the way he left them, to his mind anyway.

He took a turn and let the headlights of the van burn their way through the falling snow ahead. The path he cut through the night gave him a sense of inner peace. As if the darkness were his to navigate alone.

Azrael wasn't exactly sure why he left his victims this way anymore. It had started as a calling sign on some of his hits when something special was in order. The more he did it, though, the more he found he enjoyed it. There was some sort of primal ecstasy he found deep within himself when he totally dominated his victims. Something that broke the last human parts of him when he had run from his old life so long ago. To him, whether it was the former or the latter didn't matter. His sociopathic tendencies had warped the truth far beyond any normal moral standards, to the point where even he didn't know what honesty meant anymore.

He craved the carnal satisfaction of killing and the sense of power it gave him. The control was the most empowering thing he had ever felt in his life. The kill was, of course, the ultimate act of control, but it was the sense of submission in their eyes when they realized it was hopeless and the end had come that he truly savored. The sense of stability it provided to his fragile sense of reality seemed to ground him and keep the OCD under control. It was all he had.

Azrael reflected on none of this on the way back to his warehouse. All he knew was that his mission was almost accomplished. All he had to do was sit back and ready himself for the coming storm.

62

Senator Rand's Apartment

"Any updates from the Echo Team?" asked Senator Miller with a hastily disguised hiccup. He was still seated in the leather arm and beginning to strain against a very full bladder of coffee and alcohol.

Rand looked over at the man, who was clearly becoming very drunk, with the air of a father seeing his son get too drunk for the first time. "I've been sitting here with you the whole time. You know all the updates," Rand replied. His southern accent seemed to get more distinct the more he had to drink. At the moment, that had only been three bourbons mixed with the strong black coffee, not enough to truly affect someone of Rand's practiced hand when it came to drinking. Miller had more than twice that amount and had long since started excluding the coffee from his drinks.

Such a waste of the good stuff, thought Rand, reflecting on the three-quarters of the bottle that was now gone from his family's private reserve. He had more, of course, but he viewed the contents of each bottle as precious and deserving of being savored.

"I know that. But we both know you have your sources, and I've seen that phone of yours lighting up all night." Miller pushed a slight slur to his words.

Rand sighed. "They've apparently linked up with an FBI team that was investigating the same thing. It looks like they were under orders from a deputy director who they just found dead of suicide in his condo. His note says that Attorney General Mark Poole was his accomplice. Exactly as we suspected all along. I imagine they'll move to arrest him shortly now that they have the evidence in hand."

"Jesus, Rand, this shit is playing out like a spy novel. I mean, things like this don't just happen. What the hell is going on?"

"You'd be surprised how crazy the world is that we live in," said Rand in his characteristic southern drawl.

"What about Walker and the threat against us? What are we supposed to do about that?" Miller demanded.

"Once Poole is in custody, I imagine they'll question him to glean the location of Walker and hopefully take down the threat against us. Perhaps they'll offer him a deal to take capital punishment off the table in exchange for information. I'd say most likely the threat against us will disappear once Poole is in custody. The other conspirators will want to cut their losses and run once they see the direct line back to them."

"What about Walker? If they cut bait and run, what will happen to him?"

Rand turned back and stared at him for a moment. The flames from the fireplace danced on the walls, giving the room an iridescent glow. "What do you think will happen?" Rand asked back.

Miller's head fell to his hands. His mind was slowed by the alcohol consumption, but he had read enough books and seen enough movies to guess what would happen. "If Walker knows anything about them, they'll kill him. If not, maybe they'll just let him go."

Rand raised his eyebrows. "Is that what you think?"

Miller nearly fell apart. It was far more emotion than a man should ever properly display, Rand judged. "They can't just kill him, can they? He's a sitting U.S. senator!" Miller exclaimed.

"Did that stop them before?" Rand asked. Miller went quiet at that, keeping his head in his hands and slowly rocking back and forth in his chair.

Rand sat back and looked at his phone, which had just buzzed again. He turned his gaze to the fire, watching the flames twirl and burn their way through the air, wondering what would happen next.

63

Colin found it difficult to search the condo in the dark, even with the aid of a flashlight. The assistant director was extremely clean and well-organized, making nothing obvious. What surprised Colin most of all was the fact that Mullins had two children, both mysteriously missing. One appeared to be an older boy, likely near college age, and the other looked to be a younger girl, possibly in elementary school.

Colin gleaned this from the few photos around the apartment, the two extra bedrooms, and the various school items on the refrigerator. Still, for all of their searching, they had found nothing as of yet. Charlie was busy remotely attempting to break into Mullins's work computer, which was in his bag near his body, while Colin and the others were looking through drawers and cabinets.

Smith walked into the master bedroom of the apartment, where Colin was looking through pictures of the man and his family under the light of his flashlight. In truth, he had been taking out the backs of the photos, looking for hidden pieces of paper, keys, or anything else that would have helped them learn more about what was going on here.

"If you were a father involved in a conspiracy, where would you hide something?" she asked Colin.

He thought about this for a second. "Probably at work."

"Imagine that was a non-starter. Your workplace is filled with nosey people who figure things out and suspect people for a living."

"Like the FBI?" asked Colin.

"Exactly."

"Well, I guess I'd keep it in my bedroom. Kids are too inquisitive, and they tend to figure things out for themselves eventually."

"That's exactly what I was thinking. Have you found anything yet?"

"No. This place is clean, at least on the surface."

"Where have you looked so far? I'll help."

"Drawers, closet, under the bed, and these picture frames," said Colin, holding up one of the frames he was looking at. Smith proceeded over to the window and started feeling the curtains for anything irregular. When she was satisfied nothing was there, she moved over to look in the closet where Colin had already searched. Colin briefly panned his flashlight over to follow her across the room when a silver glint caught the corner of his eye. He panned the light back across the room to see where it had come from but got nothing. He stood this time from where he had been sitting on the corner of the bed and panned the light back across the room. The glint came from the air vent near the dresser across from the bed.

Colin walked over to the vent and ran the light across it again. The screw on the bottom right of the white-painted vent seemed to be nearly stripped, its white paint no longer covering up its shiny metallic insides. Colin knelt down, examining the vent. Each screw looked to him to be perfectly painted like they had never been touched, except for the one. "Smith, come look at this," he said. She walked over from the closet and knelt down next to him. "Why would this screw be stripped?"

She thought about this for a second. "Well, it's not in a good spot to have been damaged by someone," she replied.

Colin pulled the Yarborough knife he got when he became a Green Beret from a sheath at the small of his back. The small canvas micarta handled knife with a dorsal tapered blade was only available to Green Berets upon graduation from phase five of special forces training. Colin's went with him everywhere, without exception. He placed the blade in between the flat screws and slowly turned each of them to the left before they each fell out. The last damaged one was a bit trickier, but after a few minutes of finagling, Colin managed to remove it.

He reached his hand into the vent and felt around, finally feeling something when he was up to his shoulder. He pulled a small, cheap-looking laptop from the vent and held it up, a look of triumph on his face. They got up and took the laptop to the kitchen, not bothering to put the vent back where it was. "Got something here!" Smith said as they went.

Colin tapped his earpiece. "Charlie, I've got another laptop on this network I'm going to need you to break into."

"Roger that, boss. Ready and waiting for it."

Colin placed the laptop down on the kitchen table away from the body that was beginning to smell and opened it. He hit the power button and waited as it slowly booted up. He was greeted with a password screen. He sighed and waited for Charlie to acknowledge that he saw it. It took another few moments. "Got it. I need a few to break in."

"Why do you think that screw was messed up? I mean, he's the assistant director of the FBI's counterintelligence directorate—he knows how to hide something better than that," Smith asked.

"Maybe he wanted someone to find it," said Colin.

"This whole situation feels weird to me. Like we're missing something," Smith replied.

"I know what you mean. That's why I wanted us to wait before making a move on Poole. Odds are, we'd be walking right into some kind of trap. We need more," Colin said, pondering what he was saying while he spoke.

Savarese walked into the room. "Whoa, laptop, nice find. Is there a password?"

"Yeah, I've got my guys remotely accessing it while we speak," replied Colin.

"Good," said Savarese. "Does any of this feel weird to you guys? I know it looks bad—the note, the dueling investigations, the lies—but I knew Mullins. He's a real straight shooter, a total white-knight type. I'd be shocked if there wasn't more to this that we're not seeing."

"We've been talking about the same thing. Did Mullins seem like the type to kill himself?" asked Smith.

"No, but he didn't seem like the type to betray his country, either," replied Savarese. They stood silently staring at the laptop, thinking about what secrets it might hold, while Colin wondered what dark twist of fate had brought Mullins to this gruesome end. All the while, the thing that troubled him most was that they might never find the truth.

64

The bags under Charlie's eyes were darkening by the keystroke, it seemed. It was dark in the hangar, and the blue light from his screens flickered off of his face in the near-freezing dark and dim light of the expansive room. Two remote control windows sat open on his computer of the two different laptops he was currently accessing.

The assistant director's work laptop had been a simple exercise to get into. Charlie simply pulled his Single Sign-on credentials from the FBI's IT infrastructure Department, commonly referred to as ITAD. The secret laptop found in the vent was an inexpensive Dell laptop likely bought at a pawn shop with cash that the assistant director likely knew wouldn't have working security cameras.

Breaking into this laptop was a slightly different story, but still not something overly complicated for someone like Charlie or any common hacker. In this case, Charlie was in the process of accessing an NSA-installed back door in the operating system that was available to them on all such laptops, provided they knew where it was. Whether or not it was strictly legal to do this didn't really matter in Charlie's case, and he very much doubted anyone would ever find a trace of him having accessed this computer anyway. It essentially functioned by allowing Charlie to create a new administrator account for the system, where he could demote the other account on the computer to a regular user. He could then change their password and gain access to all of their data.

He was just finishing changing the password to Kerrigan, as he always did, which was a reference to his favorite video game series, StarCraft. He then shut down and restarted the computer to ensure that his new credentials were now firmly in place. It took the computer only seconds to reboot, and Charlie typed in his favorite video game character to get started. Once the credentials were in, it took another moment for the system to fully initialize. When it did, Charlie instantly saw what he was looking for in the form of two files on the desktop. One was labeled Poole, and the other was labeled Jack and Emily. Charlie knew from Mullins's personnel file that Mullins had two children named Jack and Emily and also that he was divorced.

Charlie opted to click on the Poole file first, figuring it to be the juicier of the two bits of information. He was greeted with several documents, and he typed in a key command to open all of them. What followed was a series of unremarkable investigative documents that looked to Charlie like they had been sent over to Mullins by the FBI team now with Colin. Charlie felt Sarah softly breathing over his shoulder, reading the documents he had open.

"So, he just had this thing to hide his misleading investigation?" asked Sarah.

"Maybe," said Charlie. "The FBI Cyber Crime Division is really good. If it was completely off the books, then he would want to keep it on a totally separate machine. Either way, this guy was no cybersecurity expert," said Charlie with a slight laugh. Sarah gave him a reproachful look that said he's dead, which Charlie instantly cowed at. "I just mean this guy launched an off-the-books investigation at the direction of the AG to throw everyone off their scent. Couldn't they have just gone through official channels and classified the investigation? They were clearly going to frame someone for all of this. Wouldn't that have been easier if the investigation looked legit?" he asked in return.

Sarah noticed he was rambling like he always did when he was nervous, but she had to admit he had a good point. "I don't know. This whole thing is fucked. Open the other file." Charlie nodded and opened the file with the names of Mullins's children. There were several videos. Charlie entered the same command and opened all of them, which instantly began to play. "My god." Sarah gasped.

The two of them were horrified at what they saw.

65

"Boss, you need to see this right now," chimed Charlie into Colin's earpiece.

"What's up?" Colin asked. He was standing in the kitchen with Savarese, Smith, and Jester. The rotten stench of decay was beginning to permeate from Mullins's dead body in the other room, and Colin couldn't help but stare at the strange assortment of colorful glassware sitting on the counter opposite him.

"Look at the second laptop's screen." Colin snapped back to the screen from the purple glass he had been staring at and couldn't believe what he was seeing. Both of the children he had seen in photos around the house were tied to chairs and looked to have been severely beaten. The video showcased a gun being held to each of their heads and someone screaming at them.

The boy looked to be a teenager, but the little girl couldn't have been more than six or seven years old. She had a cut lip and a black eye, and she wore an innocent but terrified look. The boy looked to have taken the worst of it, which was saying something considering the look of the little girl—her blonde hair was matted to some dried blood on the side of her face.

The room was dead silent except for the measured breathing of all of the calm professionals it held. Colin didn't feel calm, though.

He felt a blistering rage growing within him that someone would do this to children. He had seen many young men dead across the world involved in fights for one cause or another. He'd even seen child soldiers fighting in person in Africa. But a little girl like this was senseless.

Maybe it was the fact that this was happening in the United States, or maybe it was the fact that she looked so much like his sister when she was younger. Colin decided it wasn't either of these things. It was anyone who chose to hurt those who could not help themselves. Especially children. Within his soul, he knew he would not allow those responsible to see another sunrise.

"Oh my god," gasped Smith.

"Sick fucks," said Jester.

"Charlie, where are they?" Colin asked, his voice barely more than a whisper.

"I'm working on it, boss," he responded.

"Those videos had to have come from somewhere. Find them. Now," Colin said, his voice brooking no argument.

"On it, boss."

"So Mullins was coerced," said Savarese.

"By a bunch of fucking psychos," said Jester.

"We need to find these guys yesterday," replied Smith.

"We have a bigger issue here. What kind of guy who is doing something to save his kids kills himself before it's done?" Colin asked.

"Holy shit. They're going to kill the kids," whispered Smith.

"*If* they're still alive. Local HRT will never reach them in time," said a defeated-sounding Savarese, referring to the FBI's vaunted Hostage Rescue Team.

"Then we'll go and get them ourselves," responded Colin flatly.

"And how do you propose we do that? We have no idea where they are and no training on how to rescue people from a hostage situation. Not to mention the fact that we'd be going in blind and probably getting everyone killed in the process. No, I'm not taking that risk. I'm calling this in—we need proper resources to make this happen," Savarese nearly yelled, growing angrier with every word.

"You have no training in hostage rescue and no resources. I think you'll find that my team has plenty of both," stated Colin, his voice barely rising at all to greet Savarese's challenge.

"I don't even know who the fuck you guys are—why the hell should I trust you?"

"Have we lied to you yet?" Colin asked in return.

Before Savarese could respond, Charlie came back over their earpieces. "Boss, I think I know where they are."

"You think, or you know, Charlie?"

There was a momentary pause. "I know where they are, boss, and they're close! Don't ask me how. All I'll say is thank God for AI image recognition. It's actually pretty cool—the wooden arches behind the people in the images are from an architect who..."

Colin cut him off. "Get us the address, upload it to our GPS, and get the drone overhead now so we can see what we're working with."

"On it, boss!"

Colin turned to Savarese, whose mouth was hanging slightly open. "Listen, we know where they are. Now my team is going after the kids. It's your call whether you want to come and help or not, but make no mistake—we could use your help," Colin finished, turning and heading for the door.

66

Colin was shocked at how dark it was in the city. Nearly all lights were extinguished by the blackout, and the only thing visible was what fell within the beams of the four convoy vehicles headlights. Which at the moment was snow. Driving had become more like crawling, and though their destination would normally have taken ten minutes to get to in normal conditions, it would now take nearly thirty if they were moving quickly. The problem was twofold. The snow was so deep the vehicles could barely get any traction, and the snow was falling so thickly they could barely see twenty feet in front of them.

The impatience within the four vehicles was thick in the dry, heated air. Everyone was so anxious to get to their destination that the drivers were perhaps pushing things a little too far, but no one said anything except Jester, who always seemed to have something to say no matter the situation. Colin wasn't surprised the FBI team had accompanied them to try and rescue the hostages. It was the kind of thing that those in law enforcement, specifically the FBI, had hard-wired into them. They were there to catch bad guys, but more than anything else, they were there to keep bad people from hurting good people.

Colin had dealt with Savarese's type before. He was the kind who thought he would do anything to get the job done, no matter what the rule book said. What Savarese hadn't counted on was just how far away the rule book could get when one was in this deep. To his credit, he had come along without saying another word. The truth was, though, that he couldn't have called for help even if he wanted to. Charlie had seen to that, not that Savarese would ever have realized this.

Despite all this, Colin was happy to have them along. Provided they could even rescue the children, Savarese's team would be the ones to get them out. Colin's team couldn't babysit them until this was resolved—it would be too dangerous, and they didn't have the resources. Regardless, it would be nice to have the extra shooters as well.

The building in question was an old club that hadn't been used in many years. It had been under construction after an apparent fire twenty years ago, and little progress had ever been made. It was an old property that had been built in the early 1920s as a swing dancing establishment. Charlie had sent over more information about the building than Colin could have possibly ever read in the short half-hour drive, but he was thankful for the distraction. The drone was nearly overhead of the target building. It was taking longer due to the intense storm winds it was currently battling.

It arrived a scant fifteen minutes before the teams did and began probing the area with its normal and thermal cameras. The normal cameras were useless in this whiteout, but the thermal ones painted them a clear picture, regardless of how bleak it was. The main dance floor of the old club was sunken into the ground before a stage. A long L-shaped bar ran the length of the wall behind the dance floor, which would provide them some cover when they went in, but there was no furniture. Colin was piecing this picture together from building plans and the thermal imaging feed coming in from the drone. The real problem was that the ten or so moving blips Colin saw appeared to be packing up a van at the rear of the building. If they were packing their things up, that either meant the children were dead, or they would be dead shortly.

"Charlie, are those fuel drums?" asked Colin.

"It looks like it to me, boss," replied Charlie. That really wasn't good. They were going to torch the place to get rid of the evidence.

Colin relayed this information to the rest of the team and had Charlie text it to Savarese. Moments later, Charlie connected a call from Savarese into Colin's earpiece, where they began to work on a plan. They would all breach as one through the rear of the building by the loading dock. This would be done because the snow would conceal them until the last possible moment and muffle the sounds of their movement. Colin's team would do all of the initial shooting with silenced weapons to help reduce the risk of being heard by the men in the building. Breaching through the front door, which opened directly onto the dance floor, was a non-starter and would likely have gotten many of the team members and the hostages, if they were still alive, killed.

From there, they would proceed down the loading dock hallway and split into two teams split with Team Alien and FBI shooters, one clearing the kitchen and the other clearing the dressing rooms for the band. Both would emerge at the same time on either side of the dance floor and try to catch the remaining bad guys by surprise. Colin dictated this to Savarese more than had a conversation with him about it. He had a more complete tactical picture and actual training on how to carry out a mission like this. Jester would lead one team, and Colin would lead the other.

"Boss, they're moving those fuel drums inside," said Charlie in an exasperated tone.

"Fuck, step on it," he said to Sheriff. Colin knew that this was going bad quickly. If they were taking the fuel inside, they were likely nearly ready to leave. Either the children were already dead, they would be shortly, or the men doing this didn't intend to kill them at all. In fact, Colin now deemed it likely that the men who had taken them didn't intend to kill the children at all. Bullets left evidence of a murder...

But burning them alive could be made to look like an accident.

67

Colin slammed a new magazine into the MP7 as his earpiece started squawking. "Colin, the thermal readings are spiking on that building—they're lighting it up!" Charlie nearly screamed into Colin's ear.

"One minute out, boss," said Sheriff from the driver's seat next to Colin.

"Fuck parking a block away, pull right up to the loading dock!" Colin ordered pulling the MP7 from the floor between his legs. "Jester, we're doing this shit on the fly—follow my lead," Colin said into his earpiece. The vehicles slid around the corner the building was on, and Colin heard the engine roar as they accelerated toward the loading dock. Sheriff killed the lights as they went. A faint orange glow was beginning to emanate from the warehouse, illuminating the falling snow.

Sheriff slammed the brakes, and the SUV slid nearly twenty feet in the accumulated snow. Colin saw the loading dock slide into view as the Suburban decelerated. Several men were throwing the last of their supplies into the waiting truck, too busy to notice the arriving vehicles in the dark. Flames licked the garage-style door open on the loading dock as Colin hopped out of the nearly stopped SUV. A Chinese man getting into the passenger side of the truck looked up just in time to see Colin raise his MP7 and fire. He didn't even have time to blink before the 4.6-by-thirty-millimeter cartridge slammed into his head, killing him instantly.

Colin didn't waste any time, moving as fast as the deep snow would allow, and he felt the MP7 snap twice in his hand as he pressed the trigger, dispatching two more men. Colin felt Sheriff behind him now, moving along, and heard the similar whisper of two more shots from MP7s to his right as Jester and Witch took down two more targets. The sound of the flames coming from the building was now at a dull roar, the heat mixing it up with the cold in a similar firefight to the one taking place outside between men. Colin heard the unmistakable sound of an AK-47 rattling from the other side of the truck and heard the scream of a man somewhere to his right as the 7.62-millimeter rounds tore into his body.

Colin heard several more silenced rounds leave MP7s, and the Kalashnikov's owner did not respond again. Colin ran forward along the white truck and heard the rattle of more gunfire from the other side of it. He turned around the back of the truck and found one more man preparing to turn and fire on Jester's team. Colin shot him once in the back of the head, spraying blood and brain matter all over the back of the white truck and the snow, which was rapidly turning gray with ash from the raging fire.

The heat was immense, even standing fifteen feet from the building. "Smith, get this truck away from the building! I'm going in for the kids!" yelled Colin to be heard over the wind and flames. Smith tried to object, but Colin didn't hear her. He charged into the building, his only thought on saving the two children he knew must be somewhere inside. If they were alive and Colin didn't get them out, they would endure a fate worse than most. The heat seared Colin's freezing face from the cold outside, and the smoke stung his nostrils. Colin ran down a hallway that was half-covered in billowing flames, feebly holding a hand in front of his face to try and shield his eyes from the relentless assault of heat and ash they were enduring.

He made it to the kitchen and started screaming the two children's names to get a response. "Jack! Emily! Can you hear me?" he yelled. There was no response. Colin continued yelling undeterred, doing his best to keep his eyes open and looking for them. Colin coughed and sputtered from the yelling. He was inhaling too much ash and smoke, and breathing was becoming extremely difficult. He pushed through two swinging doors from the kitchen and emerged into the main club room just in time to see a support beam fall and crush the bar at the far end of the room. Flames streamed up the walls, rapidly turning the room into a massive convection oven. Colin stumbled forward, screaming the children's names again, "Jack! Emily! Are you here?" There was no response, but Colin thought he saw two chairs in the middle of the dance floor.

He kept moving when suddenly something crashed into him from behind, pushing him forward and pinning him to the ground. At first, Colin thought a support beam had fallen on him, but he then heard Jester's voice. "Don't you know snowmen melt in the heat!" he yelled.

A support beam had nearly fallen on Colin, but Jester had followed Colin into the building, tackling him out of the way at the last second. Colin was momentarily stunned but recovered quickly. "I owe you one!"

Jester and Colin picked themselves up off of the burning floor and ran to the two chairs in the middle of the room. Two figures were slumped in each one, a little girl and a teenage boy. Colin saw no trace of bullet wounds and didn't have time to check to see if they were breathing. All he could do was pray. He pulled his knife and sliced through the plastic flexi-cuffs securing the little girl to the chair and picked her up, burning the top of his wrist on the metal chair as he did so. Jester, ever the CrossFit maniac, had the teenager up and over his shoulder in a fireman's carry with little trouble at all. Both of them ran for the kitchen where they had come from.

A tremendous crash ensued as a large portion of the roof fell in and crushed the kitchen. Their only way out was blocked. There was little the men could do but back away, stunned at their sudden turn of fate. Colin coughed as the burning dust kicked up from the collapse entered his lungs. *Work the problem,* he thought in his head.

"Boss, where's the exit?!" Jester yelled.

Colin knew he needed to make a call. "This way!" he yelled. They stumbled for the front entrance to the club near the bar, trying to keep as low as possible as they went. Colin could hear Jester coughing the whole way. The heat burned every inch of Colin, and he sweated through his now unbearably hot clothes. They reached the front door, and it was boarded shut.

"Shit, how the fuck do we get out of here?" Jester yelled.

"Look for something to pry open the door!" Colin yelled back over the roaring fire. Colin saw a hammer on the ground and tried to pick it up, but it was so hot that it burned a hole through his Oakley tactical glove. Jester couldn't find anything either, but Colin wasn't about to give up. Sheltering the little girl's face in his jacket, he threw himself against the door shoulder-first, trying to bash it open. It didn't move an inch. He kept trying, and Jester joined him, both of them repeatedly slamming into the door. But it wouldn't move.

68

A massive crash from their right made Colin look up to see what had fallen now. To his shock, he saw two headlights and a massive hole in the wall near the bar. The two headlights rapidly began exiting the building, and Colin turned to Jester, coughing. "Let's go!"

They moved for the new exit as quickly as they could, both of them exhausted from the ordeal. Finally, after what seemed like an eternity spent inside an oven, they burst into the freezing air of the blizzard outside.

They both moved across the street, collapsing into the deep snow with their rescued hostages. Colin wasted no time, still coughing but turning the little girl over to check and see if she was still breathing. It took him a second, but he heard the faintest breath coming from her small mouth.

"Thought you guys might need a hand," called out Witch, running over to them.

"My guy's breathing, but he's gonna need to get to an ER quick, or he's not going to make it," said Jester, his voice sounding hoarse.

"Thanks for saving our asses, Witch. Can we get the FBI to get these kids to the ER?" Colin asked.

"Already on it. One of the FBI guys took a round through and through to the shoulder. Looks like he'll be all right. They just loaded him in a vehicle, and they're bringing it around now to grab the kids. Should be here any second."

True to his word, the Dodge Durango showed up a minute later, and two FBI agents loaded the two children aboard. Then they took off for the nearest hospital.

"What was in the truck?" Colin asked.

"Glad you asked, boss. You're not going to believe this shit, but a whole bunch of paper files, among other things. Signed out by Attorney General Mark Poole. It looks like they're all related to the DOJ leaks. Sheriff's uploading photos to Charlie now, but it looks like we've got him cold now. I mean, honestly, paper files—you couldn't make this shit up, Snowman," said Witch, sounding very pleased with himself.

Colin nodded, feeling slightly murderous after the AG's goons nearly burned himself, Jester, and two innocent children alive. His face felt like it had just been rubbed raw with sandpaper, and Jester looked a bit terrifying without eyebrows. "We need to get out of here before the fire department shows up," said Colin. His breathing was finally starting to slow down, but he suspected that his throat would take some time to feel better.

"Charlie says the call hasn't gone out yet, and Sheriff needs another ten to get the files photographed and uploaded to Charlie," replied Witch.

"Copy that," said Colin.

It took a few moments, but Agent Smith and Sunderland finally pulled the SUVs around to their location. She got out and trudged through the snow to them. "Are you both okay?"

"A bit more well-done than I'd like, but fine," said Jester.

"The FBI is securing the scene till the fire department arrives, and Sheriff is almost done getting what he needs from the files," she said.

"Looks like you'll finally get to use those shiny handcuffs," quipped Colin.

"I'll just be happy when this is all over. This has been the longest day of my life," she replied.

"Most of the good ones are," Colin said sarcastically. It was gallows humor, but Smith didn't seem to mind. "How do we go about arresting Poole?" Colin asked.

"Well, we have enough to arrest him and hold him on suspicion, but formal charges will have to wait until all of the evidence is gathered. Typically, with something this high profile, we would need to bring the directors in on it and gain approval from them, but obviously, we can't do that in this situation. We also need to figure out where he actually is," she finished.

"I know just who can help us with that," Colin said.

Colin walked a few steps away from the group and had Charlie connect him with Senator Rand through his earpiece. "Sorry for the late hour, sir, but we have everything we need to arrest the attorney general. It appears he had his associates holding Assistant Director Mullins's children hostage and forcing him to investigate the leaks. It looks like his intention may have been to frame someone through that investigation to take any suspicion off of him. It looks like Mullins may have been taking steps to get around all of this when someone found it and decided to pull the trigger on his children. Mullins likely thought they were already dead and killed himself. We just secured his children—they're on their way to the hospital now. It is our determination that we need to arrest the AG before he attempts to flee or to finish the job against the rest of the senators in the committee. If he thinks he's cornered, he will likely give the order to have Senator Walker, who we believe he has taken, killed. We need to locate the AG ASAP to keep the worst from happening."

There was a brief pause from the other end of the line. "Good work, Snowman, you boys have certainly lived up to your reputation. If I know Poole, that man's in his office still. I'll have to make a call to the VP to ensure everything goes smoothly at the DOJ when you go in, but I should have it all handled within a half hour or so. Do you need a warrant? I can make a few calls if so, which will take a few minutes longer," Rand finished, his southern accent abounding.

"Actually, we'd prefer not, sir. Our FBI liaison assures me we have enough to detain him while they prepare charges. My guess is the AG has enough contacts to be warned pretty quickly if a warrant were ever issued for his arrest. I'd rather that come after he's in custody so we don't spook him," replied Colin.

"He's always been clever. Whatever you all think is best, then. Good hunting," said Rand as he killed the connection. The sudden silence in his ear and a particularly strong gust of wind left Colin feeling cold and uneasy. Now he and his team just needed to detain one of the most powerful people in the world.

69

C olin and his team jogged up the snow-covered steps of the building and into the door between the columned arch that covered the front entrance to the building. A security guard was waiting for them inside and directed them to a bank of elevators down a short hallway. The team passed through a set of metal detectors on the way in, and the security guard begrudgingly ignored the fact that every single one of them set it off.

It took the elevators a few moments to bring them to the proper floor, and when they emerged, it was mostly dark. This wasn't because the power was out; the building had a large bank of backup generators. This was because there was no one they could see still working at this late hour.

They proceeded down a hallway, which brought them to a set of glazed glass door that said "Office of the Attorney General," and they opened it to proceed inside. Agent Smith led the way through the door, keeping her weapon holstered but a hand near her hip, ready to rock in case things went bad. Colin didn't think that they would. This was the attorney general, after all, not some street-level thug.

The tired-looking executive assistant sitting at the desk in the waiting room looked startled to see the group of people at this late hour. She looked even more startled by the haggard appearance of the two FBI agents and four members of Team Alien.

"Hello, how may I help you?" she asked uncertainly. She was petite, with black glasses that clashed with her pale face.

"We need to see the AG. Now," demanded Smith.

"Do you have an appointment?" she asked, looking very confused.

"This is my appointment," Smith replied, pulling out her credentials and showing them to the woman. "Please step aside, ma'am."

"Am I supposed to be impressed? This is the attorney general we are talking about—he sees folks from federal agencies all day long," said the woman, recovering slightly.

"People who are here to arrest him?" asked Agent Sunderland. The executive assistant looked even more stunned now. Her eyes darted from the agents to the bearded Team Alien members behind them. They lingered for a moment on Colin's seemingly frozen blue eyes. Just as she was about to speak, Attorney General Mark Poole stepped out of the heavy wooden door of his office.

"What the hell is going on out here?" he demanded. If he was surprised at the dirty, ashen, and injured appearance of many of the people in front of him, he didn't show it.

"Sir, I-I, um, well," the executive assistant stammered. Colin could tell she was scared of him.

"Dammit, speak English. What the hell is going on?" he barked again.

"Attorney General Mark Poole?" Smith inquired smoothly.

"Yes," said the man cautiously. The man reminded Colin more of a coiled snake ready to strike than of a bureaucrat.

"Sir, we need a word with you in private right now. It's a matter of national security," Smith said.

The man glared back at her. Colin could see the cogs working behind his eyes, trying to decide what to do. The thing that struck Colin even more than that was the genuine curiosity that seemed to be percolating from him. He unquestionably knew something, Colin judged, but there was something else there, and he didn't like it. "And you are?" Poole asked.

"I'm Special Agent Alexandra Smith; this is my partner, Agent Sunderland, and my investigative team," she said, both of them flashing their credentials as she motioned a lazy hand toward Colin and his team.

Colin saw Poole's eyes connect with his own. They locked together, both trying to pierce the other in some kind of alpha male struggle to discern the other's intentions. Poole didn't take his eyes off Colin's. "This way," he said, motioning them through the door behind him. He turned and led them into the office. Colin was on guard. He didn't like the vibe he was getting from this man. It wasn't that he thought anything would happen. It was just a general feeling of unease being in his presence. His poor executive assistant looked like she might faint from the exchange as Colin passed her.

The office was one of ornately crafted wooden paneling with a richly upholstered blue carpet, cases of leather-bound books, and a fireplace to the left of the door that was painted white and looked like it had never been used. There was a small sitting area in front of it with dark brown leather sofas, a cluttered walnut desk, and several windows that ringed the office that were completely dark at the moment. Colin suspected that during the day the view must have been excellent. The AG motioned for them to sit, but none of them moved toward the couch or armchairs. They stood rock-still, staring the man down. He stared back impassively, sizing them up.

Smith broke the silence first. "Mr. Attorney General, in a minute I'm going to arrest you on suspicion of conspiracy to commit treason and murder of the first degree, among numerous other charges. I assure you that the evidence against you is vast, and you will await formal charges at a federal justice facility in the city. The only way for you to help yourself now is to give up your co-conspirators and tell us where Senator Walker is being held."

This did surprise the AG. Colin saw it in his eyes. It was the look of something between surprise at the insolence of the people in front of him and pure shock at what they had just said to him. Colin wondered if it was shock that he had been discovered or shock of a different kind.

"I fucking knew it," he said, beginning to pace back and forth.

"Mr. Attorney General, I'm not here to play games with you. You need to give up your compatriots and tell us where Senator Walker is now."

"You need to stand down, Agent Smith. You are meddling in something that is very far above your pay grade."

Colin stepped forward. "Listen, I have had a very long day, buddy. My team has been shot, blown up, nearly burned to death, and now has to endure talking to someone so fucking twisted they tried to burn children alive. Now, Agent Smith might have rules," said Colin, advancing on the AG, "but my team does not. So tell me what I want to know, or I'm going to disappear you down a hole so deep and dark that no one will ever find you. And when we get to that hole, you are going to spend the rest of your life wishing you had never been born. So start talking now, or get a fucking bag thrown over your head and see where this goes," Colin finished, poking the man hard in the chest twice with his last point.

The AG, to his credit, hadn't backed up much when Colin had advanced on him. However, his demeanor had definitely changed. No one talked to him like this, and someone who had the power to— well, actually, Poole had never quite seen anything like that before. It was incredibly alarming and more than a bit terrifying. Poole believed the man poking him in the chest, he believed every word he said, because the blue fire burning in his eyes spoke only of rage and honest intention. As the attorney general, however, he did not get this far cowing under threats.

"I'm not exactly sure who you are, but you might want to listen to me before you—how'd you say it?—throw a fucking bag over my head. I assume you animals are investigating the leaks coming from high up in the Department of Justice. I also assume a rather convenient trail of evidence has led you here. What you don't know is that I am being set up. The leaks are being made to look like they are coming from this office. I have launched my own counter investigation to find out where they are really coming from."

"Really, Mr. Attorney General, you're being framed?" Smith cut him off. "How stupid do you think we are? I'm sick of playing games with you," she said, pulling out her handcuffs and letting them dangle from one finger.

"If you don't believe me, then see for yourself, Agent Smith," said Poole, gesturing to a stack of paper files sitting on his desk. "The inspector general of the DOJ has his own investigation going on, and he's cleared me. Take a look for yourself. Better yet, tear this place apart. I've got nothing to hide."

The worst part was that Colin couldn't discern any lies in the man's eyes. Politicians at this level were generally sociopaths, in Colin's experience, but this was something more than that. He intended to find out what exactly that was.

70

Poole launched into his story for Colin and Agent Smith while the rest of the team began digging through the files on his desk. He spoke as a practiced politician who had accomplished something and was finally presenting it to the audience to get the credit they deserved, at least in their own minds.

"Several months ago, when it started to become obvious there was a high-level leak in the government, it seemed obvious where it was coming from. Plain and simple, it was Justice Department counterintelligence operations that were being disrupted and our assets being blown and killed. I knew it wasn't me, but I wasn't sure who I could trust. Leaks pointed to possible accomplices in multiple federal agencies, so I couldn't go to any outsiders for help. Typically, when it's a matter of internal corruption or malpractice, we turn to our own inspector general for help in identifying the culprit, but truthfully, the evidence was so murky I didn't know if we could trust him." Jester coughed from the corner, interrupting him, and Poole shot him a daggers-like glare.

He took a breath and continued, "So, I embarked on my own investigation off the books to clear or convict the inspector general. I figured this was the best starting point for getting my house clean. Finally, a few months ago, I was able to confirm that he was clean and had no idea what was going on. I then tasked him to clean up his own office and launch a full investigation into the leaks. After months of work, his team concluded that the leaks were not internal." Poole paused a moment for effect. The only sound was the creaking of the old radiators near the window and the steady turning of pages by the rest of the team looking through the files.

"If you want me to believe you, Mr. Attorney General, I'm going to need more than that," said Smith.

"I thought so." Poole reached into his blue suit's jacket pocket and produced a thumb drive. "Here are records of all of the leaked case files and all of the internal and external ports they were accessed from. If the files and the inspector general's investigation don't clear me in your mind, then ask your tech guys if this will." He handed the drive over to Colin, who, in turn, handed it to Sheriff, who pulled out a tablet from his bag and began the process of uploading it to Charlie.

"We'll look into that," said Agent Smith.

"You seem to have a lot of evidence on hand. That's pretty convenient, if you ask me," said Colin.

"That is because my team is in the final throes of their investigation. We were hoping to have it wrapped up this week, but this snowstorm has thrown a bit of a wrench into things. Hence the reason I'm at the office past midnight in the middle of a blizzard," Poole stated matter-of-factly, his last point with a hint of biting sarcasm.

"If it does clear you, and I'm not saying I believe you, why would these people try and frame you?" asked Smith. Colin had been wondering the same thing.

"Isn't it obvious? My team's investigation is getting too close to the truth. If they could put together enough fake evidence against me, they could remove me and my entire extended team from our positions, thus clearing themselves and hanging all the blame on me in the process. They'd be free to do whatever they wanted with impunity because my successor would be scared to touch that kind of scandal with a ten-foot pole," finished Poole.

Colin had to admit that it made sense. As attorney general, it was Poole's job to go after this kind of thing. If whoever was behind this truly did want to clear the road of any obstacles, this would be a great way to go about doing it. "You said your team is in the final throes of their investigation. Why were you expecting it to wrap up this week?" Colin asked.

Poole smiled at this, his snakelike eyes looking like they had just sighted a very juicy rat. "Glad you asked. For over a month now, we have been not-so-quietly talking about a major counterintelligence sting to everyone who is anyone in the government. Sending out briefing documents and a variety of other digital tidbits for them to feast their eyes on, all of it fake, and all of it loaded with an NSA snooper virus that a recent update to the federal government's firewall system made possible. The intelligence calls for inter-agency cooperation on a massive scale never seen before. Essentially, we told everyone that we stole a list of Chinese and Russian spies in the U.S., and we were planning to round them all up at once. We also told them that the source intelligence was being made available to anyone with the proper clearance and set up a digital way for them to access it through the Gov-Cloud. Anyone who downloads anything related to the fake operation is instantly fed into the web, and the digital information is tracked anywhere they send it. The source intelligence was released this morning. It was downloaded three times. Only one of the hits came from an unauthorized location, using one Senator Walker's credentials."

Colin and Smith looked at each other instantly. "Walker wasn't taken! They were extracting him!" exclaimed Colin.

"Mr. Attorney General, do you have the location?" asked Agent Smith, her cheeks still rosy from the cold outside.

"Well, it was routed through several different servers. The NSA is still trying to trace the exac—"

Colin cut Poole off. "I need the raw data now."

"It's on the thumb drive I handed you," replied Poole.

"Charlie?" asked Colin into his earpiece.

"I'm on it, boss, tracing it now," said Charlie, momentarily forgetting to kill his microphone, allowing Colin to hear the rapid-fire clicking of the mechanical key switches on his gaming keyboard.

They tensely waited for another moment before Smith broke the silence.

"Mr. Attorney General, if you take down several high-level government officials in this sting, you'd be well-positioned to run for higher office."

Poole smiled. "Why the hell do you think I went through all the trouble? This country's a mess—I'm going to clean it up."

Colin rolled his eyes. *Whatever happened to doing the right thing just because, well, it was the right thing to do?* he thought.

"Boss, the trace has almost gone through. I need another minute, but there's no way Poole could have been the leak. I've been through all of the data they sent on his logs, and I got into all of his personal computers and his phone. He's telling the truth. He's an asshole and already has his resignation letter typed on his personal laptop to run for president, but he's telling the truth," said Charlie.

"Got it, thanks," said Colin. He turned back to the attorney general. "Looks like you are clean." Poole threw his hands up in a mock triumph. Colin stifled the urge to punch him.

A few moments later, Charlie came back. "Oh, this was tricky. Good news, boss. The NSA generated over four terabytes of fake source intelligence data. Whoever downloaded it must have been in a real hurry, because now they're trying to upload it back to a known Chinese intelligence server with an unmasked IP address. It's going to take a few hours to push that much data to them. Which is great news for us because now we know where they are and that they'll be there for a while!"

Colin stood quickly. "Let's roll."

71

Azrael paced back and forth methodically in front of the bank of computer monitors in front of him. He took ten steps forward each time and then exactly ten steps back. That made for an even twenty paces on one round trip in front of the computers. The even numbers helped to calm Azrael's OCD, which became worse with fatigue and stress, two things that he felt immeasurably right now.

The upload of the stolen intelligence data was taking forever. His one skilled hacker who could have expedited the process was dead, and he now relied on two of the man's underlings who sat in front of him. Azrael watched the mist of their slow breathing in the freezing warehouse with rage. They should have been breathing hard, fearing what he would do to them if they did not complete their task on time. Gone were the days of truly physical intelligence work for people like this.

Azrael cursed the laziness of this younger generation and the Nor'easter raging outside for preventing something simpler like a dead drop. The Chinese were usually more patient than this when it came to their intelligence work. This was downright sloppy. Azrael knew what the contents of the intelligence were, of course. A list of every Chinese and Russian agent active within the United States. The senator had told him this. It was understandable why the Chinese wanted it so badly that they were willing to risk everything to get it, including their most highly placed asset within the U.S. government. However, if they could have been more patient, they would have had it all without having to risk everything. Azrael was confident he could have made it so.

It was now obvious that they would face an assault by either federal agents or, more likely, the team that had been chasing him since Afghanistan. He had twenty men left, most of them thugs from local Chinese gangs paid by the Chinese intelligence service to be muscle for the operation. Five of the skillful Oriental Sword operators remained, and he would have to use each of them to lead a small force of thugs in the defense of the warehouse. Personally, Azrael knew all of them would die in the onslaught of the Americans. He was counting on this to happen while he escaped.

Truthfully, they all deserved to die. He just wished he could have done it himself, for their blind arrogance. The only real thing left for him to ensure was the upload of the source data to the Chinese. They would handle saving their assets themselves, or more likely, save the important ones and have the rest killed. They were playing a dangerous game, but becoming the most powerful nation in the world was a risky game, especially when you had to kill the king to get there.

Azrael watched as the men scurried about, making preparations for the assault. The two men in front of him were busy uploading the data, monitoring the cameras set up outside, and listening to police radio traffic to look for signs that the Americans were coming. Between the defenders, they had two dozen AK-47s and a few thousand rounds of ammunition, ten hand grenades, a few randomly assorted Glocks of various makes and calibers, and two Claymore mines, all smuggled in through various Chinese state-owned corporate interests and bought from local gangs.

The Claymore mines were being rigged to low-visibility entrance points to the building that Azrael had judged would have been primary points of entrance for any would-be assaulters. The non-skilled laborers, as Azrael had taken to calling the local muscle, were moving wooden crates and other obstacles in various patterns to both funnel assaulters into kill zones and to give the defenders cover.

All of this was important, but in truth, it was just background noise to the thoughts in Azrael's head. Azrael had a plan to exit the building when things started going south through a sewer at the rear of the building that led underground to the Metro. Azrael had actually used this tunnel as an escape route before, some seventeen years earlier when his services had been required in this city. He had used it because he was able to scrub the existence of the tunnel from the city's plans when he had gained access to the city archives. No one knew this tunnel existed except for him. Which was why he had also stored certain contingencies there as well.

In addition to extra weapons, cash, and other essentials, there was also information about the person who had hired him both times. Several documents and a floppy drive, of all things, contained damning evidence against the man who had set everything in motion all of those years ago.

Azrael was truly ready for any contingency. He didn't know exactly what would happen, only that he was prepared. The only thing he could say for certain was that he would either live or die killing every last American who walked through the doors to the warehouse.

72

Colin and his team stood huddled behind one of the Suburban's two blocks away from the warehouse Charlie had identified. They were looking over plans for the warehouse on a 12.9-inch iPad Pro, trying to decide on the best way to enter. Charlie had overlaid the plans with a real-time thermal picture of the warehouse coming from the drone that was orbiting overhead.

The pictures being returned did not look good for the team. They were seriously outgunned any way they sliced it. There were approximately twenty-four combatants in the warehouse, and only six of them. Even though the members of Team Alien were some of the most highly trained operators on the planet, this wasn't a situation they would have ideally walked into. They needed to find a way to take the initiative away from the defenders.

Ideas were tossed around by the experienced operators while the two FBI agents with them listened patiently. "We could climb up to the roof and come down through this stairwell," said Jester.

Charlie responded to this one, "I'm not sure I'd do that, Jester. This building's plans only rate the roof at twelve thousand pounds of pressure. With the foot and a half of snow that's already up there, it's well over its recommended weight. Putting six bodies up there might cave the whole thing in."

"It would certainly give us the element of surprise," said Jester.

"I'm not sure I can argue with that, but I'm pretty sure you might break a leg in the twenty-five-foot drop to the warehouse floor," replied Charlie.

"We might be able to use that, though," said Colin.

"You serious, boss?" asked Witch.

"I don't mean sending ourselves up there, but if we lob a few HE grenades up there, it might collapse a portion of the roof," said Colin, referring to high explosive grenades.

"The snow should dampen the explosions enough to keep the shrapnel from killing anyone, but the roof caving in might put them off balance," replied Sheriff with a nod.

"I'd say we'd need to lob two of them, one about here and the other here, over the entrance to this rear loading dock," said Colin. He was pointing to two separate rooms. One was the much larger main storage facility, and the other looked to be a set of offices.

The warehouse was shaped like an *L*, with the offices representing the lower horizontal line and the main warehouse being the longer vertical rectangle. Off of the vertical rectangle, there were five loading docks that ran the length of the facility. On the other side was one very large walk-in freezer, by the looks of it. Colin guessed that the facility had been used to move perishable food to local grocery stores, but it was no longer active.

"That freezer's got to be their strong point," said Sheriff. "If the senator's with them, he'll be in there. It also looks like there's two stationary computer terminals." Sheriff pointed at rectangular heat signatures that were most likely the computer terminals that were fainter than the rest of the facility. "Those walls are going to be thick, judging by how faint the thermal signatures are relative to the rest of the building," said Sheriff.

"I've seen warehouses like this before. The entrance to it shouldn't be much more than a garage door. Still, let's make sure we have an explosive solution ready if we need it," replied Colin.

"Got it," said Jester. He was the team's explosives expert for all practical purposes, though everyone was competent.

"I say we make entry through the front offices here. The roof will be the easiest to cave in judging by the construction in these plans, and it looks like they aren't defending it too heavily," said Colin. There were only four heat signatures located within the office portion of the building.

"If we do that, it looks like we could possibly gain the high ground here and set up an overwatch position," replied Witch as the team's designated marksman.

"That should give us a bit more cover through the warehouse and allow us to move a bit more intuitively. Good thought, Witch," said Colin. "Jester and I will then lead two separate teams through either of these entrances into the main warehouse," said Colin, pointing to the two entrances that led from the office into the main warehouse portion of the facility. "My team, consisting of myself and Agent Smith, will clear along the left wall to the strong-pointed freezer. Jester will lead his element of Agent Sunderland and Sheriff along the right wall down to the far side of the warehouse, then loop back around and meet us at the strong point. Any questions?" Colin asked.

"How are we hitting the other side of the facility with the grenade?" asked Jester.

"We'll use one of the M32A1 launchers and hit it from a distance first. Witch, that's on you. That should draw any roving defenders to the rear of the facility and make them think the focal point of our attack will be there. You'll then haul ass to meet us, where we will launch the second grenade onto the roof of the office one minute later. We'll make entry there with Nine-Bangers and follow the plan as prescribed. Sound good?" asked Colin.

Everyone nodded. "Now, I don't need to remind all of you that this is Azrael we are dealing with. Expect the unexpected and be ready for our good friend Murphy. These roof explosions could be fairly volatile, and who knows what added obstacles we'll encounter. Keep your head on a swivel. Remember, we need to take the senator alive to identify any other leaks. Azrael I'll settle for dead or alive, but my preference there is alive as well. The man has committed untold crimes and is undoubtedly a treasure trove of intelligence, but don't risk your own safety for that. Alexandra, Kyle, I know this isn't necessarily your normal day at the office, but stick with my guys— they'll keep you out of trouble."

Everyone nodded and turned to move out with their assembled weapons and gear. Colin secretly wondered to himself if Azrael wound up in his crosshairs, would he be able to refrain from killing the man who had done so much damage to his family?

73

Senator Rand's Apartment

Both Senator Rand and Miller sat in somewhat stunned silence. Snowman's last update to them had left them both more than a little confused. How could it possibly be that Senator Walker, of all people, was somehow mixed up in all of this? Miller wondered.

"You know, in a twisted way, it does make sense," said Rand with a more pronounced drawl than ever due to the alcohol he had been steadily consuming all night.

"How does any of this make sense?" asked Miller in an upset tone. "Walker was our friend, and he had our other friends murdered, all for what? A couple of bucks. He was a good man. I mean, hell, he was vetted enough to get onto the committee—how did we possibly miss this?" Miller continued.

"Well, he would have known enough to have the man leading the investigation, then all of us, murdered. He must have somehow found out about Poole's investigation and decided to try and frame him, and when he realized how far along Poole's investigation was, he decided to use this whole serial killer charade to disappear himself," said Rand matter-of-factly.

"No, no, it just can't be. All of this is too crazy. We know Walker.

Christ, he's been at my family's Christmas party the past few years. I can't believe he would do any of this," said Miller.

It was dark in the room, and the two men had consumed more than their fair share of the amber-colored small-batch whiskey that Rand's family had made themselves. Rand had long since decided to throw caution to the wind and drink as much of the alcohol as he could. The thought of Miller swilling it all down himself and not appreciating it upset him too much.

"Well, people aren't always what they seem. I would think after today, you might appreciate that a bit more," replied Rand.

"And what about his seat in the Senate?! Not to mention his family. The scandal alone will kill them. The shame, my God. I can't even imagine what they'll do to him for this."

"He'll get what's coming to him, as all traitors must," replied Rand. Loyalty was important to him. More important than this man could possibly understand.

"It's just… I've never known anyone who did something this serious. What if he dies of old age in prison? His children. My God, his children."

"Well, when I was a prosecutor, I used to always go for the most high-profile cases to make the biggest statement. Scoring a slam-dunk and a huge sentence against a giant like a U.S. senator is every prosecutor's wet dream. It would make anyone's career. I imagine our old friend will never see the outside of a prison or a courtroom again in his life. That is, if he survives the raid without doing anything stupid," Rand replied.

"But the committee—how did he manage to get on the committee? Members are supposed to be thoroughly vetted to prevent things like this from happening," exclaimed Miller.

"Well, as you know from being a politician, we all have a few skeletons in the closet that we do our utmost to prevent from getting out. I imagine Walker had more than a few tricks up his sleeve to get past all that. Not to mention the one vetting him could easily have been working for him and the Chinese. And, well, think about that," said Rand, sitting back in his chair and crossing his fingers. "Imagine getting a highly placed mole on the committee of a foreign government designed to ferret out espionage. There'd be no limits to the secrets you might be able to obtain at that level. It's all really rather ingenious," said Rand, a slight smile creasing his lips at the thought.

Miller sat thinking about that for a moment. Something about the statement didn't sit entirely right with him, even in his inebriated state. His mind, however, was working too slowly due to the alcohol, and this frustrated the man. He sat up as if he had something to say, then sat back in his chair, rubbing his eyes as if trying to rub the drunkenness away. Rand watched in near amazement as the man sat up and repeated the same exercise again.

"Cat got your tongue?" asked Rand, sounding more southern than ever.

"Whose job is it to vet junior members of the committee?" Miller finally blurted out.

Rand stared back at him. "What do you mean?"

"Whose job is it to vet junior members of the committee? It's not done by outsiders due to the sensitive nature of the appointment. It's done by the second most senior member of the committee. It's the senior member's job to select potential candidates, and the second most senior member's job to personally and off the books vet them."

Rand answered, "Well, that would have been me. I assure you, I was thorough—the man had nothing on him that I found."

Miller snapped back, "I know that, Rand! But as the second most senior member of the committee, it would also be up to you to set up all of the clearances and authorizations he would need to see the highly classified materials we work with to vet out other high-level members of the government."

"Your point?" Rand asked, starting to get annoyed with the belligerent man to his left.

Miller had a mad look on his face, like he was possessed. The flickering orange of the firelight made him look downright deranged. "Walker only joined the committee a month ago. It takes four weeks to get back credentials to access that kind of information. Meaning the credentials could have only come back today. Walker never had them in the first place!" Miller stood up as he finished, backing away from Rand, suddenly scared. Rand stood up, staring at the man. His look of surprise at the belligerence displayed by him was suddenly gone, replaced by something else.

Replaced by hatred.

74

Colin heard the soft thump of the M32A1 grenade launcher faintly through the peacefully falling snow, and everything seemed to slow slightly. Much like a child anticipating Christmas in early November, the time to combat typically passed slowly for soldiers; then suddenly it arrived without warning. Taking the sinking feeling in the pit of one's stomach with it and replacing it with pure adrenaline.

The deafening explosion that followed ripped through the cold air as it rolled off of the surrounding concrete structures of the industrial style park. Loud cracks, twisting metal, and thundering crashes were heard next as a quarter of the roof of the dilapidated warehouse gave in to the crushing weight and extreme pressure caused by the high explosive concussive blast of the grenade from the launcher. The falling beams and snow caught five of the defenders beneath them and buried them alive and dead. A sixth man, one of the Oriental Sword commandos, was just far enough out of the way to have only his right leg crushed by the debris. A moment later, a shot from his commander's pistol silenced his screams.

Two more grenade rounds followed in short succession. One another high explosive round blasted a hole through the furthest loading dock garage door. The second, a smoke round, followed through the door shortly after. Smoke began to fill the far end of the warehouse just as the lights began to flicker. A piece of shrapnel torn from the garage door had partially torn the belt on the generator, which had been placed at the far end of the building to keep the noise low. Jester had decided to add the two extra rounds at the last minute to help sell the ruse that they were coming in through the back. It paid off.

Commander Chen of the Oriental Sword commandos saw the smoke filling the warehouse just as the generator belt tore, completely stopping the flow of power to the overhead lighting. Darkness filled the warehouse as Chen frantically shouted orders to his men in Mandarin to relocate their forces to defend themselves from an assault in the rear. In the chaos, one of the hired guns from the local gangs forgot about the tripwire covering one of the doors from the office into the main warehouse and ran through it.

The shaped charge blew his right leg and arm off, killing him instantly and collapsing the doorway completely, making it impassable. This was both good and bad for the Chinese team defending the warehouse. On the one hand, it sealed one of the entrances completely that the claymore was supposed to seal anyway, thus funneling any would-be attackers into the kill zone of the other doorway. On the other, they had lost another precious defender.

Jester arrived back at the team near the front entrance a moment later.

"What the fuck did you hit?" asked Colin, referring to the secondary explosions.

"Added two more rounds through the rear loading bay to sell 'em that we were coming that way," Jester said, out of breath.

"Looks like it worked. Power's out, though, so NVGs on,"

replied Colin. Hitting the generator was a real stroke of luck. The team hadn't decided to try and kill the power because the building wasn't drawing any from the city, and they didn't have the time to try and locate the generator and destroy it. The four members of Team Alien flipped down their four-tubed GPNVG-18 panoramic night-vision goggles from their Gentex Ops-Core helmets.

Instantly, infrared lasers from their modified MP7s and the HK-417 with five times optical zoom ACOG that Witch was now carrying for his overwatch duties became visible. All weapons were equipped with silencers, but none of them had opted for subsonic rounds due to the longer possible shooting distances inside the vast warehouse. Agent Smith and Sunderland had only their Glocks and would follow the other operators inside.

A minute after the first grenades had hit the far side of the warehouse, Sheriff tossed a nine-banger flashbang grenade through the glass of the front door of the office. Seconds later, nine consecutive blasts overwhelmed the senses of the two men left in the office to guard against any rear assault. They were thugs from local gangs—their Oriental Sword commander had already headed toward the rear of the warehouse, where they thought the assault was coming from.

Both of them dropped their weapons and grabbed their heads to stop the ringing in their ears. Seconds later, Team Alien was inside. Rounds fired from Colin and Jester killed both men instantly, entering their brains via their foreheads.

The team split into two, Colin and Smith heading left and Jester and Sheriff heading right. Witch took the stairs to the second level and found the executive office overlooking the floor empty. He grabbed a desk and pushed it into the center of the room, keeping himself farther back from the window so as to give himself some measure of cover and concealment, then closed the door, propping it shut with a chair to give him some warning of an incoming hostile to his overwatch position.

He didn't bother knocking out the glass, knowing it would alert the hostiles below to his presence and confident that the larger 7.62

variant of the HK-416 he was carrying would have little trouble shooting accurately through the thin glass.

The two teams below moved swiftly to the doorways they were assigned, the members of Team Alien moving with experience and poise and the two FBI agents a little more awkwardly behind them. Murphy, it seemed, had other plans for them, though. Jester's voice came through Colin's earpiece within moments. "Boss, this way's blocked. Looks like one of these idiots blew themselves up. We're circling around to your position now."

"Copy that," Colin said as he crept toward the doorway. He heard frantic yelling in Mandarin from the other side of the door in front of him, echoing off the walls of the warehouse. In the bluish-green glow of his NVGs, he could see the infrared laser from his weapon probing the area in front of him. He kept moving forward toward the doorway.

"Snowman, this is Witch. I'm in position to provide overwatch. Recommend you hold your current position. I see significant enemy movement in front of you and what looks like a prepared kill zone through your doorway. Jester's distraction seems to have moved most of them to the other side of the warehouse, but there are a few still holding tight."

"Copy that, Witch. Take them out so we can proceed."

"Acknowledged," came Witch's reply. Colin heard three muted thwacks in rapid succession and the clatter of at least one weapon onto the concrete floor of the warehouse. "Clear to move forward, Snowman."

Colin heard Jester moving up behind him, and he motioned him forward through the doorway. Jester moved forward, and Colin watched his infrared laser bounce forward as he went. Jester got three feet and was passing Colin when he threw out his arm to stop him. Jester's laser had just moved over a long, thin wire running the length of the bottom of the doorway.

75

"Hold!" said Colin, more to Jester than the earpiece he had on. Colin pointed down with a free hand and moved the infrared laser on his weapon up and down. Jester and Sheriff saw the wire and nodded.

"Cover me," whispered Jester. He pulled a set of needle-nosed pliers from the right thigh pocket of his cargo pants and slowly crawled forward toward the wire.

"Witch, be advised, we've got a booby-trapped door down here. Attempting to disarm now. Hold overwatch—we can't hit shit from here," said Colin.

"Copy, way seems clear for now. Standing by."

Charlie came over their earpieces next. "Boss, looks like you've gotten eleven of them so far. I'm still seeing thirteen hostiles left. They seem to be surging back in your direction."

"Good copy. Witch, open up on them. Need you to slow them down so we can get through this door or we'll be fucked," said Colin.

"Roger, Snowman."

As if in answer, the thwacking sound of the silenced HK-417 started at somewhat regular intervals again above them. The soft tinkling of falling broken glass from the window above started on the concrete floor outside of the door. "Team, call your kills, we're going to need an accurate count of the opposition in front of us," said Colin into his earpiece.

Jester very carefully arrived at the wire running the length of the doorway in front of them. He flipped up his NVGs and pulled a small red penlight from his jacket pocket. He put it in his mouth, shining it on the wire, and very carefully repositioned himself to steady the arm that was holding the pliers. He brought it up slowly, breathing steadily to keep from moving too much. The real trick to cutting trip wires was not moving the wire at all laterally while you cut through it. If you did, you died. Very slowly, he brought the pliers to the wire, and hovering very carefully, he slowly brought the pliers to within an inch of the wire. Sweat was dripping down his head, but he ignored it, knowing the movement would likely trip the wire. When he was within less than a quarter of an inch, he closed the pliers rapidly and felt the line go slack. Either he had done it right, or his own personal version of heaven was very different from what he had imagined.

"Traps clear," Jester said.

Colin surged forward, with the rest of the team in close succession behind him. He cleared right, while Sheriff, who was behind him, trained his weapon left. They ran to a large shipping container fifteen feet in front of them, which had at least one dead guy hanging off of it that they saw.

"Two down," said Witch.

"Copy," replied Colin. There were only eleven hostiles left now. "New plan," he said to the team once they arrived. "Smith, Sunderland, you two stay here and guard our six—they will likely try and circle around us from this direction. Jester, Sheriff, on me—we're going to sweep and clear to the strong point and see what we've got left then." They all nodded, and Colin took off toward the left side of the warehouse. The unmistakable clatter of fire from an AK-47 sounded some twenty-five yards away from their new position. Two more thwacks from the HK-417 silenced it.

"Another down," said Witch in a calm voice. Colin's internal count of hostiles dropped to ten.

They pivoted around an aisle of crates and began proceeding at a fast walk down it, Colin followed by Jester in the front and Sheriff leading up the rear. The team kept their guns up and sweeping, only dropping their sights to the floor when their weapons' line of fire crossed another team member. The first hostile pivoted out from behind a wooden crate twenty feet in front of them with a flashlight attached to his weapon. Colin fired three shots at him, but the man dove back behind the crates. Colin saw the rounds tear into and splinter the wood above his head. Jester moved left and parallel with Colin while they advanced on the crate. The man poked his head out again, spraying them with fire from his AK-47.

Jester dove backward on seeing him and narrowly avoided getting shot, while Colin hit the man with three rounds from his MP7 center mass. When they reached him, Colin dead-checked him by putting an additional round in his head. He wasn't taking chances in case the hostile had been wearing body armor. The count of hostiles was now at nine.

Colin could see snow falling through the massive hole in the roof, which was bathed in brighter green light through his NVGs as he moved. Shots sounded from Glock pistols well behind them, followed by what sounded like the blast from a twelve-gauge shotgun. Then more silence. Colin dropped to a knee and motioned for them to hold. "Witch, who was shooting?"

It took him a few seconds to respond. "Agent Sunderland's dead. I don't see any sign of Smith. Looks like they took two more hostiles down."

"Fuck. Okay, Witch, you're our six now. We'll look for Smith."

"Copy, Snowman."

Colin dropped his mental count to seven hostiles. They moved forward again, now closing to within fifty yards of the strong point. It was deadly silent. Colin could feel the wind from the storm coming through the twisted wreckage of the ceiling. A woman's piercing scream echoed through the warehouse ahead. It was blood-curdling as if in horrible pain. Colin quickened his pace, knowing it must have been Smith. A sudden sound from overhead drew his green-tinted vision upward in time to see a man firing his weapon down at them.

He got off three shots before a shot from Witch's HK-417 blew off half of his head, showering them with blood.

Colin turned just in time to see two figures rushing him from a nearby alley. He shot the first man five times with a quick burst to his sternum, but the other was too quick and knocked his weapon to the side. Colin threw a vicious elbow, trying to catch the man in the side of the head, but he deflected it, throwing a kick in return. Colin caught this and drove the man backward into the crate, throwing a shoulder into his chest.

He reached for his pistol, but the man hit it just as he was pulling it from the holster, sending it clattering to the floor. Colin threw an open palm at his throat, but the man sidestepped to his right, and Colin missed, bouncing off the crate and using it to pivot away from the man and gain space. Colin pulled his Green Beret knife from the small of his back and danced forward to meet the man in combat again, just in time to see the man's right eye blow out of the front of his face from the round Jester had fired into the back of his head. Colin expected a snide comment to follow about bringing a knife to a gunfight, but upon seeing Sheriff, he understood Jester's lack of comment.

76

"It was you this whole time!" said Miller, backing into the hallway now. It was a statement, not a question.

Rand's eyes had gone hollow, as if possessed by some kind of deep-seated demon. He followed Miller, stepping forward slowly, not answering the man's hysteric statements. He paused for a moment, grabbing the Vietnam-era Ka-Bar knife from the wooden holder on the shelf by the door. Its serrated edge glinted in the firelight. He knew he would have to keep this quiet so as not to alert the Capitol Police guarding his door.

Rand intentionally stepped to his right, making Miller back further into the apartment and away from the door and the safety of the police officers outside. The man had no poise under pressure, and the alcohol wasn't helping him at all. *Disgusting that a man as weak as this could make it this far,* thought Rand.

"Please, I can keep this quiet. We can work out some kind of deal. I'll help you!" whimpered Miller, backing away to keep himself away from the man with the knife. Miller was falling back on politics to save himself now. A thoroughly useless jester in Rand's eyes, who despised pandering and weak men.

"There is no way to buy your way out of this situation with political capital," said Rand, continuing to advance.

"Please, I'll do anything!"

Rand shook his head, continuing to walk forward, determined to destroy the man's life in front of him. This idiot could have just kept his mouth shut and enjoyed the fire. He could have just stopped asking questions. He could have been scared, like the other senators were. He could have gone along. "There's only one thing left for you to do, and that's to go the way of the rest of our dear friends today," said Rand.

Miller finally hit a wall and could not back up any further. Fear took him. He went to scream for help, finally coming to his senses. "He…" He never got the rest of the word out. Rand leapt forward, sinking the knife into the man's throat, feeling the serrated edge scrape bone as it tore its way through the man's carotid artery into his esophagus. Miller's dying gasps gurgled from his mouth as he sank down the wall, Rand gently letting him down. He wasn't sure what he would do now as Miller bled out on the floor. *I could make it look like it was Azrael, or like he tried to attack me.* The thought was cut short when there was a knock at the apartment door.

"Senator Rand, is everything okay, sir?" he heard the Capitol Police officer calling through the door.

Shit, he thought. It was too late now. His only chance was to get out while he still could. He ran to his desk in the office and grabbed a small, snub nose .38 from the desk drawer. It was already loaded.

He grabbed his coat and headed for the door. Another soft knock came from the door. Rand opened it before the policeman could say anything else. The police officer looked momentarily surprised as Rand brought up the gun and shot him in the face from only a foot away. The carnage was spectacular as the round slammed into the man. The other officer assigned to the detail went for his weapon, but the surprise of his partner dying before his eyes at the hands of their protectee had slowed him down. Rand took aim and shot him through the throat at a distance of two feet. The man died a slow and painful death. Rand turned to the stairs and was out of the hallway before his neighbors had even been fully awakened by the gunshots.

He ran down the steps as fast as he could, cursing the amount of alcohol he had drunk and its slowing effect on him. He pulled a phone from his jacket pocket and texted the word "FIRE" to an unmarked number he had memorized. It was his codeword from his Chinese handlers to get him out in a hurry if he was discovered. He then texted the letter *C* to them. Which had been their code for the location they would meet. C, in this case, stood for Union Station, which was five blocks from his current location. He reached the street and took off into the deep snow as fast as he could move.

77

S heriff was bleeding profusely from a bullet wound to his upper right arm. Colin could see in the dim red penlight that Jester had pulled out that he had been hit at least twice more. Both shots seemed to have been stopped by his Mithril Body Armor.

"Looks like it's a through-and-through to the upper shoulder," said Jester. He had just finished checking underneath Sheriff for more signs of blood on his hands from possibly undiscovered wounds. Many died on the battlefield from wounds that weren't initially found by comrades in arms. "Talk to me, buddy," Jester said, pulling a small med kit from his other cargo pocket.

Sheriff sputtered while Colin knelt down to pull security to protect his fallen comrade and the one treating him.

"Status," he asked.

"I'm good," gasped Sheriff. "Bullet, took, wind, out, me," he finished stammering. A shot to the right part of anybody's armor could easily knock the wind out of the one wearing it. Another blood-curdling scream came from ahead of them. "Go, I'll be fine," Sheriff stammered.

Colin thought for a second, judging the tactical picture. *Take a deep breath and make a call,* he told himself. "Jester, stay here and render aid. Keep Sheriff out of trouble. I'll handle this."

Jester was just beginning to inject the XSAT-30 into Sheriff's bullet wound, which shot ninety-two compressed cellulose sponges into the open cavity, which expanded as they absorbed blood, rapidly sealing the wound. "Copy," he said, busy rendering aid.

Colin gave them one last look before turning and running toward the strong point. "Witch, be advised, Sheriff is hit non-critically. Jester is rendering aid. I am proceeding to the strong point. Maintain overwatch."

"Copy, Snowman."

Colin kept moving toward the agonized-sounding screams ahead. He went over his dead bad guy count again as he moved. With the three more hostiles they had just killed, there were only four others left. Colin moved carefully, quickly, and as quietly as he could toward the strong point. He dropped the mag from his MP7 and inserted a fresh one. The old one he placed in the left cargo pocket of his pants, as it still had a few rounds left.

When he was ten feet from the entrance to the industrial freezer, he slowed more and cautiously crept toward the door.

It was open, and Colin could see the dim light of what must have been flashlights of some kind coming from inside. He flipped up his night-vision goggles to keep from being blinded when he stepped into the light. Colin advanced forward and pivoted into the freezer. What greeted his eyes was pure chaos.

Two men sitting at computers saw him enter out of the corner of their eyes and went for pistols by their keyboards. Colin shot both of them before they could pick up the weapons. To his right, Agent Smith lay on the concrete ground. Her blonde hair was splayed out, floating in a pool of her own blood. Her throat was slit, and there were holes where her eyes had been. Beyond her, Senator Walker was tied to a chair with a blood-soaked knife to his throat, whimpering through the gag that covered his mouth.

Behind him was a face that Colin had seen only a few times in his life, mainly in nightmares of that terrible night in his childhood. The same baseball cap was hiding the deranged smile of yellowed teeth grinning at him from the shadows cast by the dim lights of the camping lanterns nearby.

Colin was sickened with rage and fear that only came from something that had been built up since childhood.

Alexandra was dead—someone that he hadn't known well but had done so much for him in such a short period of time. The one that had gotten him close was the one that had to die in order for Colin to get justice. Azrael had gotten his last thrill. Colin would make sure the only other one he ever got was his long fall to the depths of Hell. This was the man who had taken his family, friends, and colleagues from him. This is the man who had savaged his dreams and haunted his memories for a lifetime.

Colin was ashamed at himself for letting this happen to Alexandra, but for now, he had to focus on the present. "Drop the fucking knife and get on the ground," Colin demanded. Azrael's smile grew wider at Colin's words, as if they were all he wanted to hear. "Do it, or I'll fucking kill you. I swear to God, I will fucking kill you."

Azrael's face suddenly changed, like he recognized something. Like he recognized Colin. It would be hard to forget those eyes. They were the same Azrael had taken from his sister seventeen years ago.

"You couldn't save your sister, and now for the rest of your life, you'll have to live with the fact that you couldn't save them either," Azrael croaked as if speaking in a voice that hadn't been used in many years. He spun the knife in his hand and brought it up to plunge into the senator's throat. Colin didn't hesitate. For all the fear he had felt over the years, this was the time for action. He pressed the trigger of his MP7, sending the 4.6-by-30-millimeter round careening into Azrael's forehead at 735 meters per second, killing him instantly. Colin ran forward and flipped the selector switch to full auto, emptying an entire magazine into Azrael's chest in a pure rage to ensure that the monster never rose again.

Colin didn't even know why he did it. It was like some kind of preprogrammed response from popular horror movies where the killer always came back for one last scare. But Colin knew Azrael would never rise again.

He stood there, breathing heavily, staring at the man lying on the ground in front of him. Everything seemed to be quiet, a slowly expanding pool of blood forming under him. The twisted yellowed smile still creased his face until the moment he died. Colin was somewhere between blood lust and relief at having killed Azrael. He felt somewhat sickened with himself for emptying his magazine into him, but not nearly enough to ever apologize. Yet there was relief in finishing a job years in the making.

The flood of emotions he felt brought a chill down his spine, and he nearly cried. Because though he knew his journey was nearly complete, he had lost so much on the road. Images of Susan's young face flooded his mind, her blue eyes always present and reassuring. He wiped a tear from his eye and turned his head, catching full sight of Alexandra's corpse. The sound of the senators whimpering returned, and the world seemed to come back into sharper focus. The rage returned as he stared at Alexandra, and he knew this wasn't over.

78

"**B**oss, I show you and one other individual still alive in there. The rest of the warehouse looks clear," said Charlie in Colin's earpiece. It took Colin a second to snap out of it and begin to untie the senator.

"Copy, that's Senator Walker. I believe he was set up. Azrael was going to kill him when I came into the room. Azrael is dead. Agent Smith is KIA as well."

It took everyone longer than usual to reply. When they did, their tones were solemn. "Copy, moving to your position."

Colin pulled the gag from Senator Walker's mouth. "Senator Walker, are you okay?" he asked.

The senator looked like he was in shock. He had seen something truly terrible. Something far darker than he ever had while serving in the military. "I am," he replied, not taking his eyes off of Agent Smith's body. "I... How could somebody do something like that?" he asked in terrible disbelief.

Colin wasn't sure how to answer. "This world can be a dark place, Senator." The two said nothing as the senator got to his feet. Witch arrived with Jester, helping along Sheriff in between them. They placed the wounded man in one of the chairs. The group stood silently for a moment, looking at Smith, before Colin pulled a blue tarp off of a nearby box and put it over her body. He couldn't look at it anymore.

When he looked, he saw that part of the tarp had been covering a large circular hole in the ground. Colin grabbed a flashlight from his pocket and looked to see what was in it. All he saw was a ladder. His curiosity got the better of him, and he decided to investigate. It took him a few moments to squeeze down the hold and into the cavern some ten feet below their feet. He shined the light around and saw boxes of clothing, food rations, water, and a more mysterious green plastic box with no clear contents. Colin approached it and opened it to see what was inside.

There were a few thousand dollars in cash, three passports from the U.S., Nevis, and China, and a box of what looked like compact disks. Colin grabbed the box of disks and flipped through them until he arrived at one with a name he recognized. Frost. It couldn't have been a coincidence. Colin ran to the ladder and took the rungs three at a time to the top. "Is there an optical drive on that computer?" Colin asked, running over to the two computers on the foldout card table.

"Ah." Witch checked one while he checked the other. Witch's had one. Thankfully, the computer hadn't yet locked since Colin had killed its owner. Colin clicked the button to eject the CD tray in case there was anything else in it, and seeing that there wasn't, he slotted the disk in and waited for it to spin up.

A moment later, the disk popped up on the desktop. Colin opened it. Thankfully, the files were in English because the rest of the computer was set to Mandarin as its main language. The CD, it seemed, was loaded with text documents. Colin opened one. It was a file of carefully typed notes. It looked like it was related to some kind of murder.

Colin clicked on another document, then another, all of the notes on murder cases, all of them with the same name on the top. A name that made Colin's blood run cold.

79

17 Years Before

It was a cold, dark afternoon this close to Christmas. Inside the Department of Justice, only a few office lights remained on. Most employees had already left for vacations before tomorrow's Christmas Eve. The assistant U.S. attorney for the District of Columbia was still there, though, even if it wasn't work-related. In fact, what he was doing would have had him tossed out of this place and directly into a cell. *So much for trying to do something nice,* he thought to himself as he went through the logs on his computer.

Some people are simply too curious for their own good. Always looking to bite that hand that feeds them. What would her father have told the silly girl? Likely that she was on the right path. He was a meddlesome fool even at the best of times, his internal monologue ran.

He had decided to let the girl run with her hunches in the end, though, allowing her to follow his trail as far as she could so he could learn where he was most vulnerable. She had a talent, he had to admit. More so than anyone else who had tried to come after him, and a drive he couldn't help but admire. But that was all in the past now. She had come too far and made him vulnerable.

Well, as vulnerable as he ever really got. In truth, she had been under control from the start. His dark angel had followed her since the inception of her investigation. If she had simply stuck to her normal administrative work and kept her nose clean, she likely would have moved up quickly, perhaps even earning herself a job when she graduated.

The opportunity, however, to use her talents against her had been too good to ignore. Now, however, it was time to pay the girl for her services. He had just finished arranging it with the one the Chinese had sent to keep him protected from potential interference. He was valuable to them, perhaps more valuable to them than any they had ensnared into their service before. Especially now that he would be pursuing a new position soon—one that would give him access to far more people, programs, and, above all else, knowledge. They called the man they had sent to him Azrael.

He wasn't quite sure if he was a man. More of a monster, as far as he was concerned, but very effective when it came to sending a message—that he couldn't deny.

The hit was set for the following night, on Christmas Eve, when everyone's guard would be down. Not his idea, of course, but he saw the merit in the plan.

He turned his attention to the manila folder he had brought with him to the office and thumbed it open. Samples of what his next life might hold were emblazoned on various cardstock pieces of paper. They set an exciting, vigorous, but measured tone for what he would be to his constituents. Everything he had been since he moved to D.C. from the deep south. His campaign manager even told him the southern drawl would help calm and reassure his potential constituents that he was a steady guiding hand. He picked up one of the fliers and read the words in the new font they had picked for this run of them.

Elect Patrick Rand for U.S. Senate

80

Colin ran to the parked Suburban a block away from the warehouse his team was in, moving as fast as he possibly could in the two-foot deep snow. He left his team there to secure the site and wait for the FBI to arrive to treat Sheriff and retrieve both the senator and the bodies of their fallen brother and sister. Colin knew now that they had been tricked, and he wasn't about to let the man who did it get away. The morning was approaching. Colin could tell from the slight increase in light. The snow hadn't let up at all. "Charlie, where's Rand?"

"I'm not sure. His detail isn't responding to my calls. There was a police call of shots fired to his building twenty minutes ago."

"Track his phone!" yelled Colin, hopping in the Suburban.

"Hang on."

Colin put the car in gear and started driving toward the senator's apartment anyway.

"Okay, his phone is off, but it looks like another phone may have pinged his when you were at his apartment, I think…"

"I don't care, just do it now!" Colin cut him off.

The SUV looked like it was a sled gliding on the snow, kicking up a hurricane of swirling snow in its wake, as its tires were buried. Colin slid around a corner and accelerated to dangerous speeds in his pursuit of the senator. "Boss, he's almost at Union Station. That's seven blocks from you. Uploading it now."

"I know where it is," said Colin. He accelerated faster, knowing it was a nearly straight shot to the station. This was taking too long, and Colin knew it. The trains wouldn't be running, but if the senator was getting out of the city, he could be picked up by another vehicle or possibly killed by the Chinese to protect themselves. Rand had to stand trial for the crimes he had committed. The people he had killed in the pursuit of his power had to have their justice, but only if Colin reached him in time.

"Boss, I've routed Agent Savarese's team to Union Station as well."

"Copy," said Colin. In the distance, Colin only saw the descending snow. All he could do was envision the white marble structure that was Union Station and pray he got there in time. After what seemed like hours but was really only minutes, he saw the white-columned building that was Union Station. Massive, darkened circles hung from the columns. Colin recognized them as Christmas wreaths without any lights on.

He saw the black columns with golden eagles on top and the huge roundabout circle that led up to the station. He took his foot off the gas, hopping the first curb, then another, then another, using the curbs buried under the snow to slow his speeding vehicle. Ahead, he saw a dark figure running under the massive arch that was on the side.

Realizing he couldn't stop in time, Colin opened the door of the SUV and rolled out of it into the falling snow. He hit the ground hard but was cushioned by the thick blanket of frozen precipitation. It still hurt like hell, though. A second later, the SUV crashed into one of the stone pillars. Colin stood and tried to run after the figure, but the snow was so deep it was more like wading. Ahead he heard shouting in what sounded like a mix of southern accents and Mandarin. Colin pulled out his pistol and moved as quickly as he could.

When he got under the archways, the faint glow of emergency lights lit the white marble in a soft yellow glow. The snow tapered off here, and Colin saw what he was looking for. Rand was cornered by a man and a woman, both with guns raised. Rand was on his knees on the ground, yelling at them that he was one of them. The man raised his weapon toward the senator. Colin shot them both from a distance of twenty feet with two shots each in a rapid tap-tap motion. His grouping was tight, hitting both targets' center mass and sending them to the ground. Colin moved forward toward the senator, kicking the weapons away from the two he had just shot in the process.

"Snowman, thank God you're here. These two just tried to kill me," said Rand, trying to play it cool.

"It's over," said Colin.

"What's over?" asked Rand, acting bewildered. Colin grabbed him by his coat and lifted him to his feet. Rand tried to grab for something, but Colin punched him hard in the gut, knocking the wind out of him. The senator fell back to his knees, and Colin grabbed what the man had been reaching for. It was a KaBar combat knife. Colin threw it in the snow a few feet away.

He lifted the man back to his feet. "You killed a lot of people today."

"I didn't kill anyone," replied Rand in his southern drawl. Colin put his pistol to the senator's head, pulling his face close to his own. "If you're going to kill me, Snowman, then do it. If not, I'll remind you I'm a sitting U.S. senator and can make your life very miserable."

"I don't give a shit who you are. Let me tell you why. My real name's Colin Frost. Ring a bell?"

Comprehension suddenly dawned on Rand's face. "Ah, we come to it then."

"Come to what, Rand?"

"The reason you were so hellbent on catching Azrael. It was never about senators or counterintelligence. It was about your ridiculous sister and her nonsensical crusade for the greater good. But I guess you'll have to take comfort in the fact that you and she are on the same path."

Colin nearly hit him. "Oh, yeah? What path is that?"

"When I'm done with you, you'll never see the light of day again, either."

Colin wound up and punched the senator as hard as he could in the face. He felt the man's teeth shatter and his left orbital bone crack under the plastic-knuckled gloves he wore. The senator crashed back to the ground a few feet away and was spitting blood by the time he landed. Colin ran forward and grabbed him again by the coat.

"Stop!" yelled a voice from behind him. It was Agent Savarese, and his weapon was out. Colin raised his hands, slowly.

The senator sputtered and spat blood again. "Typical Frost. None of you could ever finish the job," said Rand.

Colin looked down at him and seriously considered killing him, but he knew it wasn't what Agent Smith or his sister would have wanted. They would have wanted justice, and true justice was having Rand answer for all of the crimes he had committed, not just the ones Colin could think of. He looked back at Rand. "I *have* finished the job."

Colin Frost will return in Book Two: Echoes of Deception

THANK YOU FOR READING CAPITAL MURDER

We hope you enjoyed it as much as we enjoyed bringing it to you. We just wanted to take a moment to encourage you to review the book. Follow this link: Capital Murder to be directed to the book's Amazon product page to leave your review.

Every review helps further the author's reach and, ultimately, helps them continue writing fantastic books for us all to enjoy.

There books in the series:

COLIN FROST
Capital Murder
Echoes of Deception

Check out the entire series here! (Tap or scan)

You can also join our non-spam mailing list by visiting www. subscribepage.com/AethonReadersGroup and never miss out on future releases. You'll also receive three full books completely Free as our thanks to you.

Facebook | Instagram | Twitter | Website

Looking for more great Thrillers?

In a daring act of piracy, Yemeni terrorists have not only seized a special oil tanker but they've also captured a high-value asset. With President Lewis desperate to save his biggest donor's assets and protect his deepest secret, he orders Director of National Intelligence Camille Banks to deploy her secret team to recover the asset. Garrett Knox, along with his hand-picked team members of elite operatives, must attempt the impossible: infiltrate the treacherous Yemeni mountains and bring the asset home alive. Battling hostile terrain and relentless attacks, Knox and company close in on their target only to have the tables flipped on them as a far deadlier plot emerges. The terrorists offer a chilling ultimatum—the asset in exchange for a notorious bombmaker in U.S. custody. With time running out and the world watching, Knox and his team embark on a pulse-pounding mission to retrieve the bombmaker. But when a shocking betrayal threatens everything, Knox must make an unthinkable choice to save Rico and save the president. **From the Oval Office to the explosive climax, Terminal Threat is a non-stop thrill ride packed with jaw-dropping twists. As a sinister conspiracy tightens its grip, will Knox's team prevail, or will the President's dark secrets destroy them all? The clock is ticking in this electrifying novel by R.J. Patterson.** *This action thriller is perfect for fans of Tom Clancy's **Jack Ryan**, Vince Flynn's **Mitch Rapp**, Robert Ludlum's **Jason Bourne** or Stephen Hunter's **Bob Lee Swagger**!*

ACKNOWLEDGMENTS

To my family and friends, thank you for your unwavering support in this dream I've had since childhood. You've made this process much easier. To all the folks that helped me with research, I won't name you here, but know that I am incredibly grateful for you helping a first-time author pursue his dreams. To my constant four-legged companions in writing, your loyalty makes a complicated world seem simple. I would also like to thank Aethon Books for taking a chance on me and helping to bring my stories out of my head and into the world. And finally, thank you to my readers. I'm immeasurably grateful for you.

Made in the USA
Monee, IL
04 September 2024

65143506R10184